Praise for
TWO OUT OF THREE, A Meagan Maloney Mystery

Named to Kirkus Reviews' Best of 2012.
"Silva sustains a solid mystery that manages to keep readers engaged throughout the many plot twists and turns.
A well-constructed story that lays a promising foundation for the rest of the series."
—Kirkus Reviews (starred review)

"Two Out of Three is one of the best debut novels I have ever read... just enough blend of mystery, suspense and a fun new main character in Meagan Maloney."
—Deb Adams

"A fun, brilliant mystery that everyone should read... the plot is clever and the writing witty."
—Joanna Hinsey

"What a wonderful and suspenseful mystery!"
—Sarah Koletas

"I loved the book...the twists and turns of Meagan's case kept me reading for hours at a time."
—Nancy Michelson

"I found this book to be very exciting, intriguing and a page-turner... this is going to be a great series and I wait with much anticipation for the next novel."
—Patty Nowicki

"Meagan follows in the footsteps of hapless heroines such as Stephanie Plum!I loved the twists and turns in this book and all the quirks!"

—K. April Holgate

"This is a good mystery that keeps you guessing right to the end and surprises you with a twist in the plot. Easy to read but hard to put down."

—Elaine Bush

"Thank you for writing a book with characters that are so "relatable". Meagan left me wanting to know more..."

—Amy Muscatell

"The development of the characters made me feel very close to them, like they were best friends or relatives.
From cover to cover, the suspense captured my attention...
for this to be a debut novel, it's a first game home run!"

—Lee Smith

THE STAIRWELL

M. M. SILVA

Cover design: BEAUTeBOOK

Original Cover Photography: Artybrad at the English language Wikipedia and Eric Harrison

Author picture by John P. Silva ~ location was Pleasant Valley Country Club in Sutton, MA

*To the victims, their families, and all
of the everyday heroes of the
Boston Marathon bombing on
April 15, 2013*

PROLOGUE

Friday, November 1st ~ Present Year

JEFF GEIGER FELT LIKE A KID IN A CANDY STORE, and it wasn't only because last night had been Halloween. This afternoon he was purchasing a vacation home, and he had a spring in his step as he approached the entrance to the glimmering skyscraper in downtown Boston. The John Hancock Tower was a glassed modern marvel, with its silver-blue tint reflecting the buildings all around it. His closing would be held at the law firm handling the estate of the late Ava McGraw, a woman he'd never known but with whom he would now have a common address.

Jeff entered through the revolving door of the massive building and checked in at security. The uniformed young woman squinted and studied his license thoroughly, which made him feel like he'd done something wrong when he absolutely hadn't. She glanced up and scrutinized him, and Jeff gave her a tight smile. She looked back down at his ID and then, evidently satisfied, directed him to the turnstiles. He pushed through the metal arm of the first one he came to and made his way to the bank of elevators that would take him to the twenty-fifth floor. He smiled at the knowledge of the building's elevators, how only certain cars went to certain floors above; efficacy was a wonderful thing.

He arrived at the plush suite of offices and checked in with the attractive receptionist. She picked up the phone, quietly announced his arrival, and seconds later, he was greeted by Jolene O'Hara, the attorney who would handle the transfer of the property. She escorted him to a large conference room, where a wall of windows showed off a spectacular view of the Boston skyline. The long mahogany table in the center of the room, polished to a beautiful sheen, held a gleaming silver tray with a glass pitcher of water and floating lemon slices, alongside four crystal tumblers. The massive table looked to seat about thirty, but today only three people were scheduled to be at the meeting.

Jolene took a seat at the far side of the table and removed assorted paperwork from her briefcase. Jeff sat across from her, appreciating that she'd given him the side of the table with the wonderful view of the city.

While they made small talk about the warm fall weather, the Patriots, and the latest political scandal, Jeff studied Jolene. She was probably in her late-fifties and wore a white, low-cut business suit that was one size too small for her stocky frame. Jeff wasn't an expert on women's fashion, but he thought there was some rule about not wearing white during certain times of the year. Silver bracelets dangled from her thick wrists, and a couple of silver chains disappeared into the tunnel of her cleavage. The makeup must have taken at least an hour, and talon-like fingernails almost perfectly matched her red hair-from-a-bottle. Her gravelly voice hinted at many years of smoking, and Jeff briefly wondered how many times a day she took the long elevator ride downstairs just to light up.

He was also beginning to wonder how much longer they would have to chit-chat when Bill McGuire entered the conference room. Leave it to Bill to saunter right past the receptionist and come in unannounced. Jeff swiveled in his chair to greet his real estate agent and friend. Bill was a typical Irishman, with light red hair, freckles, and pale skin. He was over six-feet tall with a quick wit and a twinkle in his bright, blue eyes. He was the type of guy who had a smile that mothers warned their daughters about, but the daughters never listened. And eventually he won over the mothers, but never the fathers.

Bill exchanged pleasantries with Jolene and took a seat beside her, across the table from Jeff, and they began. The meeting progressed without much fanfare, and forty minutes later, Jeff Geiger owned a home in Jamestown, Rhode Island, a small community just outside of scenic Newport. After some final small talk, Jeff gathered his things to leave. Jolene momentarily looked panicked and made a not-so-subtle attempt to stall his departure.

"So, Jeff, it's not often we have people at such a young age paying cash for a home. That's quite impressive." She attempted what he assumed was meant to be a demure smile, but she really just wound up looking constipated. She stood and stretched across the large table to pat Jeff's hand. Her palm lingered there, and Jeff's right eyebrow shot up, looking to Bill for some help.

"It's a *second* home, too," Bill threw in, enjoying the spectacle way too much to not pile on. Jeff shot him a glare that spoke volumes, as he preferred to keep his personal life just that: personal. Now he had to say something.

"Uh, thank you, Jolene, it's a great little property that has a few projects I can work on. I'm excited to get down there and get my hands dirty." At the mention of his hands, Jeff pulled his out from under hers, leaving her half-sprawled across the massive table. He had to get out of there before they could delve any further into his second house, his age, his money, or especially his lack of a wedding ring.

After escaping Jolene and scampering out of the building, Jeff hit the sidewalk with a renewed bounce in his step. "God bless you Ava McGraw, I'll do you proud," Jeff whispered, looking up at the fluffy white clouds. He briefly wondered about her life and hoped she had enjoyed her many years of living on the coast of Rhode Island. He jingled the new house keys in his hands and nearly skipped down the crowded street to the parking garage.

After walking down several flights to his vintage Porsche 911, he unlocked the door, started the engine, and spiraled up the parking garage loop. Digging in his pocket for his wallet, he was careful not to bump the car against the narrow cement walls as he circled around toward the ticket-taker. The man working the booth was probably in his mid-sixties, and he wore a light blue cardigan sweater and a gray, newsboy cap. A disgusting, unlit, chewed-up cigar hung out of his mouth. He held out his hand and didn't even look up from his newspaper to acknowledge Jeff. Sticking the ticket in a little machine, the green neon numbers revealed what Jeff owed.

"Forty bucks, mac," the man said, with a heavy Boston accent.

"Holy cow, I was only in there for about an hour." Jeff was just messing with the guy, but he wanted to see if he could get him to glance up from the sports page. He wasn't disappointed. The man looked up and narrowed his eyes as he pointed his slimy cigar at Jeff.

"Listen mac, it's highway robbery, I agree. But I don't set the rates; I just collect 'em. And I don't make no commission on it, either, so don't bust my stones. Just gimme the forty, and you'll be on your way. Or don't gimme the forty, and we'll getcha towed. Makes no difference to me."

Jeff smiled. Only in Boston. He gave the man a fifty and told him to keep the change, which merited a small grunt and a barely audible thank you. That didn't faze Jeff, though. Nothing was going to get to him today. It was Friday afternoon, the weather was beautiful, and he was heading to his new digs. Life was good.

The traffic getting out of Boston was slow going but steady, a small miracle on an early Friday afternoon, and Jeff had crossed into Rhode Island in no time. He had friends in the Midwest who could never understand how someone could zip through a portion of all six New England states in a matter of hours.

The drive through the Ocean State was effortless and beautiful, and the gold and orange leaves on the trees lining Interstate 95 made him feel like he was driving through a Thomas Kinkade painting. He made the trip in less than two hours, another great feat for a Friday. He pulled onto his new property and proceeded down the curvy, gravel lane to his house. His land had a huge, open meadow with grass that blew with the ocean breeze. Jeff pictured the wildflowers that undoubtedly grew here in the springtime and was once again thankful for the good fortune life had sent his way.

He took a moment to admire the view of the ocean and the Newport Bridge. Smelling the salt in the crisp fall air, he inhaled deeply and smiled. He was on cloud nine and tried to etch the moment in his brain, because everything was absolutely perfect.

Right up until the point when he opened his front door and saw the dead body at the bottom of the stairwell.

CHAPTER 1

Sunday, November 3rd

I WOULDN'T NECESSARILY SAY AUTUMN SUCKS; I actually wouldn't say that at all. It's simply knowing what comes next that sometimes makes your hair hurt if you think about it too hard. Opting to *not* think about it too hard, I made a conscious effort to focus on the fabulous whipped caramel concoction sitting on the table in front of me. I'd taken the lid off the lovely creation, in order to inhale the wonderful smell and watch the steam come off the magic liquid I love.

I have a *thing* for coffee, specifically the deliciousness just mentioned. My morning routine involves visiting a wonderful coffee house on Boylston Street in my home city of Boston, and I'm better acquainted with some of the shop employees than some people are with their own family members. I'm way beyond the stage of having to place an order. When they see me come in, they immediately start in on my beverage; it's that easy.

"Are you thinking about winter, Meg?"

Doobie, my neighbor and best friend, had accompanied me on my coffee run, and I looked at him with surprise.

"Doob, I swear you're a mind reader more often than I'd like you to be. That's exactly what I was trying to *not* think about. How did you know?"

He shrugged. "You're staring outside with that glazed, faraway look, and your bottom lip is protruding like one of those aging celebrities who just had 'em done."

"I do not!" I protested. Planting my upper row of teeth firmly over my lower lip, I eyed Doob with curiosity. "You're an expert on celebrity collagen implants now?"

Doob nodded. "Yes, I am," he said with no shame. "I almost always have a television on, and I like the shows about all of those movie stars making spectacles of themselves. I've picked up my vast plastic surgery knowledge from their shenanigans. And it's gross, but some of them have their work done right on television; it makes me queasy, but there's some type of sick fascination with it, too. Someone is always getting poked or prodded or having something sucked or tucked. Fluffed or buffed. Brightened or lightened. Chiseled or drizzled. Waxed or shellacked—"

"I got it, Doob," I said, putting my hand up.

But he persisted. "I'm not kidding; it's high pressure for these people, Meg. They gotta bring home the bacon, and it's a dog-eat-dog world out there. You think it's easy." He shook his head slowly.

Fortunately, I didn't have anything in my mouth just then because I would have spit it out with laughter. "Doob! Like you know anything about a dog-eat-dog world. That's classic."

"True," he quipped. "But if I had to get by on my looks..." He framed his face with his hands, "...I'd have me a nice 'frigerator box and shopping cart with at least two bad wheels. So I see why they do what they do. I'm just grateful I'm not under that type of pressure."

That was the understatement of the year. Doob was a trust fund baby and originally from Iowa. When Doob was a kid, his dad had developed some type of fertilizer or pesticide that he'd sold to a huge conglomerate and had made a fortune in the process. Doob's parents love to travel and are usually off ziplining through jungles in various parts of the world, but Doob made a home in Boston after a kind-of-semester in college, and I was glad for it. He now spends his days computer hacking and feels no remorse about it whatsoever. His claim is that he's done more good than harm with his questionable *hobby*, and I can't argue the point. He's been a tremendous help to me with many of my cases, but I often tell him to refrain from sharing the illegal help he's given me. Denial is one of my shortcomings. Or talents. Whichever.

As for me, I'm a private investigator. My partner, Norman Switzer, and I have been in business for a while now. Our firm has been growing at a nice, steady pace. Norman brings the knowledge, experience, and the instincts of a cop with over twenty years on the force, and I have...well, I have some guts and just enough tenacity to get me into heap-loads of shit at times. It works for us. Norman won't readily admit that, but please, just take my word for it.

Our little business presently has two open cases. One is the unsolved murder of my fiancé from a few years back; the other is to find and bring to justice a psychopath named Melanie who changed my life last March. She kidnapped me during a nor'easter and murdered a friend of mine that same night. She would have also killed me if I hadn't escaped, and I've been living with the overwhelming guilt ever since.

Melanie sent me a postcard back in July, and it was postmarked Portugal. She's on a mission to kill her biological father, Vic, who's currently living with my uncle; they're roommates with a group of old guys who live in a three-story over in Southie that I've dubbed the geriatric frat house. Their setup is a hoot, but Melanie's wishes to bump off her father and me are far from funny. I've vowed to keep every hair on their gray heads safe as long as there is a breath left in me. Melanie is never far from my thoughts, and I'm confident I'll see her again someday.

Truth be told, I actually see her all the time. I see her at the supermarket, in line for a movie, at a baseball game, at the mall, at church, literally everywhere. I'm not confessing to being crazy, mind you. I'm self-aware enough to know that I'm not actually *seeing* her. But somewhere deep in me, I don't completely forget her. I can't. Even on my best day, there's a simmering at the core of me that is always on the lookout for Melanie. It's like she's attached herself to a sliver of my soul.

But for now, Doob and I are at the coffee shop for a reason that has nothing to do with Melanie. Yesterday I received a call from an old friend from high school, Jeff Geiger. He'd discovered a dead body at his new vacation home and wanted to discuss how and why it got there. It was good to hear from him, and I told him I'd gladly meet him to see if I could help.

"So how much did this dude win again?" Doob asked with a mouthful of doughnut.

"Somewhere around six million dollars," I responded, and Doob whistled lightly.

At age thirty-one, Jeff and two other lucky people hit the Massachusetts lottery. He'd been smart with the money and hadn't gone crazy like a lot of winners do. After he'd won, Jeff hadn't even told anyone about his windfall for two months, and he was still working at the security firm he opened *before* he won the lottery. I don't know if I'd have that type of discipline if six million dropped in my lap, so good for him.

While speaking with him yesterday, I learned the first big purchase Jeff made was to gift his parents a home in Aruba; the second was a fancy sports car; the third was his vacation home in Jamestown where the dead body happened to be when he strolled in two days ago. He sounded pretty freaked out about it, and I wondered if he'd end up selling the place.

The door to the coffee shop opened, and Jeff and I exchanged waves as he walked toward the counter and studied the menu, which was really just a huge, long blackboard with all sorts of colored chalk listing out the delicious coffees. He approached our table a few minutes later, toting the largest coffee known to man, along with a massive cinnamon roll. Doob didn't even wait for an introduction; rather he jumped out of his chair and bee-lined for the counter. He'd homed in on the cinnamon roll the minute it entered his nasal periphery, and he'd opted to go buy one for himself, rather than rip it from Jeff's unsuspecting clutches. I hoped Doob would have the good sense to come back with two.

Jeff and I exchanged pleasantries as I got up to give him a hug, and he jerked his head in Doob's direction.

"The computer dude?"

I smiled. "The computer dude, yes. Sorry I didn't introduce you, but he clearly smelled your roll and lost all sense of manners. He's like a puppy that way. Hopefully he won't relieve himself on the floor before we leave."

Jeff laughed. "Food first, I get it. You look great, Meagan. How are things?"

"Thanks. You do, too. I've been good. Work and my social life keep me busy, and my parents are both still crazy in a good way, so I can't complain. And what about you, Mr. Lottery Winner? I've got to imagine your life has changed quite a bit since hitting the big bucks."

Jeff nodded as he took a sip of his coffee. "That's an understatement. The money is awesome, but a lot of freaks have come out of the woodwork. I get a couple of marriage proposals a week through the mail, and a whole bunch of long lost *friends* have managed to track me down. It's bizarre."

I rolled my eyes in mock sympathy. "Poor baby."

Jeff gave me an exaggerated sigh. "I know. The tortured millionaire; it's a burden."

Doob reentered the picture at just that moment and plopped a heavenly smelling cinnamon roll on a paper plate in front of me. I love my neighbor. Then he held out his hand to Jeff.

"I'm Doobie, nice to meet you." Doob was a bit awkward in most social situations but had clearly realized he'd been a little bit rude when Jeff had walked in. It was cute watching him try to make up for it by being all formal.

"Likewise," Jeff said and shook his hand. "I've heard from Meagan you're her right-hand man when it comes to private investigating."

Doob bobbed his head from side-to-side but couldn't respond because of a mouthful of pastry he'd instantly shoved in his mouth after releasing Jeff's hand. Normally that wouldn't stop him from talking, so I knew he was definitely trying to make a good impression. I also knew his good table manners might be very short-lived, so I jumped in before he could projectile something out of his mouth and across the table.

"Doob is invaluable to me, and he's cheap labor to boot. So tell us, Jeff, what the heck happened the other day?"

Jeff blew out a big puff of air. "Just the usual dead body at the vacation home type-of-thing," he said, trying to sound casual but not quite pulling it off.

"I understand this might be hard to talk about, but if you two are all set with eats, I'd like to hear the story from the beginning. But take your time; we've got all day."

"And thank God we do, because she'll interrupt you every five seconds," Doob said as he swallowed another ridiculous-sized mouthful of cinnamon roll.

I balled up and threw a napkin at him while Jeff started his story.

CHAPTER 2

"SO, ONE MINUTE I WAS ALL EXCITED AND PROUD, and I put the key in my new door, walked in, and the next minute I was looking at a dead man at the bottom of the stairwell. I couldn't believe it."

"What did you do?" I gently prodded.

"He was dead when you got there?" Doob asked, his face all scrunched up.

"It's going to sound awful, but I didn't know if I should touch him or what. I was so freaked that I just wanted to bolt, but I also wanted to help him if I could. I checked his neck for a pulse but didn't feel anything, so I turned and ran outside as fast as I could."

"That's understandable," I murmured.

"I would have passed out," Doob added.

"So I got to the front yard and kind of started, I don't know, hyperventilating or something. I just couldn't catch my breath and was gasping like I'd just outrun the devil. But I knew I had to call 911. My hands were shaking as I dialed, and I was so flustered I couldn't even remember my new address. I had to check the paperwork in the car to make sure I gave her the right information. Then it felt like forever before the police and ambulance arrived, and all I could see was the guy's face in my mind. No matter how hard I shut my eyes, all I could see was his face."

Being haunted like that is something I'm completely familiar with, but this wasn't about me. "I'm sure it was awful," I said, patting Jeff's hand.

He shuddered. "It really was. I wouldn't wish that on anyone. The guy's pallor was kind of a bluish-white, and his neck was twisted in a way that's not natural for living, breathing people. It looked like he'd fallen down the stairwell."

All of a sudden he looked sheepish. I asked if something else was bothering him. As if the dead body wasn't enough.

His face reddened when he said, "I'm going to sound like a total ass, but I was kind of pissed. I mean, I walked in and I'm staring at a dead dude at the bottom of the stairs. In my *new* house! What the hell? But I think that little spark of anger kept me from going into shock. It was supposed to be a wonderful day with a wonderful beginning at this wonderful house by the wonderful Atlantic Ocean. I want generations of my family to enjoy this place, and it started off on a pretty crappy note, ya know?"

"It's okay to be upset," I said and Doob nodded.

"So there I was feeling all sorry for myself, but then my internal-asshole-radar went off, and I realized how selfish I was being. So I sat down on my front lawn and stared into the distance until I heard the sirens approaching. Knowing it was going to be a long night, I half-wondered if I was going to need a lawyer but figured I'd deal with that if the cops got accusatory."

"Did they?"

Jeff shook his head. "No, not at all. They were cool. A few hours after they arrived, I was alone again in my front yard. The body was gone, the EMT's were gone, the police were gone, and the sun was long gone. It was weird."

"How so?" I asked.

"The cops were great; they absolutely did their jobs and were very thorough with me and with the scene. But it's just that, I dunno...I just got the sense they wanted to wrap it up all nice and tidy. They're going to investigate to make sure it wasn't a crime, but I absolutely *know* it's going to be ruled an accident. I mean, he was an old guy at the bottom of the stairs, right? And the police don't have the time or resources to follow-up on my silly theories, especially when I've given them nothing to go on. So I get it. I get that it'll be deemed an accident, but..."

"But what?"

"All I know is I can't stay in that house if there's one millionth of a chance something bad was going on there. If they decide it was an accident, so be it. But I just can't let it go that easily."

I considered the possibilities. "I can understand you feeling that way. But let me play devil's advocate. If something bad was going on, it probably had everything to do with the dead guy and nothing to do with the house, right? I mean, what can a house do?"

Jeff shook his head. "The guy was *there* for a reason. If he died of something other than natural causes, my worry is the house did have something to do with it. Because why else would he be there? Was he meeting someone there? Was he looking for something? I probably sound nuts, but until you find a dead body at your new home, you don't know how freaked out you'll get."

I sipped my coffee. "Okay, I'm with you. So let's go back to the other night. The cops, the ambulance, the, uh, body was gone. What did you do then?"

"I stayed outside the entire time, and I was freezing to death. But I couldn't go back inside because it's still an open investigation, and I sure as heck didn't want to go back in there anyway."

"So what did you do?"

"Started up the car, and headed back home. That's when I left you the message, Meagan. The police told me it'd be a couple days before I could get back in the house, and I didn't want to check into a hotel in Rhode Island when I've got a perfectly good place here. The cops said they'd be cleared out today."

"They've obviously got all your contact information?"

"Yep."

"Did they tell you not to leave town, anything like that?"

"They just asked that I be available. Like I said, they were pretty cool. But I don't think they're suspecting me—or anyone—of foul play. It appears so open-and-shut.

"So that's why I'm here with you two. If this whole thing is deemed an accident—and I guarantee it will be—then I need your help to either confirm or deny that. I want a second set of eyes that can focus completely on this case. Even if it really was an accident, there's a reason the guy was in my house. At the very least, I want to know that reason."

I'd been thinking as he was describing the whole scene. "I know you were totally weirded out, but it may very well have been a horrible mishap. Suppose the man was simply a wanderer who'd gone into your home and then tripped and fell down the steps. Maybe he had a heart attack or an aneurysm. Maybe he had dementia and had lived there as a little kid or something. A dead body doesn't necessarily mean a murderer is wandering around little Rhode Island."

Jeff glanced at his watch. "Sure, there are all kinds of things that *could* have happened. But I want to know exactly what did happen. As a matter of fact..." He fished a card out of his back pocket, held up a finger to let us know he needed a minute, and dialed a number on his cell. As I read the card upside down, it looked like the number to the precinct Jeff had been dealing with the other night. He muttered a lot of *uh-hunhs* and *okays* and scribbled notes on a napkin as he listened. When he hung up, Doob and I learned the dead man had been identified as Charlie O'Neill, a caretaker of sorts to Ava McGraw. Charlie's wife had been a childhood friend of Ava's, and Charlie tried to help Ava out with her nephew, Rusty, on occasion, as she'd been named custodian when his parents died. Rusty had gone bad, and Charlie and his wife, Eileen, had always kept an eye out for Ava. Why Charlie was found dead in Jeff's home was still a mystery.

"Well, that's a start," I said. "It sounds like he was a family friend; it's sad what happened to him. Have they officially ruled the death an accident?"

Jeff shook his head. "Not yet. It's coming, though. First thing I'm gonna do is install a state-of-the-art security system in that place."

I winked at him. "Since you own the company, I'm sure you'll get a nice discount. Hopefully that will make you feel a little safer until this whole thing is sorted out."

"Heck, I'd pay double if I could get that visual out of my head. Anyway...I think that's it. You guys now know what I know. So if you're up for it, I want to hire you. Hiring a pro will be well worth it if I can get my peace of mind back."

"See that Doob? I'm a pro." Doob rolled his eyes as I turned my attention back to Jeff. "Given the circumstances, it's going to be tough for you, but do you know when you're going back to the house?"

"I've got to leave here around eleven, actually. My furniture is going to be delivered down there between one and five o'clock, and I'm kind of glad I have to go. Otherwise I'm not sure when I'd be back. If ever."

I glanced at Doob, and he nodded.

Jeff veered his focus from me to Doob and back again, his brow puckered. "What?"

"We do this telepathy thing sometimes," I explained. "Doob often knows what I'm thinking before I even think it. It's kinda cool."

"It's kinda scary," Doob countered, breaking into a blueberry muffin he'd purchased with the cinnamon rolls.

"Keep eating, muffin man, and your brain will be so full of starch it will stop working anyway," I chirped and looked back to Jeff. "So, how many beds and/or couches are being delivered today?"

"Quite a few. Why?"

I shrugged. "Well, I want to help you with your case, and Doob is like a dog when it comes to a road trip. Put a blanket and food in the car, strap him in, and he's ready to go."

Doob nodded eagerly.

"We'd be happy to work on the case, and it sounds like you aren't too excited about being at the house by yourself anyway. So what I'm saying is we'd be glad to stay with you until this thing is settled. That is, if you want some house guests."

Jeff eased back into his chair, his posture softening. "Serious? That would be great! I mean, I don't want to sound like a sissy, but it's just a little creepy—"

"No need to explain," I reassured him. "Anyone would feel like that, it's only normal. So if you're good with all of this, we can go over my fees, and you can give me your address; then Doob and I will head down to Rhode Island later today."

"What about Sampson?" Doob asked as he coughed out some crumbs.

Oh boy. Sampson was the Springer Spaniel I shared with my sister. Moira works a lot, so Doob and I are generally on Sampson-duty throughout each day.

"Who's Sampson?" Jeff asked and then shrugged. "Actually, who cares? If he's cool, he can come. The more, the merrier."

I held up my hands. "Whoa, slow down. Sampson is of the four-legged variety, and he's a great pooch, but some people don't like dogs, especially in a new house. So if you'd—"

"Definitely bring him!" Jeff exclaimed. "I've been thinking about getting a puppy myself. This can be a test drive for me."

"Rock on," Doob said before his next bite.

We spent the next few minutes going over particulars before Jeff left for Jamestown. Doob and I hoofed it back to our apartment building to pack, and while we walked, I found myself pretty excited about doing some business in the lovely Ocean State.

I called Norman's cell phone and left a message about what was up. Then, against my better instinct, I called and left a message at the office for our intern, Becca. Becca was a new addition to our little firm, cute as a button, but an absolute ditz. Norman's twenty-plus years on the Boston police force had made him a lot of friends, and one of his old cop comrades had a daughter in college who needed an internship. Before I knew it, we were Interns-Are-Us. Approved through her college in record time, we were "enjoying" a semester with Becca in our midst. She studied criminal law, but I couldn't, for a second, imagine her passing the bar exam. I couldn't imagine her *spelling* bar exam. Anyway, I'd let the dingbat know what I was up to because Norman would want me to. Plus, if I didn't check in promptly on Monday morning, she might put out an APB on me and then blink heavily mascaraed eyes when we asked her to justify her actions. I would be the first to happily bid her farewell before the holiday break in December. God only knew what she'd screw up between now and then.

"Meg, are you even licensed to work in Rhode Island?" Doob asked as we strolled along the tree-lined sidewalks.

I smiled. "Are you thinking of my little mishap in California earlier this year?"

"I am. You're lucky that Officer Simonetta dude was nice enough to not bust your chops about being out of your jurisdiction."

"Well, you'll be relieved to know that I'm officially licensed in several neighboring states, so we won't have to worry about that." My thoughts suddenly drifted back to California and the case that changed my life forever.

Doob sensed my mood shift and added in a low tone, "Melanie or David?"

He really can read my mind.

"David," I replied.

Doob sighed as we continued walking, our steps matching each other's stride for stride. "When's the last time you talked to him?"

I exhaled every bit of breath within me. "I'm going to sound pathetic, but can we talk about *anything* else?"

"No problem." My neighbor knows when to push and when not to push. And that's part of what makes him wonderful.

Back at the apartment, I'd been in my bedroom for less than five minutes when I heard the front door open. Doob has his own keys, and he comes and goes as he pleases.

"Meg, does Sampson have a bag?" he yelled from the living room.

Have a bag? What in the world? "What do you mean?"

"Like, does he have a suitcase or something? I know you're going to take forever to get packed, so I thought I might run and buy him a bag somewhere."

I walked into the living room where Doob was perched on a couch. He had his laptop and a stuffed pillowcase perched by the door. The once-white-now-yellow pillowcase looked like it had been made sometime during the Lincoln Administration and had at least five holes I could see.

"You're ready to go?" I was incredulous.

"Aye-aye Captain," he said with a salute. "And you'll be another hour or two, I presume?"

"I'm not that bad; I'll be ready in fifteen. And Sampson doesn't need a suitcase, but thanks for the offer." I glanced at his sorry excuse for a pillowcase. "Any chance *you* need a suitcase, Doob?"

He looked puzzled. "No. Why?"

"Oh, no reason at all," I said, shaking my head. "Anyway, if you want to take Sampson outside for pee-pees before we leave, that would be great."

"Can do," Doob said and saluted again.

"Hang on!" I exclaimed. "Watch what Sampson and I have worked out." I put two fingers in my mouth and produced an extremely high-pitched *weeaa-weet* whistle. His dog tags tinkled a split second before Sampson came bounding out of Moira's room, leash in his mouth and tail wagging furiously.

"Whoa, that's cool, Meg. I'm so gonna have to learn that." Doob then put two fingers in his mouth and spit all over himself.

Less than a half hour later, Doob, Sampson and I were on I-95 South, loaded up in Doob's new Mercedes G63, aimed toward the tiniest state in the country. The drive to Rhode Island was beautiful, and time flew. My breath caught in my throat as we wound to the end of the lane leading to Jeff's new home. It was stunning. The lawn was more like a meadow, with long, soft yellow grass swaying in the gentle breeze. Clumps of massive trees, centuries old, dotted various sections of the property. The stories those trees could tell...

Sampson's bark brought me out of my reverie, and I saw Jeff waving at us from his front door. We piled out of the car, and Sampson took off as if he'd never been let loose before. He raced like the wind and then, true to his breed, sprang in large arcs before bounding off again. Stopping and cutting and tearing up turf, the dog had moves that would make an NFL running back envious. Making huge circles as he ran toward the house, he stopped about a hundred yards from us and sniffed around. I noticed a huge puddle of water and muck, and I tried my new fancy whistle, but Sampson didn't give it a thought, charging smack into the middle of the gunk, splashing and prancing up to his belly.

Doob sprinted toward the big puddle, and I wasn't sure if he would lure Sampson out or join him in the murky mayhem. Not that murky mayhem would hinder Doob for a second. Fortunately, Doob is as smart as he is slovenly. Pulling a treat from his pocket, he enticed Sampson back to the house with the promise of a beefy tidbit.

I looked sheepish as Jeff met us at the bottom of his front steps.

"Meet Sampson," I said in my best *ta-da* voice while swinging my arms toward the filthy canine. "I'm really sorry about this. He doesn't get out much."

Jeff laughed as he grabbed my bag and shook Doob's free hand. "No worries. The second bathroom isn't all that clean yet; I don't even have a shower curtain in it, so a wet dog won't hurt anything. We'll throw Sampson in the tub and get him cleaned up in no time."

Doob said, "Let me get him tied up out here for a second while we get settled, and then we'll run a bath for him."

Run a bath? I envisioned Doob and Sampson neck-deep in bubbles in about twenty minutes.

Doob went to the car and came back with a doggy-leash gizmo for the yard, complete with a little pole that stuck in the ground and a ten-yard nylon rope attached to it. He hooked Sampson up, and the dog gave a tiny whimper as we went up the stairs without him. Being left alone outside was new territory for the pampered pooch.

Doob rushed back to him and ruffled his ears in just the right spot. "We'll come and get you in no time, buddy." Sampson licked Doob smack on the mouth and then turned three circles before plopping on the ground. Dogs are pretty resilient.

Jeff, Doob and I walked inside and stared at the bottom of the stairwell. Hunh. So here was the elephant in the room.

"Welcome to my humble abode," Jeff said with a halfhearted smile. "The good news is we're dead-body-free today, and the furniture has already arrived, so things are looking up."

Once again, his attempt at being casual wasn't really working, and I gave him a sympathetic look. "Jeff, are you going to be okay?"

He shrugged. "I hope so. I fell in love with this place the minute I saw it and just want that feeling back. Coming here this afternoon, I was about a mile from the house and realized I couldn't recall anything about the drive. My mind must have been on autopilot just coming to grips with being back here. It kind of sucks."

"It does," I agreed.

"And when I drove down the lane, I scanned the exact same amazing view that was there two days ago, but it just wasn't the same. I had to force myself to get out of the car and was a little shaky when I went to unlock the door. I had to take the crime scene tape down, which didn't help. But like I said, no dead bodies. No *remnants* of a body, no carnage whatsoever. Hopefully someday I'll be able to get the mental picture out of my head. However, that's probably wishful thinking, at least for now."

"I'm sorry. But it should help when we figure out what happened." I turned my attention to the beautiful, open floor plan. "This place is fantastic! It looks brand new."

Jeff smiled broadly. "Yeah, Ava re-did the downstairs a couple of years ago, and it's completely up-to-date and modern. What I like is the upstairs still feels like an old house, with creaking floorboards and even some disgusting wallpaper in a couple of the bedrooms."

"I love it," I said and gave him a hug. "So let's get this place looking like it's yours. We'll unpack some things, put up a few pictures, light some candles, wash some bedding, and get it feeling a little more homey."

Both men looked at me like I had two heads.

"Or we can hook up the TV and eat some chips," Doob suggested.

"I like that," Jeff agreed while I groaned.

"Fine. After we take care of Sampson, you two couch potatoes can get the TVs operational. Then, Jeff, if you've got some boxes for the kitchen, let me at them, and we'll at least get this place functional."

We spent the next couple of hours getting Sampson cleaned up and making Jeff's house feeling a little more like an awesome vacation home and a little less like a big coffin. I was unloading the dishwasher when I heard my cell phone blare out *It's Raining Men*. That song gets my hips gyrating every time, and sometimes I miss calls because I get into full dance mode before I answer. But I saw it was my sister's number on the Caller ID, so I postponed the full dance-a-thon for a less important caller down the road.

"Hey, Moira, how was the shopping?"

"Hi Meg. It was fun. I found some great sales at that boutique on Boylston just down from your coffee house. You really should come with me one of these days. I could get you all glammed up."

There aren't many things in life I dislike more than shopping. And glam? I don't think so. "Fat chance, sis. But I'm glad you had a good day. What's up?"

"Well, a couple of things. First, I got your note. Is Jeff that cute guy who was a good basketball player in high school?"

"The very one," I replied.

My sister has always been attracted to pretty boys, with the exception of her last asshole boyfriend who looked like a bulldog-faced troll. Hopefully at this point in his stunted life he was now in a creepy fairyland far, far away and living under a rickety bridge. With smelly goats as companions.

A girl can dream.

As for me, I generally like a man's man. Muscles, some scruff on the face, a baseball hat, and a cat-that-ate-the-canary smile. I don't care to ever have a man in my life who's prettier than me. Moira will never have that problem, as she's gorgeous, so good for her.

"So what's this about a dead body or something?"

I filled her in on the events of the past few hours. "Jeff is weirded out, and it's a shame because it's an incredible house. Hopefully we can figure out what happened and help him feel better about everything."

"Aren't the police working on it?" she asked.

"Well, yeah," I replied. "But money isn't exactly an issue with Jeff, and he's asked me to help out, so Doob and I are mixing a little business with pleasure."

"Holy cow! That's right, I forgot all about the lottery. Cute and money. I should drive down and join you."

"The more, the merrier," I echoed Jeff from earlier, but I knew she was kidding. "Anyway, you said there were a couple of things. Did you need something else?"

I heard her take a sharp intake of breath. "Yes, there is, and I guess there's no easy way to say this."

My heart plummeted. "What's going on? Tell me Ma and Pop are okay!"

"My God, Meagan. If it had been something with Ma or Pop, I would have started with that."

Good point. "What then?"

"Well, let me start by saying for the billionth time that I hate your job."

I rolled my eyes. "Duly noted."

"So, that said…I'm sorry, but you got another postcard."

A chill ran through my entire body. I knew it was from Melanie without even having to ask.

"What did it say?"

"All it said was 'Thinking of you, Meagan.' It was postmarked Holland."

"Holland? What the hell?"

"I have no idea," Moira replied.

"Were any letters underlined?"

"Yes, I was just going to tell you that. The H was underlined."

"The H," I repeated.

"Exactly."

When Melanie sent me the postcard from Portugal, she had underlined the letter O. I hadn't really noticed it until Doob was studying it one night and pointed it out. I hadn't been completely convinced at the time, but if she'd underlined another letter in this postcard, then it had to be intentional.

"She's sending me a message," I said simply.

"Possibly," Moira said. "And it spells...um...oh or ho."

"I doubt if it's the word oh," I said. "And why would she send me a postcard to call me a ho? That's juvenile."

"I have no idea, other than to say maybe it's the beginning of a word and not an entire word," Moira said. "I'll think about it and let you know if I come up with anything. I'm sure Doob might be able to help as well."

I didn't say anything. There was a sinking sensation in my stomach.

"I hate to dump this on you, Meg. But your note didn't say when you were going to be back, and I thought you should know."

"No worries, kiddo. I need to call Vic," I said. Melanie's father had received a postcard similar to mine last time, and I was guessing he'd probably received one today, too. Melanie wanted to stay in both of our thoughts.

"Probably," Moira replied. "I'm sorry. You shouldn't have to be looking over your shoulder for this psycho every day."

"Yeah, well..." I didn't have a response to that.

"Are you going to be okay?" She sounded like I had when I was worried about Jeff in the entryway earlier.

I smiled. Wasn't *I* the older sister? Wasn't *I* the one who was supposed to have the shoulder to lean on? "I'm good, sis. It'll all work out in the end."

Moira sighed. "Okay, well let me know if you need anything. I'll just put the postcard on your bureau in the meantime."

"Okay, thanks. I'll take a look at it when I get home. And—" A lump formed in my throat, thinking about Moira at our apartment by herself.

"I'll be careful, Meagan," she said, reading my mind. "She's in Holland hopefully."

God knew where Melanie was, but I didn't want to alarm Moira. "Yeah, if she's smart, she'll stay far away from Boston for a very long time."

"Speaking of, do you have any idea when you and Doob will be coming back? Not to mention my *dog*?"

Whoops. She had a bit of a tone when she asked about Sampson. I did kind of dog-nap him, I guess.

"Yeah, sorry about that, but we're home more than you are, and Sampson friggin' loves it out here. I would guess we'll be gone for a few days, but I don't really know. I'll keep you posted, obviously."

"Just keep him out of any tall grass or water, please. I don't want him getting fleas or an infection or anything. I don't really trust that stuff we give him every month to keep all those nasty things away."

Whoops times two. Time to get off the phone. "Thanks for calling me, kiddo. I'll give Vic a call to see if he heard anything from Melanie."

"Be careful, Meg. I just wish she was out of our lives," Moira said softly.

Before I hung up, I had to ask, "Are you worried about being home by yourself? I'll come back in a heartbeat if you want me there." I love my job but sometimes don't love its effects on my family.

"No, I'm fine. I'll let you know if I change my mind, I promise."

"Fair enough, and please stay alert. I know Jeff wouldn't mind if you joined us down here, so give it some thought. You should take a few days off anyway."

"I just started working on a huge lawsuit with the top partner in the firm, so I've got to keep my nose to the grindstone for a while. But I'll be fine. Let me know when you're coming back."

We rang off, and I tried to reach Vic, but one of the old dudes told me he wasn't home, so I left a message. Hopefully he was out enjoying his day instead of being tormented by a postcard.

After my call, Doob, Jeff and I reconvened in the living room, beers in hand. They plopped down on each end of a spectacular soft, muted brown couch, and I settled in a matching chair across from them. We sat in silence, admiring the lovely furniture as well as our handiwork, and I felt like our few hours of effort had been a success. The house was taking on a beachy-vacationy-relaxing-yet-classy type of vibe, and I hoped Jeff was getting more comfortable in his new surroundings.

As things always did when it came to Doob and me, we quickly decided food needed to become a part of our immediate future. Jeff had only a few bags of chips and some remaining beers, and while that would suffice for certain occasions, this wasn't one of them. So we piled in Doob's Mercedes and headed for Newport. The drive over the scenic Newport Bridge was gorgeous, and the twinkling lights from the quaint little town looked like something straight out of a postcard.

Not that I wanted to be thinking of postcards at the moment.

Twenty minutes later we spotted an adorable little mom-and-pop diner in downtown Newport. Like many of the buildings in town, it looked small from the outside because of its narrow width. However, upon entering, we saw how long and deep the establishment ran. There were all kinds of tables with red and white checked tablecloths, and each of them had a small vase with two or three decorative flowers in them. It had a sweet, inviting atmosphere, and I liked it instantly.

A young girl with a long, blonde ponytail greeted us and said to sit wherever we liked. A moment later she came over to the table, gave us waters, and left some plastic-covered menus. Her name was Shelley, and she relayed the specials that were also scrawled on a vertical blackboard propped up by the entrance. Shelley said she'd be back in a couple of minutes to take our order.

After fully gorging ourselves to maximum capacity, we decided that a trip to the grocery store was in order. It's better to grocery shop when you're not hungry, right? Yeah, right. Tell that to Doob, who is perpetually hungry.

Jeff picked out a lot of the typical things needed to start a kitchen—milk, bread, butter, eggs, salt, sugar, cereal, fruits, vegetables, salad dressing, cheese, steaks, ground beef, chicken, some condiments, potatoes, soup, soft tortillas, tuna, three boxes of penne and pasta sauce, paper towels, napkins, toilet paper, and finally some paper plates, cups, and silverware. He said that he'd buy some *real* table settings another day.

While Jeff was being sensible, Doob and I grabbed our own cart and were on a completely different mission. We loaded up on Pop Tarts, Doritos, barbeque chips, frosted mini chocolate doughnuts, powdered sugar doughnuts, M&M's, Hot Tamales, hot chocolate packets, Diet Coke, Red Bull, assorted lunch meat packets, Frosted Flakes and Cap'n Crunch cereal, beef jerky, Snack Pack puddings,

Fritos, Double-Stuff Oreos, cake mix and frosting, three different flavors of ice cream, six frozen pizzas, several bags of assorted Lindt truffles, French fries, and ten boxes of macaroni and cheese.

After wheeling two overflowing grocery carts out to the parking lot, we barely managed to wedge all the groceries into Doob's truck, despite its massive size. As we loaded bag after bag, I seriously considered strapping Doob to the top of his own rig because he whined like a three-year-old that the ice cream would melt before we got back to Jeff's house. I told Doob that both the ice cream and he could use some cooling off in the crisp, November air, and held up some Bungee cords from the back of his truck for effect. That shut him up for a little bit, but his lip protruded during the entire drive. I thought his worry over the ice cream might actually make him consider going one mile over the speed limit, but Doob is nothing if not slow.

We each made several trips from the Mercedes to the house once we arrived at Jeff's place, and we quickly found a home for everything. Doob was thrilled to see all three ice creams still intact, and in celebration, he had one scoop of each.

As the Ben & Jerry's spectacle was unfolding, I glanced at my phone to see I had a voicemail. *Hunh?* My ringer was on, so I shouldn't have missed a call, but maybe it happened in the bunker of the grocery store. Or maybe the Mercedes had been so jam-packed with crap it blocked all cell coverage.

I smiled when I heard the voice, but then my stomach lurched, as I realized why he'd probably called.

"Hi Meagan, it's Vic McBride. I got your message and wanted to let you know I got a postcard also." There was a long pause and then a sigh. "From Melanie. But I guess you already knew that. Anyway, your uncle is going to have lunch with Moira tomorrow, so I'll give it to him and he can pass it along to her to give to you. I hope that's okay. I really don't want it. The whole thing makes me sick to my stomach. So call if you need anything, Meagan. I'm sorry about all of this. Take care of yourself."

I hung up and stared at the phone for a moment. Anything to do with Melanie made me sick as well, and my heart rate perked up as bad memories invaded my thoughts. I hated that I could have such an immediate reaction to anything related to her, but that would probably never go away. And I definitely wanted a look at his postcard. Vic hadn't mentioned if she'd underlined any letters, and his last postcard hadn't had any underlines, but I wanted to see for myself. Maybe the underlines were just for me, her warped little brain trying to send me some clues or just fuck with me in general. I thought about calling him back to ask about underlines, but I decided not to worry him. Moira would let me know once she got the postcard from Uncle Lare. Until then, I would try to put all-things-Melanie out of my head and instead have a few scoops with Doob.

CHAPTER 3

Monday, November 4th

IT WAS VERY COOL TO WAKE UP IN THE FANCY SLEIGH BED in one of the cozy guest rooms the next morning. I'd slept like a rock and felt like I was enveloped in a huge, wonderful marshmallow. Sun streamed through the windows onto the beautiful blue-and-white-striped comforter Jeff had purchased, presumably with a nautical theme in mind. The entire bedding set with the matching chair had probably cost a fortune, but I guess you can splurge when you're a millionaire.

As I was talking myself into getting a few more winks before facing the day, my cell phone sang out its hoppin' tune on the pillow beside me. I'd parked it there the previous night, as the room had a great bed but no nightstand as of yet. I'd have to complain to management. Grabbing the phone, I smiled as the familiar number appeared on the screen.

"Hey girlfriend, this is unexpected." I wasn't used to Kayla calling me this early in the morning.

"What? I need to setup an appointment to call you now?" she snapped. "Get your ass out of bed and meet me at your little coffee place in a half hour. I need some help."

"I'm doing well, thanks," I said dryly. "And I'd love to meet you for some caffeine, but I'm in Newport."

"Nice! Did you get laid?" Her tone had changed completely, and I could hear the excitement in her voice.

"No, my promiscuous pretty, I did not get laid. I'm here on a case."

"Really? What case? How long are you going to be there?" She sounded raring to go, nothing new for Kayla.

"It's hard to say. I just got here yesterday, and I'm trying to find out why a dead body showed up in a friend's new vacation home. It could take some time."

"Don't they have *police* who do that?"

I sighed. "They do, yes. But my friend has a large amount of funds at his disposal, and he's a little impatient to get this solved and to make sure everything's done perfectly. So he hired me because I'm a pro," I said with some fake bravado.

"*He?*"

I sighed again and smiled. "Yes, it's a he."

Her voice was singsong. "So *he* hired *you*? *He*, with the vacation home? *He*, with the large amount of funds? You definitely got laid! Well done, my friend. I didn't think you had it in you."

"Kayla, seriously. It's all on the up-and-up. Doob is down here with me, as is Sampson, and I'm truly working on a case. But it doesn't seem like very heavy lifting so far. I've got a view of the Newport Bridge and the water from the sleigh bed I'm currently sprawled in."

There was a beat of silence. And then, "I'll be there this afternoon."

Ummm. "Kayla, I'm sure we'd all love to see you, but..."

"But what? If you're not screwing Richie Rich, you can bet your sweet ass I'll give it a go. Plus, I need to see you ASAP."

"We can't discuss whatever you need over the phone?"

"Meagan, it sounds like you don't want me down there. What exactly is the problem?"

"Of course I'd love to see you, but it's not my invitation to extend. I can run it by Jeff and get back to you. He just moved in a couple of days ago, and he's already encountered one dead body, two overnight visitors, and a stinky dog."

"Boo-fucking-hoo. Here's the thing, Meagan. I'm coming unless you call and tell me I absolutely can't. With your wit and charm, I'm sure your client will be fine with me joining the party. So make room in that sleigh bed of yours until I can be a ho-ho-ho on *his* sleigh bed. Get it? Sleigh? Christmas? Ho ho ho!"

Ho could only make me think of Melanie, but it didn't matter because Kayla was forging ahead.

"What's his name?"

God help me. "His name is Jeff Geiger, and again—"

"Well, tell him to batten down the hatches and put on some cologne."

This was going nowhere good. "Kayla, don't forget Doob is here as well. You'll break his little Iowa heart if you fawn all over Jeff."

"I'll slip him a roofie, and he'll never be the wiser."

"Kayla! You're not drugging Doob. I'm not really sure you coming down here—"

But she wasn't listening. "Email me the address, Meagan, and I'll be there mid-afternoon. Also, let me know if you want red or white wine. Oh, forget it. I'll just bring both." With that, the line went dead.

I rolled my eyes and then rolled myself out of bed. Anticipating Kayla's arrival was kind of like waiting for a big storm. You knew things could get ugly. You might lose electricity. You might sustain damage to your home. You could possibly encounter loss to life and limb. And yet, in a weird, almost perverse way, a tiny part of you looked forward to the excitement of it all.

After brushing my teeth and emailing Kayla from my phone, I shuffled downstairs to greet the men, who were both loafing on separate sofas and watching cartoons. *How* old were they? But really, who was I kidding? After grabbing a frosted strawberry Pop Tart and Diet Coke, I plopped down beside Doob and joined in on the animated mayhem.

During a commercial, I relayed my conversation with Kayla to my housemates, and thankfully Jeff was more than happy to have an additional guest. And Doob? Let's just say Doob lit up like a lighthouse and then sniffed at his armpits. I was certain he'd mix in a shower before her arrival.

"I know we have a ton of food here," I announced after a particularly violent cartoon came to its bloody end. "But it looks gorgeous outside, and I wouldn't mind running into Newport again to grab a bite and do some sleuthing. I'd like to grab a newspaper and possibly swing by the police station to see if I can learn anything about this dead body of yours. I'll pick up the breakfast tab, if you guys want to tag along."

Evidently, telling a multi-millionaire and a trust-fund baby that breakfast would be on me wasn't very motivating. They both continued to stare at the television. I wondered if they'd even heard me.

Jeff finally said, "I'm pretty cozy right here, Meagan, but thanks. There's a special on ESPN coming up—"

I held up my hands. "No explanations necessary." I glanced at Doob and smiled. "I assume you'll be keeping Jeff company here at Casa Relaxa?"

Doob nodded. "I'm going to save my energy for Kayla's visit," he said with a grin and raised his eyebrows twice.

"It's good to know you have some energy, Doob," I said and tromped back upstairs to get cleaned up for the day.

I'd enjoyed last night's diner so much that I ended up at the same place. There was a cute little stand-up chalkboard on the sidewalk outside of the restaurant that advertised brunch and a bunch of other assorted goodies until 2:00 PM.

Shelley was waitressing again and greeted me like an old friend. She showed me to a table, slapped down a menu, relayed the specials, and went off to retrieve some coffee. *Thank God.*

After perusing the menu and deciding on the biggest omelet possible, I scanned the other patrons at the diner and spotted an elderly man just a couple tables over. The man looked to be eating a very light breakfast, and I noticed Shelley spent some extra time paying attention to him. The man asked Shelley if he could look at the newspaper another customer had left behind, and she immediately grabbed it and gave it to him. The man smiled broadly, and I concluded he had a little crush on the pretty waitress. It was sweet. Meagan Maloney-Spotter-Of-Crushes-From-A-Mile-Away-Extraordinaire.

Suddenly the man's blue eyes locked onto mine, alert and not completely friendly. It seemed he read my mind and communicated he didn't have a crush. Rather, he was just a lonely old guy who appreciated a kind waitress, he conveyed with his sharp look my way. Heat rushed to my face, and I then nodded deferentially at the old man. Since I couldn't wish myself invisible, I decided to be proactive.

"Good morning," I said politely.

His gaze softened a notch. "Good morning," he replied with a slight nod.

We looked at each other for an awkward moment before I resorted to the topic *everyone* resorts to during awkward moments.

"It sure is a beautiful day, isn't it? Feels more like September than November."

"That it does, young lady." He studied me for a moment. "Are you new to town or just visiting?"

"Visiting. I'm from Boston and staying with a friend of mine who just bought a place by the water. I've got some errands to do today, so I decided to fill up on some good food before running around." As if on cue, Shelley arrived at the table with my omelet, home fries, sausage, bacon and toast. She then grabbed my empty coffee cup and chocolate milk glass and said she'd be back with refills.

The man looked at my food and cocked his head. "You must have a pretty large appetite in that little frame of yours."

I looked down and said, "This is just the first course." That finally elicited a smile from the old man. He pulled a flask out of his jacket pocket and poured black liquid into his coffee. I stifled a giggle. He didn't seem nearly as menacing with his little container.

"It's not what you think, young lady. I don't mind having a nip or two during the day, but I generally wait until late afternoon. Since you're from Boston, I'll ask that you pardon the molasses. It's just a habit that's been passed down through my family, despite the great flood."

Pardon the molasses? Great flood? "Uh, sorry. I'm not familiar..?"

He grinned. "You're far too young. It happened back in 1919. Heck, even *I'm* too young, if you can believe that. But I've heard the stories."

Before I could help it, I heard myself saying, "If you'd like to join me and tell me about it, I'm always up for a bit of history." I gestured to the other side of the table.

He said nothing for a few seconds, and it struck me this would be the ultimate rejection—getting blown off by a guy about forty years older than me. It wasn't like I was hitting on him, for God's sake. I was simply being polite. Oh well, adios self-esteem. I focused on my breakfast and pretended I hadn't extended the invite.

Digging into my eggs, I sensed him sliding out the chair across the table from me. I smiled and saw Shelley looking over at *us* with a tender look on her face. He had two girls half his age looking out for his welfare. Good grief, this guy was probably a player. Or, a *playa,* to be accurate. I'd have to introduce him to my Uncle Larry. They'd be breaking hearts up and down the east coast in no time.

Before he sat, the man held out his hand. "I'm Gus, and I accept your breakfast offer."

Hunh. He reminded me of Doob the day before, all formal with the introductions, but it was cute. I shook his hand and said, "I'm Meagan. Thanks for joining me."

He opened his paper while I attacked my plate with reckless abandon. Shelley clucked and doted on us, and it was surprisingly comfortable. When I'd finally inhaled my last bite, I realized Gus and I hadn't exchanged a word the entire time I devoured my meal. This moved Gus up a notch in my book. He seemed to intuitively understand my complete focus on my food.

I leaned back and patted my stomach like some overfed king at the head of his over-packed table in his overdone castle. Sampson and I would have to go on a long walk later if I wanted to shed any of the billion calories I'd just ingested.

"So Gus, do you live here in Newport?"

He folded his paper and took a sip of coffee, as if transitioning to conversation mode. "I do. I've lived here my entire life and feel like it's the best place on earth."

I nodded. "You sound like me. I've been up in Boston my whole life, and I don't think there's anywhere better."

He tilted his head to one side. "Boston is a great city, but it's got too much hubbub for me. And the damn traffic and one-way curvy streets will drive you batty inside of an hour, pardon the language."

Pardon the language? Oh boy. I'd have to watch my mouth around this one if he considered *damn* offensive. But again, it was cute.

"That's okay, Gus. You're absolutely right. That's why they call Boston a walking city. No one in their right mind drives there on a regular basis. But as far as hubbub goes, Newport gets a little hectic during the summertime. Plenty of hub and bub," I said.

"Very true, young lady." He added a bit more molasses to his coffee and gestured at it. "I'll be glad to fill you in, if you're still interested."

The molasses story. I was intrigued, because I couldn't figure out why Gus putting molasses in his coffee today had anything to do with a flood in 1919. *The Titanic maybe?* But that wasn't a flood. *A tragedy, but not a flood.* And wasn't that in 1912 or 1913? *The White Sox throwing the World Series?* I'm pretty sure that was in 1919. *Again, not a flood.*

My food coma had clearly started. "Yes, the molasses. I'm definitely still interested."

Gus sipped his coffee and snapped his napkin. He seemed to relish having an audience. "Well, my father was born in Boston and was a little boy back in 1919. He, along with my grandparents, my aunts and uncles, had seen some hard times in years prior, because of World War I, the supposed *war to end all wars*. How I wish that was true." He took another drink from his cup. "Do you remember when that war ended Meagan?"

Oh great. Trivia questions on a full stomach. *Okay, think Meagan*. Flashing back to grade school, I remembered something about the eleventh hour of the eleventh day of the eleventh month. "November of 1918 was when the ceasefire was signed," I responded like a game show contestant, with much more conviction than I felt. If he started asking me about the Treaty of Versailles, I was screwed.

Gus smiled. "Someone paid attention in history class," he said.

As if. "It's just easy to remember that many elevens," I shrugged.

"So in January of 1919, the war had recently ended, but the nation was getting ready to enter a new era—Prohibition. I'm sure you're familiar with that?"

I shuddered in mock horror. "I'm grateful that experiment failed long before my time." A life without wine and margaritas was not one I wanted to experience.

"What's key to this story is the vote that would eventually ratify Prohibition was scheduled for January 16, 1919. There were forty-eight states at the time, and thirty-six were needed to ratify the 18th Amendment."

"Okay." I didn't know where he was going with this. but hoped it would be somewhere interesting.

"So, Meagan, do you know which state voted on January 16th?"

No amount of flashing back to any grade in any year whatsoever would help me with that question, so I shook my head. "No idea." Then, I held up a finger as if I'd just remembered something crucial. "But I do know Utah was the thirty-sixth state who voted to ratify the 21st Amendment, which *repealed* the 18th. So, God bless Utah," I said and held up my refilled coffee in a toast.

Gus clinked his coffee cup against mine. "Okay, you get half a point for that one. It was Nebraska who voted on January 16th."

"And this matters because..?" I wasn't trying to be a wise guy, but molasses and Prohibition and Utah and Nebraska just weren't doing it for me.

One side of Gus's mouth curled into a slight smile, and I knew he could read my impatience. I further sensed he wasn't going to rush his story because of it. In fact, I was pretty sure he was going to slow down.

"Back then in Boston, there was a storage tank on the water side of Commercial Street. Do you know the area?"

Cocking my head, I thought about that for a couple of seconds. "I do, but I'm not remembering a storage tank, unless it's small. I think there's a park in that neighborhood, isn't there?"

The curl of Gus's mouth enlarged. "There's a park now, yes. And no storage tank anymore. But back in the day, there was definitely a tank that had been built by the Purity Distilling Company, and it was massive." Gus spread his arms wide to emphasize his point. "It was fifty-feet tall and about ninety-feet in diameter, a monster of curves and steel. The bottom plates were set in a concrete base and pinned together with a stitching of rivets. The whole structure was built to store molasses and could hold two and a half million gallons of the brown stuff."

My eyebrows shot up. "Whoa."

"You bet *whoa*," Gus said.

"So what happened?"

"The short version of the story is that it collapsed, exploded, take your pick." He took another swallow of coffee.

I scrutinized Gus for a moment or two. *Exploding massive storage tanks of molasses*? Hunh. I began to wonder if Gus really had some spirits in his tiny flask and would next be telling me tales of little green men in spaceships.

"Look it up if you think I'm off my rocker." He motioned with his chin to my phone resting on the table.

My cheeks flushed. "You're a mind reader in addition to a molasses instructor?"

He winked and nodded but didn't say anything. Then he blew on his coffee, and waited to see if I wanted to hear anymore of his story.

"I hadn't completely decided if you were off your rocker or not."

"He's not," came a voice from behind me.

Shelley skirted around the different tables, and she smirked when she saw me looking at her.

Good grief. "Okay, I'm officially interested. But if little green men ride out of that tank on a wave of molasses—"

Gus laughed a full-belly laugh, and it echoed like music in the little café. I noticed several people look over at us, but not in an unpleasant way.

"There are no little green men, Meagan. But it was like something no one had ever seen before. When you think of a flood, you generally think of the ocean, a lake, or the great one in the Bible, but this was an actual flood of molasses that got up to three feet deep in certain parts of Boston.

I raised an eyebrow. "What in the world? How have I never heard about this?"

Shelley zoomed by to refill our cups and chuckled. "Don't feel bad. I didn't know about it, either."

Pretty impressive. She definitely had some rabbit ears on her because she seemed to have heard our entire conversation even though she'd been zipping around from table to table.

I turned back to Gus. "What happened? How did this tank, uh, explode or whatever?"

"Well, here's where we get to the scientific part of the story."

"Oh joy," I muttered.

Gus ignored me. "Back in 1919, molasses was the standard sweetener in this country. It was also fermented to produce rum and ethyl alcohol, an active ingredient in other alcoholic beverages.

"So on January 15th of that year, the temperature had quickly climbed over the single-digit temperatures of the previous few days. It got up to about forty degrees, and it's believed to be one of the contributing factors of the tank's collapse."

"How so?" I asked.

"Well, the rising temperatures would have increased the pressure within the tank. Couple that with the fermentation process, and that would have created a great degree of stress."

"Carbon dioxide?" I asked.

"Very good," Gus said.

I am such a scientist.

"But Gus, those two things had to have happened in countless other tanks as well. Temperatures rise. Fermentation occurs. Tanks shouldn't just explode."

"True. But it was proven later the tank had also been built poorly. It had been filled to capacity only eight times since its construction, which put the walls under an irregular, cyclical load. The force exerted in a full tank would have been the greatest at the base. Sadly, there was a manhole cover near the base of the tank, and it's believed a fatigue crack started there."

I nodded. "And with all that pressure building..."

"It was just a matter of time," Gus said, his voice tinged with sadness. "Of course, there was an inquiry done after the tank exploded. The people responsible said it had been blown up by some anarchists, but that was a bunch of hooey. As it turns out, the man who oversaw the construction of the tank didn't do the basic safety tests, like filling the tank with water to check for seepage. It's said the tank leaked so badly it was painted brown to cover up all the dripping goo. The local residents would actually stand under the holes and collect molasses for their meals."

"That's gross," I said.

His eyes narrowed a bit. "Life wasn't as easy then, young lady, and free molasses was free molasses."

I flushed but still thought it was pretty disgusting. "So I assume people were hurt as a result of this explosion?"

He nodded. "It *killed* twenty-one people and many horses as well. Over two million gallons of molasses flooded the streets, and they say the wave was over fifteen feet high. In addition to the deaths, Bostonians were injured by the hundreds."

I covered my gasp with my hand. Okay, so now I felt a little bad for saying collecting the molasses through seepage was gross. "What a way to go," I murmured.

"You can say that again. It wiped out houses as well as the structure supporting the elevated train. It literally destroyed everything in its way."

I slowly shook my head while picturing the scene. "Molasses seems thick and, well, it just appears like it would be slow-moving, doesn't it? Do you think some people outran it?"

Gus shook his head. "If you think about a jar of molasses, you're right. But over two million gallons? Think of it. The speed was estimated at thirty-five miles per hour. And many didn't see it coming; you don't exactly expect something like that to happen as you're walking down the street. It swallowed children coming home from school. Houses collapsed on the people inside, killing them instantly. One man who was eventually found was compared to a preserved body from Pompeii."

I shook my head. "How awful."

"That it was." We sat in silence for a few moments until Gus spoke again. "To bring this full circle, the rescue workers and cleanup crews who were laboring in the streets on January 16th were suddenly surprised at the ringing of church bells all across the city of Boston."

"In honor of the victims?"

He shook his head. "No. Nebraska had just voted on, and ratified, the 18th Amendment. Prohibition had become law, and the churches who'd lobbied for it were celebrating the victory. Those poor men and women who were literally up to their ankles in the making of rum had to wonder at the irony of it all."

"My God. Adding the ultimate insult to injury."

"Despite months of cleanup, it's said you could smell molasses in that section of the city for decades afterwards, especially on hot days."

"Which would have been a constant reminder to those people. There must have been lawsuits?"

"Yes. United States Industrial Alcohol was eventually found liable and paid out somewhere in the neighborhood of a million dollars. Each of the victims' families got about seven thousand dollars."

"Pennies in today's world," I mused.

"It was a good bit of money back then, but I'm sure those folks would have rather had their family members with them."

"Of course," I said sadly.

Gus toyed with the pages of his newspaper and glanced out the window as if he needed to ground himself in the present again. "So how long are you visiting Newport?"

I shrugged. "I'm not sure. It's kind of an open-ended thing." And then I remembered the reason for my visit. "Gus, if you've been here your whole life, did you happen to know Ava McGraw?"

His blue eyes grew wide, and it was clear I'd struck a nerve. I wondered if I'd upset him. *In town less than twenty-four hours and already terrorizing senior citizens. Nice job Meagan.*

"Why do you ask?"

Answering a question with a question. Hunh. "Ava McGraw owned the house my friend bought. That's where I'm staying."

Gus's posture stiffened. "That's where Charlie O'Neill died a couple days ago." It was a statement, not a question, and I wondered if Gus had known Charlie.

I realized I'd barely thought about the victim, but that was the name of the man who'd been at the bottom of Jeff's stairs. "Yes, that's right. Did you know him?"

Gus rubbed his face with his big left hand. "I did know him, and I knew Ava as well. She was a peach of a woman; they don't make 'em like her anymore. I hope your friend appreciates that beautiful house and the view."

I nodded. "He definitely does, Gus, but he was pretty upset about finding a body the minute he walked in."

"Well, I should think so," Gus responded. "Would you mind talking about it for a little bit?"

I cocked my head and quirked my lips. "You're not a reporter, are you?"

Gus roared with laughter, lighting up his face and making him appear ten years younger. "At my age, Meagan? Fat chance, I couldn't keep up with all the computers and cell phones and gadgets those people use. I'm not here to ask the questions. I'd just like to give you another little history lesson if you're up for it."

"That would be great," I said and genuinely meant it.

Eyes twinkling, Gus motioned to Shelley that we'd both like more coffee. She plopped a kiss on the top of his head before she walked away, and that's when I saw their profiles were nearly identical.

"You two are related," I said.

Gus beamed. "Shelley's my granddaughter. She's looking after me while going to school full-time. She's a good girl, that one. She's going to be an attorney and lock up assholes like the person who killed poor Charlie, pardon the language."

Okay, that was quite enough. "Gus, let's get a couple of things straights. First, I've heard and used words like *damn*, *asshole*, and much worse during my lifetime. So please don't apologize when you let a bad word slip out. It makes me feel like I have to be on my best behavior, and that's a tremendous effort for me."

Gus chuckled.

"Second, you think that Charlie was murdered? Why?"

Humor fled from his face. "I do think that. Charlie was in good shape; he didn't fall down some stairs. Something bad happened to him."

"I'd love to hear your thoughts."

"Are you sure you want to be bored by an old man when you could be running your errands?"

I leaned forward and lowered my voice. "Believe it or not, Gus, I'm a private investigator, and I'm here in town because of what happened at Jeff's—well, at Ava's—house. And something tells me you're going to be way more helpful than anyone else I might speak with today, especially the cops."

His eyes narrowed. "You don't like the police?"

"Oh, I love the police! And I respect what they do; don't get me wrong, please. I just seem to have a way of irritating them with my questions and then end up with no information. All I manage to do when I'm around the police is tick them off." I spread my arms wide. "Please, Gus, by all means—tell me your story."

He studied me for a moment and licked his lips. "Let me begin by telling you about Ava McGraw's nephew, Rusty, who spent most of his adult life in prison."

CHAPTER 4

THIRTY MINUTES LATER, I FELT LIKE I'D DISCOVERED A GOLD MINE. Ava McGraw had never married but had become the guardian of her nephew when his parents died in a car crash. She'd done her best but didn't really know how to relate to a ten-year-old who was mad at the world for taking his parents so abruptly.

Rusty muddled through school as a less-than-average student. He didn't participate in sports, and he also didn't really seem to have any close friends. He was introverted and kept to himself.

While raising him, Ava was always worried about finances. Toward the end of Rusty's senior year of high school, it was clear he had no desire to go on to college, for which Ava was quietly grateful. She didn't have the funds or the knowledge to help him further his education, and she'd always worried he'd get even more lost if he unsuccessfully attempted the world of higher education.

The summer after Rusty's graduation, Ave spoke with a neighbor who was a groundskeeper at an exclusive country club in the area to see if he might be able to take Rusty on for a while. He didn't have any room for the boy on his crew, but he was able to secure him a job as a caddy, even though Rusty had never hit a golf ball in his entire life. The man explained Rusty wouldn't need to do much more than carry the clubs, be deferential to the players, and keep his mouth shut. He'd have to learn the layout of the course and the greens, but that wouldn't be hard for him. Ava had thought it the perfect match.

"That summer turned Rusty bad," Gus said with a shake of his head.

"How so?" I asked.

"I don't know who it was, but he met someone at the fancy country club who sent him down the wrong path. And it was tough to blame the kid. He hadn't had a father figure in a long time, and someone took him under their wing, but it was to use him rather than help him."

Father figure? "It was an adult who got him in trouble? From a fancy country club? That seems odd."

"It's sick," Gus said flatly. "Rusty went to prison and would never say who was paying him for their little schemes. But I need to start at the beginning..."

Once the weather turned and the golf course closed for the season, Rusty started doing odd jobs around town. Even though he'd always struggled in school, he was a self-taught handyman who could do just about anything around a home. From repairing leaky plumbing, to replacing hardwood floors, to finishing abandoned electrical work, to building additions to the already huge residences the Newport elite owned, Rusty could do it all.

"You said he wasn't good in school. Was he licensed for any of those jobs?" I asked, ever the practical one.

Gus chuckled. "No, he didn't bother with that. But the funny thing is, a lot of the rich folk like to do things under the table, so it was never really an issue."

"So what happened?"

"Well unfortunately, the access to those fancy homes finally led to Rusty's demise. A series of break-ins occurred in Newport, and rumor had Rusty being behind most of them. On one fateful night, the family Rusty was robbing returned early from an overseas vacation, and the father caught Rusty in the upstairs office. The father had a gun on him, and after some type of struggle, the gun went off and killed the man instantly. The wife and kids were at the bottom of the stairs and started screaming when Rusty ran out of the room with blood all over him. They thought he was going to kill them as well, but he didn't. He froze. Rusty would have never dreamed of killing someone. He was a thief, not a murderer. He didn't even try to fight the charges. And the rest was history."

"What was he stealing?"

"Anything and everything, but he never stole any money. It was mostly...what should I call it? Trinkets. Collectibles. Antiques. That type of thing."

"Why would Rusty want stuff like that? You'd think he'd take money if he wanted to help out with finances. It doesn't sound like he'd have any black market connections to unload his wares."

"Exactly right, Meagan. That's how everyone knew someone was financing his small-time operation, but nobody ever figured out who it was, and Rusty never told."

Rusty had gone to jail over twenty years ago and was in his forties now. Ava McGraw and Charlie O'Neill's wife, Eileen, had always been friendly, so Charlie had been checking in on Ava ever since Rusty had gone to prison. Charlie would visit Rusty regularly as well, and he had his suspicions about the person behind Rusty's thieving activities, but Rusty never ratted out his backer. It drove Charlie nuts.

"But why would a rich dude hire Rusty to take...well, *stuff* from other rich people?

Gus shook his head. "I wish I knew what made people tick, Meagan. Some rich folks have to make sport of things like that because they're bored. Or because someone has something they want, so they just decide to take it. Who knows what goes through the minds of certain men?"

I was intrigued by the wealth of information Gus had unloaded on me, but it didn't seem to relate to Jeff's house just yet. "So why on earth would Charlie end up dead in my friend's house?"

Gus pursed his lips. "Maybe Charlie was looking for something," he said.

I tilted my head to the side until my left ear almost brushed my left shoulder. "Such as..?"

Gus reveled in the attention, and the animation in his expression again erased a decade from his face. "Supposedly, one of Rusty's final heists landed him quite a bounty."

I burst out laughing. It felt like I was sitting in a bad spy movie from the 1950s. "I'm sorry, Gus. I just haven't heard the word *bounty* in a long time."

"You won't be laughing when I finish. As the story goes, Rusty got to know the complete layout of the homes he worked in; he knew the alarm codes, and he got to know the owners' schedules and vacation habits. Prior to finishing his work at each of the homes, he would always leave a window in a neglected room unlocked. Nine times out of ten, those rich folks never changed their alarm code, and they never noticed they had an unlocked window in their house. Rusty would usually wait about six to eight months before he'd ever go back to a place to rob it. I guess he didn't want to be too obvious or something. Word has it he could crack a safe in less than two minutes, but usually what he took was wide out in the open."

"Who taught him how to crack a safe?"

Gus shrugged. "Wouldn't I like to know? He was definitely a handyman. Maybe he was self-taught, but I doubt it.

"So anyway, you know about the heist that got him busted. But it was the second to last job he did that has some people still wondering."

"Still wondering what?"

"Evidently he'd been given some type of tip about some valuables in a safe. Because on this job, it's said he had to crack the safe."

"Looking for valuables? Jewelry? What?"

"For coins."

"Ummm, okay? They must be some special coins," I said.

"If they even exist," Gus countered. "These accounts are a couple of decades old. You know how stories grow and get exaggerated."

"Do you know if the owner of the coins ever reported them missing?"

Gus smiled. "Not that I know of, but that's got an interesting twist, too. Rumor has it these coins came from the *Whydah*."

"The Who-dah?"

"A ship called the *Whydah*. It's the only pirate ship that sank off of Cape Cod, back in 1717, I think. It was initially a slave ship, but a pirate named Samuel "Black Sam" Bellamy overpowered the crew of the *Whydah* and then wreaked havoc along the east coast. Legend has it the ship was supposed to finish its voyage in Maine, but it was diverted to the Cape so Black Sam could see his mistress. As fate would have it, the ship ran into a nor'easter and sank before it made it. Only two of the crew of well over one hundred survived, and it's been said the ship carried at least 180 bags of gold and silver coins, in addition to all of the other loot that was stolen.

"Anyway, as the story goes, the man who Rusty robbed came across those coins in a not-so-legal way, and if that's true, then it might explain why they were never reported stolen. The guy couldn't very well admit the coins he had stolen had, in turn, been stolen from him. That would have left a lot of explaining to do. But the thing is...they've never been found."

Wow. So maybe Charlie had been snooping around the house looking for some type of long-lost treasure. Wouldn't that be something?

I smiled and had never been so glad to have invited someone to lunch. "Gus, this has been amazing. I could sit and talk all day, but I've got to go meet someone at my friend's house shortly. The guest list is an ongoing thing," I explained. "Is there any chance we could meet here again tomorrow morning?"

"Are you buying?"

I laughed. "Of course. And I'll probably be bringing my friends, if that's okay." I thought of Kayla and thought I should try to prepare him. "One of them is a girlfriend of mine, and well...it seems you're pretty conscientious about bad language. Let's just say she *isn't*, so I'll apologize in advance. She's a great girl, but she doesn't hold her tongue at all."

There was a twinkle in Gus's eye. "She sounds like a pistol. I'll be fine, but I appreciate you telling me."

"Then we'll see you at 11:00 tomorrow morning?"

Gus nodded. "I'll look forward to it, Meagan. It's been nice talking with you."

After leaving breakfast money and a hefty tip for Shelley, I got up to walk away. But I heard Gus utter something after I'd taken a few steps, so I stopped and turned around. "Did you say something, Gus?"

"I said Mrs. O'Neill might be able to shed some light on the situation."

"Who?" I frowned.

"Charlie's widow."

My stomach dropped. I felt terrible I hadn't wondered about Charlie O'Neill's life or family. I'd been so focused on Jeff and the house I hadn't thought of someone who was undoubtedly going through terrible pain right now.

"You're right, Gus. Thanks for the advice. I should have already thought of that." I headed out the door, enveloped in thoughts of pirate ships and widows and dead bodies.

CHAPTER 5

I WAS BARELY AT JEFF'S HOUSE FIFTEEN MINUTES WHEN Kayla's car tore down the lane, kicking up dirt and sand behind her on the twists and turns to the house. She even managed to fish-tail the vehicle before coming to a stop and then had to wait for the swirling dust to subside before getting out. Tropical Storm Kayla had arrived.

I turned to let the men know the newest houseguest had arrived. Doob bounced from foot to foot, looking past me out the window and craning his neck so hard I thought it might snap off. If it hadn't been for Jeff's new furniture, Doob would have jumped up and down on the couch, screaming in glee.

"Please don't wet yourself," I said dryly.

"Too late," Doob replied and waggled his brows.

"My goodness, this girl must be something else to get that type of reaction," Jeff said good-naturedly. "Thank God I bought some real dinnerware earlier."

"Calm yourselves, gentlemen. If you're too obvious, she'll have you rubbing her feet and hand-feeding her grapes within five minutes of crossing the threshold."

"I'm in!" Doob scampered toward the door. "I'm going to go help with her bags."

Jeff and I waited in the doorway while Kayla saddled Doob down with various bags and suitcases in all shapes, colors, and sizes. Jeff leaned into me and whispered, "How long is she staying?" Thankfully he had a grin on his face.

"I tried to warn you," I whispered back and giggled.

"This is fucking gorgeous!" Kayla squealed as she walked up the steps. She looked adorable. Her long blonde hair was pulled back in a ponytail, and she had on huge, round Coach sunglasses. Her ensemble was a chocolate-colored suede jacket, coupled with khaki pants tucked into a pair of knee-length brown leather boots, and a scarf elegantly tangled around her neck. She looked like she just stepped out of a fashion magazine. I gave her a huge hug and introduced her to Jeff. She gave him an oh-so-obvious once-over and smiled coquettishly. He turned a million shades of red while Doob waited patiently at the bottom of the stairs like a forgotten hotel valet.

"Shall we move this inside before Doob collapses?" I suggested. He looked at me appreciatively as he hauled Kayla's belongings up the front steps.

After getting her bags deposited alongside my things in the guest bedroom, we all gathered in the recently-renovated white and chrome kitchen. The stainless steel appliances and chef's stove, complete with six burners, were intimidating. The room had a *presence* and made you feel like you better do it justice, should you dare to cook anything. There was a huge island in the middle, with a beautiful black and gray granite countertop, and Jeff had purchased some gorgeous bar stools to surround two sides of it, with a built in wine rack on yet another side.

I glanced at my watch and said, "It's five o'clock somewhere, right?"

"Break out the booze," Kayla agreed. "I've got something heavy to discuss, and a couple of pops will probably help."

Odd. My friend was never one to get rattled; she never had *heavy* things to discuss. She was unflappable, wild and carefree, and threw caution to the wind at every opportunity. And I loved her for that. So this statement, coming from her, concerned me. But I didn't press.

"First things first," I said. "Are we eating in tonight? If so, we don't need to pick a driver, but if we go out—"

"I'd love to fire up this kitchen," Jeff said, looking around excitedly. "I can do some steaks, chicken and baked potatoes if you guys want to fill in the blanks with a salad and garlic bread. We'll figure out dessert later. Sound good?"

We all voiced our approval while Kayla leaned toward me and whispered, "And he cooks, too. Holy shit, you've hit the jackpot."

I rolled my eyes. "No jackpot, Kayla. He's a friend. But I've got to say I know something is on your mind because you actually lowered your voice just now."

She wrinkled her nose. "So?"

"So…that shows *tact,* a trait you never exhibit. You're going to need to tell me what's wrong very soon so I can get my friend back."

"Well, fuck you too!" she boomed. "Get me something to drink before I shove some tact right up your ass."

I looked over to see Doob's massive smile. "Doob, there's not going to be a catfight, so calm yourself."

His happy expression crumbled.

I got up and opened the enormous refrigerator. "Okay, please submit your drink orders, and I'll get us started."

Fifteen minutes later, I'd made a pitcher of sangria for Kayla, a margarita for myself, and I'd set Doob up with a rum and Coke while Jeff downed some Guinness. Blech. Even looking at that dark beer sends my taste buds into a tizzy. While I mixed drinks, Jeff busied himself with the main course and Kayla threw together a big salad with the healthy food Jeff had purchased the day before. Doob showed off his Iowa-cute by setting the table and putting glasses of water at each of the place settings. He even added slices of lemon to the waters and then started a fire in Jeff's massive stone fireplace in the middle of the living room. The open floor plan allowed for a view of the crackling flames from the kitchen, and I relaxed, thinking how Jeff's new place was feeling more like a home every minute.

Dinner was wonderful. Everything from the presentation, to the delicious smells of the food and the fire, to the company was just right. Comfortable. Warm. It was safe to say Jeff did right by his magnificent kitchen. The conversation flowed easily, and while I was the common denominator of the group, the four of us chatted as if we'd all known each other for years.

After polishing off some ice cream and clearing the table, we moved our overfed selves into the living room and each found a cozy spot to stare into the flames. There's something peaceful and mesmerizing about a fire, and I thought we all might fall asleep in our respective locations without another word.

As my eyes grew heavy, I heard Kayla's voice from the other end of the couch we were sharing. "I don't mean to be a buzzkill with this whole Zen scene we've got going, but I really need to talk with you about something, Meagan."

I willed my eyes open and straightened in my chair. "Do you want to go upstairs? If so, you might need to carry me."

She hitched a shoulder and said, "I dunno. If the guys don't mind, maybe this is something we could all hash out."

I looked at Doob, head flopped back on the oversized leather chair and light snores emitting from his wide open mouth. I glanced at Jeff, who looked back at me and shrugged as if to say, *why not*?

"Well, it looks like Doob is down for the count, but Jeff, if you don't mind, we'll stay parked here by the fire. It's too comfortable to move."

He nodded. "If it gets way girly, I reserve the right to remove myself from the room," he said with a grin. But I think he was only half-kidding.

Kayla shook her head. "It's not girly at all, I promise." When she didn't elaborate after the promise, I'd had enough.

"All right girlfriend, spit it out. I can't deal with you being morose and cryptic. It goes against nature. It breaks laws of the universe. It's counterclockwise, it's—"

"Meagan, shut the fuck up."

Call me crazy, but that somehow made me feel better. I watched as Kayla took a swig of her sangria and a deep breath.

"So here's the deal. Jeff, I bored you with my life story earlier, so you both know I opened my own insurance company after quitting my bullshit job last spring."

We nodded.

"Well, early on when I worked at that other shit-hole, there was an insurance claim that came in on a four-year-old girl." Kayla took another sip of her drink, and I noticed her hand shook, the ice cubes tinkling against the glass in the silence of the room. I glanced at Jeff, who studied her closely. We both stayed silent and waited for her to go on.

"They say cops and detectives—you'll probably understand this, Meagan—always have a case in their careers that never leaves them. That's what this claim was like for me.

"This beautiful blonde-haired, blue-eyed little girl drowned in her family's pool..." Her voice caught, and I actually thought my strong-willed, loud-mouthed, bigger-than-life friend was going to lose it. But she didn't. She kept talking. "...and the mother had a $250,000 life insurance policy on the sweet thing."

She stopped and stared down into her sangria, but she didn't take a drink. It didn't feel like she was done with her story, but it also didn't seem like she planned to say anything more.

Sliding down the couch, I put my hand on her free one. "I'm sorry," I murmured, hoping to prompt her back into story-telling mode.

"That's a horrible tragedy," Jeff added from his couch.

She nodded. "It was terrible. And I'm afraid it's going to happen again. At least he's going to try to do it again."

Hunh?

It was completely out of character, but I managed to remain quiet for a few moments. I glanced over at Jeff, and he slowly hitched a shoulder and tilted his head as if to say he didn't know what she meant, either.

"Okay sweetie, you're going to have to fill in a few blanks. You're clearly upset, and I want to help. But you've got to tell me why you think something like this will happen again, and who is the *he* you're referring to?"

She shook her head in disgust as she continued to gaze into her drink. "*He* is the asshole who was engaged to the lady who filed the claim. *He* is the one who convinced her to take a $250,000 life insurance policy out on her little girl. And..." Kayla's voice cracked, and I squeezed her hand. She suddenly tossed her head in the air, as if to proclaim that tears were not going to get the better of her. "...*he* was the one who found little Cassie in the pool at three o'clock in the morning."

Something twisted in my gut. "Kayla, what are you saying?"

She gave me a hard look. "What I'm saying is that fucking asshole had something to do with Cassie's death, probably *everything* to do with her death."

I studied her intently. "Okay, that's some heavy stuff, my friend. I'm not saying I don't believe you, but that's a big accusation. Wasn't there an investigation?"

"There was. They determined Cassie got up by herself in the middle of the night, got herself outside through a locked door, got herself through the locked fence that surrounded the pool, and drowned."

I sighed. "Okay. So if that's what the investigation determined, why do you think otherwise?"

"Because number one, he was fucking creepy when they came into our office—"

"You can't suspect someone based on the creepy factor," I interrupted.

She held up a finger. "And, number *two*, he and his *new* girlfriend strolled into my agency two days ago to inquire about life insurance for her three-year-old-son."

I narrowed my eyes. "*Sorry?*"

"Yep. I about shit."

"Well obviously he and Cassie's mom didn't work out?"

"Evidently. Because of the engagement, I'm sure he thought he'd be in on a big payday, but I heard Cassie's mom packed up and left town after the drowning. And she left his sorry ass behind."

"So he just moved on to the next single mom?"

"They met online," she said. "I'm sure the asshole purposely scrolled through all the eligible females, looking for one with a kid. Most jerks run from single moms. This guy is preying on them."

"Poor lady," Jeff said sympathetically.

"This is a little off-topic, but you saying they met online made me think of something. Don't most people buy insurance online nowadays?" I asked.

She shrugged. "Some do, some don't. Depending on the company they eventually go through, they might need to see an agent because of the amount of money involved. Other times there are underwriting factors where an in-person visit makes the most sense. It can help with the rates."

I nodded and steered her back to the story. "So they walked into your office, you managed to keep your composure, then what?"

"Okay, so they were supposedly inquiring about insurance on both the mom and son, but I knew what he was up to. The asshole did most of the talking and said his girlfriend wanted to provide for her son if something ever happened to her, and he went on to talk about how it might make sense to buy insurance on the kid since life insurance on children is inexpensive. He was trying to not act too pushy, but I could see through his bullshit. The woman was completely swept up in his nonsense, and all I wanted to do was scream for her to get the fuck away from him as quickly as possible."

"What did you do?" Jeff asked, beating me to the punch.

She sighed. "I tried to take it all in stride and not act too rattled. I took their information down and said it would take me a couple of days to research some quotes and I'd let them know what I'd come up with."

I cocked my head. "So the guy obviously didn't recognize you?"

She shook her head quickly. "Nope. Remember when I went through the way-too-professional phase when I first started at the other insurance place?"

I thought for a second and then laughed. "I do. You darkened and straightened your hair, and you plastered it back in a ponytail every day. I remember it looked like it was pulling your skin off. Then you did the square, black Superman glasses, too."

She smiled a little bit. "Yeah, I looked like a fucking priss, but I was trying to develop a certain image."

I looked at her free-flowing, wild, long, curly blonde hair and her glasses-less face and thought she was stunning. "I like you better this way. The other look was so *not* you."

"You look great," Jeff blurted, and both Kayla's and my head snapped simultaneously to look over at him. He shrunk inward and seemed surprised at his own outburst. "Just saying," he added quietly and did that slow shoulder shrug again.

Kayla smiled demurely and said, "Thanks. But this isn't about me. I just look different than I did back then, and I wasn't the lead broker on the account on that other claim. I was the assistant. Anyway, the asshole definitely doesn't remember me."

"Okay. What's next?"

She shrugged. "I'm not sure. But I'm going to stop him. Whatever it takes." Kayla's face had a hard edge I'd never seen before.

"Can't you go to the cops?" I asked.

She gave me a look. "Go to the cops with *what*, Meagan? They need proof. The other claim was investigated, and we paid. Case closed. But I had a creepy feeling then, and everything I've ever thought about that fucking scumbag was confirmed when he walked into my office the other day. I have nothing to go on except my gut, but I would stake my life I'm right about this guy." She paused for a moment and said, "I hope it doesn't come to that, though."

The fire popped loudly, startling me and making me flinch. "I can see you're serious, Kayla. And if you're right about this guy, I promise I'll help. We just need to use our heads."

Jeff nodded. "I'll second that. If he's as bad a dude as you think, you don't want to play in that league. There's a right and wrong way to approach this. Just promise me you'll both be careful."

I suddenly heard Doob chuckling, and his head lolled down from the back of the chair. "Kayla and Meagan, careful? Jeff, you've got a lot to learn, my friend."

CHAPTER 6

Tuesday, November 5th

THE NEXT MORNING I WOKE WITH KAYLA SPOONED UP BEHIND ME, and it was somewhat disconcerting. I slowly reached for the arm she had draped over my waist, and I tried to disentangle myself without waking her. No such luck.

"It's fucking freezing in here!" Kayla grumbled and burrowed under the covers. "Get one of those men or Sampson up here immediately. Hell, get all three of them up here; I need some friggin' body heat."

Something told me all three of them were up for the job, but logic won out. "How about I try to find the thermostat instead? And in the meantime, why don't you put some clothes on? You're sleeping in dental floss."

"I don't sleep in burlap sacks like you, Meagan. My stuff is sexy."

"Well, sexy equals cold." I found the thermostat, and it was set at sixty-nine degrees, which I promptly shared with Kayla.

"Oooh, I like that number," Kayla said with a meow in her voice. "Go get that Jeff up here, and I'll get this room up to eighty in no time."

I yanked a black Iowa Hawkeye sweatshirt out of my suitcase—a gift from Doob—and threw it at her. "Calm yourself, Horny Hornster, you're not disrupting this house. We've got work to do today."

Kayla groaned. "Always working, no wonder you never get laid. Are you going to make breakfast?"

"Lovely segue," I replied.

Both Doob and Kayla were bottomless pits when it came to eating, and I couldn't fathom how they both stayed so skinny. "This morning we're meeting a guy for breakfast. I met him in town yesterday, and I think he might help solve the dead body issue."

Kayla stretched her arms and yawned. "Is he hot?"

Good grief. "He's probably in his late sixties or early seventies, and he's a sweet man, Kayla. Try not to terrorize him, please. I already warned him about your foul mouth."

She wrinkled her nose. "I need aspirin and a *lot* of water. How much did we drink last night?"

"More than enough," I replied. "Jump in the shower, and I'll find you some aspirin and a bottled water. We're meeting Gus at 11:00, and then I'm going to try to meet with the dead guy's widow after that."

Kayla harrumphed as she got out of bed and threw one of the pillows toward the headboard. "This vacation sucks," she grumbled.

My eyebrow shot up. "Vacation? Kayla, you invited yourself out here, and I told you I'd be working. This is not a vacation, it's my life."

"Well, your life sucks," she said and went across the hall into the bathroom. She's a smidge bitchy in the morning.

I padded downstairs to find Doob and Sampson sprawled on the floor in front of the television, remnants of food all over the new, beautiful rug that covered Jeff's hardwood floors.

"Doob! What the hell? This isn't my place! Get off the floor and go find a Dustbuster or something."

A voice from behind me said, "No worries, Meagan. At least half of that mess is mine, probably more. It'll clean up, no big deal." I turned to see Jeff looking almost as scary as Doob, with his mile-high hair, and stubble mixed with crumbs all over his face. He had a full glass of chocolate milk and a box of Hot Tamales. "I love how you guys eat. This is living."

I looked back at Doob, who stuck his tongue out. Shaking my head, I went into the kitchen and grabbed some crap of my own—a frosted strawberry Pop Tart and a Diet Coke. Then I remembered Kayla.

"Does anyone have aspirin?" I yelled, digging for a bottled water out of the massive refrigerator. I really needed to win the lottery. I'd never seen a bigger refrigerator, nor had I ever seen a *full* one. It was a thing to behold.

"Advil, Midol, and Tylenol are in the half bath," Jeff replied.

Wow. A full medicine cabinet, too?

Doob mumbled something, but I couldn't understand him, undoubtedly because his mouth was full. Walking back into the family room, I asked him to repeat himself.

"Where's Kayla?" Doob repeated as he turned a brilliant shade of red. Jeff sat up straighter, and Sampson's ears even perked up a little.

My *God*. Every male in the house was in the throes of anticipation.

"She's in the shower, and the bathroom door is bolted shut, so stay the hell away from the upstairs. It wouldn't hurt you guys to mix in some soap and water, either. We're meeting a friend for breakfast at 11:00."

"You buying?" Doob asked.

I threw my arms in the air. "Of course I am, Doob. It's not like anyone else here has any money, right?" Jeff chuckled as I headed toward the bathroom to get some aspirin for Kayla.

Jeff called after me. "A friend?"

"You'll like him, I promise," I responded over my shoulder.

At 10:30, we all piled into Doob's Mercedes and headed to the picturesque little town. We found a parking spot easily enough, which would never happen in the peak summer months, and read the specials on the chalkboard outside the diner before going inside.

Shelley greeted me warmly, and I introduced her to the group. She showed us to a table and said Gus hadn't arrived yet. Doob and I ordered super-duper-maximum-sized coffees, Jeff ordered an orange juice, and Kayla ordered a hot tea.

We were perusing the menu when I saw Gus make his entrance. He was adorable and looked like he'd dressed in his Sunday best. Shelley gave him a hug and peck on the cheek, and walked him over to our table.

After the introductions, Gus pulled up a chair beside Kayla and gave her a wink. She rewarded him with a big smile and said, "What's shaking pops?"

Good grief. He looked over at me and tilted his head toward Kayla. "You weren't kidding about this one," he said with a gleam in his eye. Add another male to the list of Kayla's admirers.

Kayla sighed. "I'm sure Meagan warned you I will seduce you with my feminine wiles and then leave you to blow in the wind." She leaned in and feigned a husky whisper. "But you'll have a great time along the way."

Gus's laughter boomed through the café as Shelley deposited beverages for everyone at the table. After ordering our food, Gus brought the rest of the group up-to-date on what he'd shared with me yesterday. And then he surprised me with some new information.

"I have a friend on the police force here in town," Gus said. "It sounds like they're going to rule Charlie's death an accident, so the case will probably be closed soon."

Jeff looked skeptical. "They sure wrapped it up quickly. I knew that would happen," he said with a shake of his head.

Gus shrugged as he set down his coffee cup. "He was an old man, he was at the bottom of the stairs, and his neck was broken, Jeff. It's a horrible thing, but if it looks like a duck and quacks like a duck..." But there wasn't much conviction in his voice, and I remember what he'd said yesterday about Charlie possibly being killed.

Jeff still didn't look convinced, so I jumped in. "Well, that's why I'm here. If there's something more to this, I'll find it. It really might be an accident like they're saying. And that would be a *good* thing, wouldn't it? It would be better than having a murder victim in your house."

Jeff nodded. "Of course. I dunno, it just didn't *feel* like an accident. I don't know how to explain it." He lifted that shoulder like he does when he's not sure what to think. "Heck, maybe the poor guy was just poking around and fell, and that was that."

Shelley appeared with a tray of food, and our conversation turned to lighter subjects. I noticed Kayla trying hard to be her usual self, but she seemed a little withdrawn, and I knew we'd have to revisit our discussion from last night very soon. I just didn't know how we were going to handle that situation, but first things first. There was bacon to devour.

After everyone but Gus had worked themselves into food comas, we sat around staring vacantly into space, and I found myself hoping someone had a wagon or a wheelbarrow or something to drag our gluttonous selves back to the car. As the older and much wiser one, Gus looked around at each of us and smirked.

"Should I be concerned I'm going to walk in here tomorrow and find all of you in the same seats and the same clothes? Would you like me to stop by later with some blankets and pillows?"

"Yes, please," Doob said automatically, and Gus laughed his big, full belly laugh.

I shook my head. "No, we've got to move at some point. Kayla and I are going to go see Mrs. O'Neill today." Kayla pulled a face, but I glared at her. "You're going, princess."

"I'm not good around sad people," Kayla whined.

"That's because you're out of practice. Plus, we need to talk more about our *topic* from last night."

She nodded grudgingly, and we all bid Gus farewell. After getting back to the house, Doob and Jeff changed into sweatpants and plopped down on their respective couches. I was pretty certain Kayla and I would find them fused to the furniture when we returned later in the day.

Kayla and I arrived at Eileen O'Neill's house and expressed sincere sympathies for her loss. I'd called Eileen the day before and had been shocked she'd agreed to meet with me today, since Charlie's funeral was just this morning, but she said anyone who would help find out why Charlie had been in that house was welcome in her home anytime.

Despite her grief, Eileen was a gracious hostess, saying she had more food than she knew what to do with. Neighbors and friends had been stopping by for three days straight, and casserole dishes and Tupperware were jammed to maximum capacity in her refrigerator. The smell of coffee permeated the house, and I accepted a cup as Eileen served us coffee cake. Kayla and I exchanged *we're not hungry* glances, but I would have eaten a full-grown elephant if this woman had put it in front of me. It was simply the right thing to do.

I quickly developed a soft spot for Eileen because her thick Irish brogue was so much like my Uncle Larry's, which always became heavier after a few cocktails. Eileen didn't seem to know exactly why Charlie had been at the old McGraw house, but something in her sad, earnest face made me think she was holding out on us. I wanted her to trust us, but that was a lot to expect from a woman who'd just buried her husband of forty-seven years. Blurting out I thought she was lying was probably not the way to her heart, so I let the conversation go where it might, and three little nuggets of information came out of the visit.

The first was when she gave me several small boxes of personal items from Ava McGraw's house. Charlie had kept them after her death and intended to give them to Rusty if he was ever paroled.

The second tidbit of information she mentioned was that Charlie had visited Rusty in jail the day before Charlie disappeared. Eileen reported him missing just twenty-four hours before Jeff got to the house, which I found to be curious timing. Eileen said she'd known something was wrong, when Charlie didn't come home, as they'd never once during their marriage spent a night apart from each other.

Sigh. Where in the heck were love stories like that anymore?

When I said I found the visit to Rusty to be more than coincidence, Eileen said Charlie visited him several times a year and didn't think there was anything unusual about it. I remained unconvinced but didn't want to argue with the kind woman.

The third thing Eileen shared, which I found quite intriguing, was Charlie had once been a firefighter, and he'd participated in the Boston Marathon every year for the past twenty years. Even though he was over seventy years old, it sounded like the man had been in pretty good shape, and it didn't seem like a fall down the stairs would end him.

On our way out, Kayla and I thanked the sweet lady for her time and again expressed sympathies for her loss. The feeling she hadn't told us everything was still in the forefront of my mind, and I gave her a hug and placed a business card in her hand. "Eileen, if you think of anything else—anything at all—I won't betray your confidence or get you into any type of trouble. You have my word on that."

She studied me for a long moment and gave me a smile. Kayla and I started across the porch and down the front stairs of her home.

"Oh, girls!" Eileen called after us as she stood in the front door.

Thank God.

I turned, waiting for her to continue. She tentatively stepped onto the porch and stopped, gazing at her feet. "There is one last thing, although I don't know if it'll be helpful. I probably should have mentioned it when you were inside." Her shoulders sagged. "I guess it's been a long day."

Placing my hand on her arm, I tried to sound as soothing as possible. "Of course it has, Eileen. We can come back another time. You've been more than gracious, and you should get some rest."

Eileen shook her head and gestured toward the dark, wicker furniture that was still on the front porch, despite the chill in the weather as of late. The set was comprised of a bench and two matching chairs and looked to be something straight out of Pier One, complete with coordinated outdoor pillows. I sat in one of the chairs and watched as Kayla ignored the furniture and instead plopped on the swing on the other side of the porch. Her long legs pumped just a little bit to get the swing moving at a slow, steady pace, and watching her made me smile. When had America moved to backyards and decks off the kitchen? There was something very nostalgic and sweet about a front porch.

Eileen took the chair opposite mine, wringing her hands. Despite that, I sensed she was going to soldier on. "I think I just needed to get out of the house for a little bit. It seems a lot bigger with Charlie gone."

I didn't know what to say to that, so we sat for a few minutes in the solitude while the swing squeaked slightly under Kayla's rhythmic rocking. It was a lovely fall evening, and if Eileen needed to sit here all night, then I was in for the duration.

Finally, Eileen cleared her throat and said, "It's been an eternity since I've talked about this, and I don't even know if it's relevant or not. It's been such a long time..." Her gaze shifted to the horizon, and I watched a steely glint come into her eyes.

"Take your time," I murmured, and Kayla nodded in the background. We didn't want to interfere with the fragile atmosphere.

I watched Eileen's jaw set hard, and then she looked around, almost as if to see if someone could overhear her. "Well, you've probably heard the stories about Rusty McGraw's—uh, *activities*—that landed him in jail."

"We have."

"Well, Charlie always felt a little bad for Rusty, obviously. He thought Rusty might have done some jobs for people who...well, people who didn't want to get their hands dirty. People with money." Her voice had reduced to a near-whisper when she said the last few words.

"That happens a lot," I said, trying to encourage her. "Is there someone else we might want to speak with about Rusty's *activities*? Maybe someone who could give a little insight as to what Charlie was doing at the McGraw house?"

Eileen continued to wring her hands and look around some more. When she spoke, her voice was again very soft. "Well, not that you could get near Mr. Hoity-Toity himself, but Charlie always thought Malcolm Johnson had something to do with more than one or two of Rusty's more lucrative antics."

My eyes bulged. "As in Malcolm Gage Johnson, the oil tycoon?"

Kayla's eyes narrowed as she glided back and forth. "There's no oil in Newport, dipshit." Then, in a rare moment of self-awareness, she glanced at Eileen and said, "Sorry, ma'am."

Eileen chuckled. "Well, the family didn't strike oil in Newport; you're right about that, Kayla. Malcolm Gage Johnson lives in one of the mansions on Ocean Drive, but he's only there for a few months a year. He has houses all over the world."

"Rough life," I grumbled, getting a little sick of being surrounded by money at every turn.

Eileen nodded. "His granddaddy struck it rich during the oil boom in the early 1900s near Beaumont, Texas, and the rest, as they say, is history. I don't think Malcolm has ever dirtied his hands during his entire privileged life. But he's a greedy coot, and it's been rumored that even with all of his money, he always wanted more. He's older now, but in his time he was a huge gambler and a rumored womanizer, and Charlie was convinced Malcolm used to hire Rusty to steal other rich people's trinkets just for the sport of it. Pardon my French, but Charlie used to say Malcolm would *get off* on things like that. He liked stealing precious items and taking them to one of his other homes where no one would ever know where they came from. And Charlie didn't like Malcolm involving Rusty and treating him as a pawn in his little games."

"Eileen, Malcolm sounds like a total jerk, but what does his hiring Rusty over twenty years ago have to do with Charlie's death? Do you have anything that might tie the incidents together?"

She looked tentative. "No, but you said that anything might be important—"

I nodded and told myself to quit interrupting. "You're absolutely right. Please continue."

"Well, obviously, this was all before my time, but back in the day, Charlie was a bit of a ladies' man." She sighed and looked wistful. "He was so handsome and friendly. Charlie could have sold ice to an Eskimo. He never met a stranger; he was simply the perfect man."

Watching her eyes twinkle while talking about her husband, I became strangely jealous of this woman who'd buried her soulmate only hours before. While I wouldn't have traded places with her for the world, I couldn't help but think of what life would have been like with Tom, had fate played a different card. I was envious of this woman who had a lifetime of memories while the man I had pledged my heart to had been murdered on our wedding day.

"Meg? You okay?" Kayla was looking at me tenderly, an uncommon reaction for her. Like Doob, she can sometimes read my mind.

I stammered. "Oh...um, yes. I'm sorry, Eileen. I was just thinking how difficult this all must be for you. Please go on." Kayla's eyes were full of compassion, and I wanted to cover her face with one of the decorative pillows to avoid seeing the pity.

Thankfully Eileen continued. "Anyway, Charlie dated Malcolm's younger sister way back when. Her name was Charlotte. Kind of cute, right? Charlie and Charlotte."

I smiled but didn't comment.

"She and Charlie went on a couple of dates, and I don't want to speak ill of the poor dear. But to hear Charlie's side of it, Charlotte was a little *off*."

I cocked my head. "What do you mean by 'off'?"

She shrugged. "Nowadays, they have names for everything and every disorder. Today they would probably diagnose Charlotte's condition as bipolar and medicate her accordingly. But, back then, Charlie said she'd have severe mood changes, and he really wasn't interested in those types of shenanigans. What is the word the kids use nowadays? Drama. He didn't want to deal with the drama. So he broke it off with her, but it didn't go well."

"What happened?"

Eileen wrung her hands again. "Well, even though they'd only gone to a couple of dinners, Charlotte took the breakup really badly, and she ended up overdosing on a bottle of pills."

"She died?" I asked.

Eileen nodded. "She did. Charlie felt horrible, but he didn't have anything to do with it. That poor girl needed professional help; no one knew how bad it was."

"That's terrible," I commented. "Is it safe to assume Malcolm and his family held Charlie responsible?"

Eileen shrugged. "I don't know about the family, but Malcolm certainly did. When Charlie arrived at the wake, Malcolm left the receiving line and physically dragged Charlie outside. He told Charlie he'd kill him if it was the last thing he ever did."

"Did Charlie tell the police?"

She shook her head sadly. "No, he didn't. He felt sorry for Malcolm and thought his emotions had gotten the better of him. Charlie left the wake and didn't go to the funeral or gravesite service. He wanted to pay his respects, but he didn't want to make it harder on the family."

"What's hard to imagine is that Malcolm would have still been harboring that type of resentment against Charlie. How long ago was it?"

Eileen smiled sadly. "Well, Charlie and I met shortly after his run-in with Malcolm, and we had a whirlwind courtship. We married within a year of Charlotte's death, and we were together for over forty-five years, so it's been a very long time, my dear."

"That just doesn't make sense to me," I said. "But I guess revenge can be a powerful motivator."

Eileen looked thoughtful. "That it can. But at this point, you only know half the story."

Hunh? "Okay, what's the rest of it?" I asked and wondered why all of this was coming up after we'd left the house.

Flitting her eyes back and forth, Eileen lowered her voice so much that Kayla and I both had to lean in to hear her. "Charlie was the oldest in his family, and there were ten kids." She glanced at me and smiled. "You're of the freckled variety, so you understand."

I felt my freckles jump to attention and smiled. "Yes, we Irish are known for our breeding."

"Charlie's youngest sister was named Patricia, and she was extremely beautiful. She was fifteen years younger than Charlie and the flower girl in our wedding. Just a precious little thing," she said wistfully. It seemed her mind had gone back to her wedding day, and I'm sure it all felt like a breath ago in time.

I smiled, and she continued.

"The whole thing was odd because it was *years* after Charlotte's suicide, when Patricia was all grown up, that it became fairly well-known Patricia had become one of Malcolm's...uh..."

"They were having an affair?" Kayla jumped in as only Kayla can do.

Eileen's cheeks colored. "They were. And Patty was a good girl for the most part, maybe a little wild. She didn't mean to get messed up in being a mistress and all of that type of thing. But she'd been recently divorced, and well, I don't know..." She started wringing her hands again, and my impatient side wanted her to get to the point, but I again reminded myself this was a sweet lady who'd just buried her husband. It's sad I have to tell myself to *not* be an asshole at times.

"It's okay," I reassured her. "Kayla and I certainly aren't anyone's judge and jury. Especially Kayla," I said with a wink.

This resulted in a middle finger from Kayla that Eileen didn't see.

I continued. "Even though Patty sounds lovely, it seems to me Malcolm was with her just to mess with Charlie. Does that sound reasonable?"

Eileen nodded. "Malcolm's wife, Barbara, has always preferred to spend most of her time in Texas. She's a southern belle at heart. Anyway, I think she's known from day one about Malcolm's little trysts but forever looked the other way." Eileen shrugged. "It wouldn't have worked for me, but everyone is different."

"Different strokes," I mused.

"Yes, well, it was over thirty years ago that Patricia became—let's say *involved*—with Malcolm. She would have been somewhere in her mid-twenties at the time. She was a redhead with stunning green eyes and porcelain skin. It wasn't surprising any man would try to woo her, but in hindsight, it was very obvious what Malcolm was up to.

"Anyway, Patty didn't come out and tell Charlie and me who she was seeing, but we could see a change in her over those months. She appeared very happy and had a lot of new jewelry and lovely clothes. We had her over for dinner one night, and Charlie figured out what was going on, and he was furious. He called her a horrible name..." Eileen's face colored.

"Slut? Whore? Harlot? Mata Hari? Concubine?" Kayla suggested, tact a non-issue as usual. I glowered at her for adding to Eileen's obvious discomfort.

Eileen cast her eyes downward. "The W word," she mumbled. "He told her no sister of his was going to be a W of a rich playboy, and Patty screamed back at him that she was having fun and being treated well for a change and he needed to stay out of it. Charlie yelled that Malcolm was just using her to get back at him and he'd never pay her any attention otherwise. Patty stormed out of the house. It was just awful."

"It sounds like it. I'm sorry, Eileen. What happened then?" I wanted her to get to the end of this story as soon as possible, for her sake and ours. She was wiped out, and I needed to find out if she had any relevant information.

"We didn't see her for a few months, at which point she'd been seeing Malcolm for about a year. But one night—it was pouring rain—I will never, ever forget it as long as I live. That night, Patty rang our doorbell. Her face was all puffy and bloody. She had a black eye swollen shut; a cut lip; and bruises on her face." Eileen shuddered, and this time, I didn't push.

Kayla even managed to stay silent, for which I said a quick prayer of thanks.

"Forgive me," Eileen mumbled and her eyes filled with tears. "It's been such a long day." Her hand went to her mouth. The tears overflowed, spilling down her cheeks.

That was enough. I grabbed her in a bear hug and said I'd walk her back to the front door and get her settled with a nice cup of tea.

But as suddenly as the emotion came, a defiant flicker flared in the good woman. "No, I'm going to finish my story, Meagan."

"Okay," I said but kept a firm grip on her hand.

"Naturally, Charlie went berserk. Never mind the fact he and Patty had fought months before. He wasn't the type to see his baby sister's face mangled and not do anything about it. Who is?"

I dubbed that a rhetorical question and let her carry on.

"To make a long story short, Patty discovered Malcolm had found himself another..." Eileen actually looked over at Kayla and waited for her to fill in the blank.

"Slut? Whore? Harlot? Mata Hari? Concubine?" Kayla spouted, as if reciting her only lines in a play.

"Yes, those things. He'd moved on to another young girl who was just as beautiful as Patricia. That's when she finally figured out that smarts and good conversation didn't matter to Malcolm. He only wanted a trophy on his arm. He'd use them and discard them, and brains were definitely not required. And sadly, she'd realized Charlie had been right and Malcolm had just been using her to get back at him."

"But who beat her up?"

Eileen looked surprised that I'd asked. "Malcolm did. Who else?"

I shrugged, my hands spread wide. "Well, he used Rusty to do his thieving. You said he didn't like to get his hands dirty."

"This time he did. Patty confronted Malcolm and his *wife* at a little restaurant on Thames Street in Newport. Patty was always one for theatrics. After she'd had a few drinks, she evidently went in and caused quite a scene. Malcolm excused himself from the table, said he'd see to it that his driver got her home. Publicly, he was polite and kind as he escorted her out of the restaurant and into the alley where his car and driver were waiting.

"Patty said Malcolm opened the back door on the far side of the vehicle—probably to block a potential witness's view— and within ten seconds he pummeled her face. He knocked her to the ground with the first punch.

Afterwards, he shoved her into the back of the car and said he'd kill her if she ever made a spectacle of him again. Then he screamed at the driver for smoking in the car. Can you imagine that? The spineless little man sat there smoking the whole time Malcolm was beating Patty.

"Anyway, Malcolm then reached across the seat, and yanked the cigarette from the driver's mouth with one hand, while grabbing Patty's face with the other. She said he nearly crushed her jaw with his fingers. Then he put the burning cigarette so close to her eye, it singed her lashes. He told her if she called the cops, they'd never find her body."

"My God," I exclaimed. "He's a monster." Kayla's eyes were huge, and her skin looked a little gray.

"Malcolm instructed the useless driver to get her out of there. Patty gave the man our address because she didn't want to be alone. When he pulled up to our house, he told her it was really too bad *she'd slipped and fallen like she had*. Patty got the message loud and clear—no police. The people in the restaurant hadn't seen Malcolm assault her, and the driver obviously wasn't going to say anything, so it was pointless.

"Patty told Charlie if he called the police she'd never speak to him again. She was terrified Malcolm would kill her as he'd threatened. And like I said, it was going to be her word against Malcolm's because that driver was never going to sell out his boss. That man has since died, and I hope he's rotting in hell."

"So Charlie took things into his own hands?" I surmised.

Eileen nodded. "That he did. He was the kindest man I ever knew, but he had this switch inside of him when someone messed with his family, and it turned him into someone I didn't even know."

I nodded in understanding. My Uncle Larry has that same type of switch; a type of dark side I generally pretend doesn't exist, which allows him to stay in my favorite-people category. I believe I've mentioned denial has always been one of my talents.

"So then what?" Kayla prompted.

"Charlie showed up outside of Malcolm's mansion bright and early the next day. He couldn't get to the front door because of a security guard at the entrance of the premises. So he waited outside the gate."

"For how long?" I asked.

"Over two days," Eileen replied with a smile. "That Charlie was a stubborn one, and he said he didn't leave his spot on the road for over fifty-one hours. He'd taken along a bunch of candy bars and what-not, and..." Her face colored again, betraying her reluctance to say something untoward.

"He pissed on the side of the road?" Kayla supplied. "Probably crapped there, as well."

Eileen blushed so hard her freckles disappeared. I gave Kayla a *what-the-hell* look and she shrugged as if to say *whatever*. Someone had to say it. Kayla was always that someone.

"Charlie's bodily functions really have nothing to do with anything," I said, and Eileen look relieved she wasn't going to have to recap Charlie's bowel movements.

"That's true," Eileen agreed readily. "So anyway, Charlie eventually spotted a dark limousine winding its way down the long driveway and through the double gates. Charlie got on its tail and followed it all the way to Logan."

"As in the Boston airport?"

"That's correct, dear," Eileen replied. "Charlie followed the car into the parking garage and confronted Malcolm right then and there. Malcolm responded by saying he had no idea what Charlie was talking about and that he had been surrounded by business guests and his wife the entire evening in question.

"Charlie got in his face and told him to stay away from Patty. Otherwise, he'd make Malcolm dig his own grave before Charlie put him in it. He told me those were his exact words." She sighed heavily and shook her head slightly. "That's what I meant by him sometimes acting like a person I didn't know. It made me sick with worry at times, this husband I didn't recognize every now and again. But in an odd way, it also made me proud. It made me feel protected. My Charlie was true-blue to the ones he loved, and I guess—in his eyes—sometimes that meant he needed to turn into something dark and sinister."

I wondered about that. Had that side of Charlie recently landed him into a boatload of trouble? Had something he'd said or done led to his murder?

"So, how did Malcolm react?" A bigshot millionaire probably didn't take too kindly to being threatened by an average Joe.

Eileen trembled. "Charlie said Malcolm smiled and placed a hand on his shoulder, like he was going to dole out some advice." She wrung her hands and shook her head.

I mentally smacked myself for continuing to push this kind woman, but I didn't want to stop now.

"Are you okay to continue, Eileen?"

She thrust her head up and took a huge breath, and I knew this would be the grand finale. Whatever she was going to say right now was all she had left in her for today.

"Malcolm's weasel of a driver came around the car and handed a package to Malcolm, who then handed it to Charlie. He leaned into Charlie and said 'You are out of your league here, sir. Watch your step, because I have plenty of people who will certainly be watching you and yours.'"

"What did that mean?" I asked.

"Malcolm and the driver walked off, with the driver toddling behind Malcolm with a bunch of fancy suitcases. Nothing more was said.

"So Charlie went back to his car and ripped open the package—" Eileen burst into tears again.

She'd just told me she wanted to finish the story, but I simply couldn't sit here and watch her sob. I looked over at Kayla, and she drew an imaginary line across her throat with her finger.

"Eileen, I know you want to finish this, but let's do it another time," I suggested. "I'm so sorry to add to your already horrible day."

"There were dozens of pictures of our family—of my *children*—in the package," she blurted. "School photos and family photos and all sorts of stuff." She pulled a handkerchief from inside her sleeve and dabbed at her eyes. "I know there's Facebook and the Twitter and all kinds of things like that now, but I don't think there was much of that—if any—thirty years ago. I don't know how or when they got so many of our personal pictures. They had snapshots of every person in my family, and even our extended family, and Malcolm said they'd be watching. I, for one, believed him."

"Did Charlie?" I asked.

Eileen nodded. "He did. His pride was wounded. He felt Malcolm bested him. Malcolm had more time, resources, personnel, things like that. He could have made our lives a living hell if he'd wanted to. So Charlie grudgingly threw in the towel. It was best for everyone."

"Do you know if they ever had any run-ins after that?" I asked.

"Not that I ever knew of, and Charlie never mentioned anything. They weren't exactly in the same social circles, and Malcolm was only here a few months each year, so the odds weren't great that their paths would cross." Eileen's face fell. "And they definitely won't cross now, with my Charlie gone." Her voice cracked on the last few words, and this time we were definitely calling it quits.

I stood up and motioned for Kayla to do the same. "Eileen, you've been so kind to give us some time today. But we need to go and let you get some rest. If Malcolm Johnson had anything to do with Charlie's death, I will get to the bottom of it. I promise you that. Do you have an idea if he's in town or how I might get an appointment with him?"

Eileen shrugged. "He's in town, yes. I really don't know about getting an appointment, dear. He lives in a bubble. Although..."

"Although, what?" I prompted.

"His wife Barbara does a lot of charity events. And she's having a party—excuse me, a *gala*—at their home—excuse me, at their *mansion*—sometime soon. I don't know exactly when. But I do know it's a very expensive event; I've heard it's about two thousand dollars a plate."

"That leaves us out," Kayla chirped. "You got anything else?"

"Not so fast," I said. "I'm thinking that Mrs. Malcolm Gage Johnson might welcome a large donation from a certain Richie Rich, of which we have two."

Eileen cocked her head while Kayla beamed and spoke out loud to our absent, unsuspecting friends. "Doob and Jeff, dust off your wallets. You're taking us to a gala!"

CHAPTER 7

THE MINUTE WE GOT THE BOXES EILEEN HAD GIVEN ME into the car, I searched for the gala info on my phone and learned the big event was scheduled for this coming Friday night. I then left Jeff a message that he needed to call me ASAP.

"Other than finding out there's a big shindig coming up, that was awful," Kayla said when we got back in her car. "I felt so bad for that nice old lady. Your job sucks ass."

I blew out a breath in shared empathy. "Sometimes it does. But doesn't meeting her make you want to get to the bottom of this? Doesn't it kind of charge you up?"

She slapped a palm on the steering wheel. "Fucking A, yes it does." Then she jabbed an elbow in my side. "By the way, we need to go shopping for this ball."

Short-lived period of conviction for my friend.

"You've turned it into a ball?" I asked. Every fiber of my being screamed at me to avoid the topic—let alone the actual act—of shopping.

"Yes, Cinder-friggin-rella, it is *now* a ball," Kayla said as she spread her right arm across the dashboard. "The word gala sounds ridiculous. But whatever you want to call it, it's sure to be a fabulous party with a bunch of rich old buzzards, and we're going to set the place on fire!"

I seriously hoped she wasn't being literal, but I could never tell. "Both hands on the wheel, please. And I don't want to shop at *all*, Kayla. You know my size, so you're officially in charge of finding me something nice and demure. I'll pay you a finder's fee or something. Just. Don't. Make. Me. Go." I banged my head on the back of the seat as I spoke every syllable.

She cut her eyes to me. "Have some fucking cheese with your whine, Meagan. If you don't go with me, I'll find you the sluttiest, most revealing dress you've ever seen. It would be a huge mistake to not go along. More importantly, I'll need you to help *me* find something amazing."

"In which case, *that* will then end up being the sluttiest, most revealing dress I've ever seen," I quipped.

"You are such a baby about shopping. We're going. You made me see the sad woman, I'm making you shop. End of story."

We drove in silence for a few minutes, which gave me time to percolate an idea. "I'll make you a deal. I'll agree to go on a very small shopping spree with you but propose we find a consignment shop here in Newport. If we shop for new gowns here, or even back in Boston, we're going to pay a fortune. These rich women in Newport have probably dropped off clothes that cost more than my monthly rent. Let's try to find something reasonably priced, considering we'll probably never be invited to another ball."

"Speak for yourself," Kayla retorted. "But fine, I can live with your deal. At least I'll agree to *start* at a consignment shop, but if the stuff sucks, all bets are off. My gown is going to make a statement."

I chuckled. "There's not a doubt in my mind. Let's hold off on getting any evening wear until Jeff calls back. We don't even know if we're going to this thing, yet."

"Oh, we are *going*," Kayla said, all bluster and certainty.

As if on cue, my phone rang, and the Caller ID showed Jeff's name and number. I relayed our discussion with Eileen O'Neill, and he good-naturedly said he'd check into getting tickets.

"Sometimes it's completely irritating, but at other times, it's very cool having rich friends," I relayed to Kayla. "Jeff said he should be able to get us tickets to the event."

"Yeah, at least he's a good guy with money, unlike that monster Les."

I cocked my head. "Who?"

"The guy I told you about—with the insurance policies and those little kids."

"Gotcha. Sorry, I don't think you said his name last night."

She sighed and stared at the road ahead, rather than look at me. "I hope you don't mind, but before we left today, I gave all his particulars to Doob. I asked him to find the articles on that lady's daughter from last time to see if he could find anything incriminating about Les."

My jaw tightened.

At last, she glanced over at me. "Meg, I'm sorry, but you don't *own* Doob. He was glad to help. It's the right thing to do if this asshole is as bad as I think he is. And I think he's really, *really* bad."

I told myself to relax. She was absolutely right. Doob would help anyone, and with the whopping dollar I pay him a year, I certainly didn't have exclusive access to his hacking. "That's fine, Kayla. I'm just used to being the one to boss poor Doobie around. So he's digging up info on Les. That's cool. The guy seems more real to me now that I know his name."

I noticed her knuckles go white on the steering wheel. "We can just stick with calling him prick or scumbag or fucking-sicko. Whatever you want, Meg. He's a goddamn-psycho-bumpkin, and we've got to stop him."

Taking a deep breath, I said, "I'm almost scared to ask, but do you have some type of plan? And if you do, and if it's illegal, then don't please don't tell me."

She gave me a sly smile. "You wouldn't perjure yourself in court for me?"

"Kayla!" I gasped. "I don't know what I would do. Just don't put me in that position. Please."

"God, don't piss yourself, Meagan. I do have a plan, and the first part of it definitely isn't illegal."

"The second part?"

Her lips twisted. "Well...that would involve your Uncle Larry."

Good grief. I don't know precisely what Uncle Larry did as a younger man to earn a living, but I've heard all sorts of stories about him and the Boston mob when they had a stronghold in Southie. Whenever those accounts came up, I jammed my fingers in my ears and started screaming Christmas carols at the top of my lungs. It's my way of keeping Uncle Lare a bright, shining star in my universe. The smart, practical me knows Larry could make some bad things happen to someone if he wanted to. And Kayla obviously knew that as well.

"Why don't you share the first part of the plan and leave my uncle out of it for now?"

"I knew you'd say that. Your uncle digs me, you know."

"God, Kayla. You really have no shame. That's just gross." I stifled a shiver and stared out the window.

"Okay, Miss Prissy Puss Pants, the first part of the plan is easy. I just need you to go talk with Alicia and tell her to dump the prick. Tell her what we suspect, show her some newspaper articles about that poor little girl, and tell her it's pretty fucking coincidental that he's repeating his pattern."

"You want *me* to speak with Alicia? I gather that's the girlfriend? How did I get nominated for this?"

"She knows me, Meagan, and so does he. I can't talk to her without jeopardizing my job. Plus, he is probably—well, definitely—a psycho. Like the word Eileen used earlier, he's a little *off*; you can see that if you spend two minutes with him. I don't know how he even lands halfway normal women, because he's all backwoods lout. You're trained with all that shit, I'm not."

I gaped at her. "Are you serious? I'm trained in backwoods lout?"

She arched a brow. "You aren't?"

"You're something else," I retorted with a snort. "So what happens when Mr. Backwoods Lout comes after me?"

"Meagan, think about it. If you do it right, and convince her he's bad news, she'll break it off with him. She doesn't need to explain why. She doesn't need to betray you. And if he does find out why she's dumping him, she could tell him someone mailed her a letter and a newspaper article anonymously."

"Which is exactly what we *should* do," I fired back. "Why don't we be the anonymous Good Samaritan? That would work."

She shrugged. "It might. But if you meet with her and say someone cared enough to hire you and have you speak with her, I think that would be more effective."

"Hire me? So you're *paying* me for this little chat you want me to have?"

"Don't be dense, Meagan. You wouldn't take it anyway."

"Funny. I always use that line on Doob, and when I'm the one saying it, I tend to believe it."

She sighed. "Fine.You need to at least *call* her."

I chuckled. "I *need* to? I'll think about it, Kayla. But I really think the anonymous route is the way to go."

"Well, even if it is, that only solves this particular situation. He could move away and start doing it all over again. But that's where your Uncle Larry comes in."

I pointed at a plaza coming up on the highway. "Pull into the liquor store, please. I am *so done* with this conversation."

"Meagan, Larry is no saint—"

"Jingle bells, jingle bells, jingle all the way!" I screamed with fingers planted firmly in my ears.

CHAPTER 8

Wednesday, November 6th

WE LEARNED THE PREVIOUS EVENING Jeff had secured tickets for the gala/ball/party, and it sounded like it was quite the process.

"Seriously, I don't mind spending the money at all; it's a great cause. But from a security standpoint, it seemed a little over-the-top."

"What do you mean?" Kayla asked from the couch, her head supported by her propped elbow.

"When I called, I had to go through three different people to get *permission* to attend. I felt like I was doing a phone interview for a job. Usually you don't have to convince people to let you drop eight grand for their event." He glanced over at Doob. "If you want to spring for a few more people, they said there are still tickets available."

"Nah, but I'll be glad to pay for half," Doob offered.

Jeff shook his head. "My treat, no worries."

"That's cool. In that case, I'll write them a fat check when I get there," Doob said with a mouthful of powdered sugar donut.

"Enough you two," I exclaimed. "Back to planet earth with the poor people. Jeff, obviously we owe you *huge*. But we're all set, right?"

"We are. I had to give them our four names, addresses, and our reason for wanting to attend. Had they started in with Social Security numbers or blood types, I would have bowed out," he said good-naturedly.

"What did you tell them about why we wanted to attend?"

"I told them I was new to the area and wanted to get involved with the community." He glanced toward Doob sheepishly. "I may have also mentioned I'm a lottery winner and bringing an entrepreneur friend who might be interested in donating to some of their future causes."

"Entrepreneur and computer hacker are fairly synonymous, right?" I teased, but Doob wasn't smiling.

"I'd donate whatever necessary if it would keep me out of a penguin suit," Doob whined.

He was in a tremendous dither about playing dress-up for an evening. But Jeff assured him he had "a guy" in Boston who could hook them both up with tuxedos as long as Doob knew his size. This sent Doob into a further dither, because all Doob knows for sure is that he's male.

It was finally agreed that Doob would head back to Boston with Kayla early tomorrow, which would allow him to go see the guy about the tux. She was going to get a little work done, and I could use Doob's Mercedes until they got back late tomorrow night.

So now I had to face the music, come hell or high water. Since we were in the Newport area, I was hoping for high water, but none came. Trying to hide my irritation, I hopped in Kayla's car and watched as she punched in the address on her GPS to the consignment store called *Second Thoughts* we'd found on the Internet.

"I'm having second thoughts about this whole thing," I groaned.

Kayla shot me a sidelong death glance. "This consignment thing was your idea, super sleuth. Suck it up. It's going to be fun."

Meagan-Maloney-Mighty-Bargain-Shopper-Extraordinaire.

About an hour later, Kayla and I had actually managed to find some pretty fabulous gowns, although I didn't readily admit that to her. She'd landed herself a long, dark emerald, skin-tight ensemble with spaghetti straps that left zero to the imagination. It fit her like a second skin, and with Kayla's willowy build, it was perfect.

At her insistence, I'd decided on a red getup. Normally I view red as a color that screams *look at me,* and I avoid it like the plague, but somehow this red didn't bother me. Like Kayla's, it was also a floor-length gown, in somewhat of an empire design. There was a pretty tiny bow just under the bosom, with a strapless upper body. Along with the color red, I usually avoid anything strapless, but again, this seemed to work. Above the little bow, it kind of triangled up in several sections, in a pointy way that resembled a row of napkins at a fancy restaurant. It looked like an outline of the Rocky Mountains in a luxurious red fabric, and it had some type of built-in foundation that actually created a little bit of cleavage. It seemed a little odd, since only *I* could see the cleavage, due to the mountain range covering my breasts. But it was nice to actually have some cleavage, so I wasn't complaining. The added benefit was I basically had a private little shelf within my dress. If the sandwiches were good at the gala, I could smuggle a couple out in my makeshift cleavage.

All in all, a good find.

Coupled with my pretty dress, I also found a great silver clutch and strappy, sparkly, silver heels that topped off the whole outfit; it was all so girly I could hardly stand it, but I was pleased that both Kayla and I found acceptable gowns for bargain basement prices.

With that mission accomplished, I decided to get back to the task at hand, which was figuring out how Charlie died. While I could hopefully confront Malcolm at his enormous soirée on Friday night, that still gave me some time to explore some non-Malcolm options. The guy sounded like an absolute piece of shit, but I wasn't convinced a decades-old feud resulted in Charlie's death last week. Maybe, maybe not. But I was going to keep turning over rocks until I figured it out.

So I needed to brainstorm. Fortunately for me, Kayla and Jeff had decided to go for a jog. It was a beautiful fall day, and a run by the ocean in the late afternoon seemed to agree with them. Doob—who barely believes in walking, let alone jogging—decided a nap would suit him just fine, and Sampson was more than happy to join him.

Which left me alone with my thoughts, a very scary place to be at times. Grabbing a pencil and notepad, as I often do, I plopped down on a stool at Jeff's beautiful, granite island in the kitchen. I started scribbling ideas that came to mind, however mundane those might be.

First of all, the death could have been an accident, just as the authorities had dubbed it. Charlie could have had a legitimate fall which ended his life in an abrupt manner. But I wasn't buying it, and several other people weren't, either.

I wondered if there was any chance Charlie decided to kill himself and dismissed this as quickly as I thought of it. Everything I'd heard led me to believe he was living a nice, peaceful life with his bride of many years. He had grandchildren; he was retired; he was healthy; he was enjoying his golden years. And even if I could force myself to believe he'd offed himself, why would he pick an abandoned house and fling himself down the stairs? It wasn't even a guaranteed death. While I wasn't an expert on suicide, my thinking was that launching one's self down a stairwell didn't make the top ten list.

So okay; what was left? If it wasn't a slip-and-fall or a suicide, there must have been something unsavory going on. Malcolm was definitely an option on the table—and I'd deal with him on Friday—but I needed to think about other alternatives. Did Charlie know something or find something or see something related to the house? Did he walk in on a squatter who pushed him down the stairs and then ran off? That was doubtful, as the police didn't uncover any evidence of someone living in the home.

Was it possible Charlie was looking for those coins or something else? But the house was completely empty when Jeff moved in. Wasn't it? I couldn't say for certain, so I circled that thought and made a note to ask Jeff about it later.

On the flip side, was it possible Charlie had planted something in the house? But what and why? Jeff had never met him, so it's not like Charlie was leaving a fruit basket for his arrival. And if Charlie was going to plant something, did he succeed? Or was he killed before he could leave it? And if so, was it on him when Jeff found his body?

While I felt myself grasping at straws, that question niggled at my brain. Who could tell me what was on Charlie's person when he was found? The police? The medical examiner? The undertaker? I decided it would be the police. My conclusion was based on my vast knowledge gleaned from *CSI*, *NCIS*, and other television shows that tidily solved their problems in an hour, minus commercials. I envied those detectives at times.

By now, it was likely Charlie's effects had been given to Eileen, and I simply couldn't bring myself to bother her again just yet. But thinking about those television shows also gave me an idea—a lot of times, the arsonist hangs in the background at the scene of the fire, or the serial killer wanders outside the police tape of a discovered mass grave. If someone had killed Charlie, I wondered if they might have gone to the wake, the funeral, or the gravesite. Besides Eileen and her children, who could tell me that?

I was thinking the sign-in book at the funeral home might be a good place to start. With any luck, Mr. or Ms. Killer would have signed in as such, and I could wrap this thing up and get back home, sans gala. That was definitely motivation to get this case solved before Friday.

The problem was I had no idea who should or shouldn't be paying their respects to Charlie. I would have to question the funeral home director to see if anyone was behaving out of sorts, although I'm sure the range of behavior at a wake is massive. Would the director know murder-behavior from regular funeral-sad-upset-behavior? Ugh.

Then I wondered if anyone possibly took a picture at the gravesite? Maybe I could get one and show it to Eileen or her kids. They would have been seated close to the casket and probably didn't notice everyone who attended.

But a picture of attendees didn't seem too likely; rather, it seemed completely inappropriate. Further, it seemed stupid. But sometimes stupid works out, and I guess it wouldn't hurt to ask.

Finally, I would have to ask Eileen and her family about the people who came to her home after the gravesite ceremony. That was typically an occasion for close friends and family, so hopefully those attendees would be easier to recall. Maybe one person would stand out—after notes were compared between Eileen and her children—who no one knew and who didn't belong there.

I looked at the scribbles on the paper in front of me and had created quite a mess but some semblance of a game plan. Tomorrow I would speak with Eileen about Charlie's personal effects, the gravesite attendees, and the sign-in book. I might also try to meet with the funeral home director to glean, well...something.

With that, my mind was tapped for ideas.

A sudden clicking on the wooden steps caused me to glance up in time to see Sampson waddling into the kitchen, where he conducted his post-nap doggy stretch. His first move involved a Nike-swoosh curl with his butt to the sky, followed by a forward stretch with one leg extended out behind him. It was the same routine every single time, and it was as reliable as the sun coming up in the morning.

Now fully limber, Sampson looked to the cabinet where we'd stashed the dog treats a couple of nights before. Quick learner. I obliged and had him go through the requisite sit, shake, and speak performance before giving him his reward. He passed with flying colors, so I gave him two.

A few moments later, the front door flew open, with Kayla and Jeff bursting in, faces flushed and out of breath. Doob appeared seconds later, face flushed and out of breath from simply walking down the stairs.

"Taxing nap, Doob?"

Doob put his fingers under his chin and flicked them at me. He then walked over to the cupboard to get Sampson a treat.

"I just gave him a couple of those," I said in a scolding tone.

"He had a bad dream," Doob said and gave Sampson two more treats before I could protest any further.

"Moira will have your ass if that dog gains so much as an ounce. You'll be assigned to walking him all over the city if he goes back home with a gut."

"Speaking of, I hope my tux fits me come Friday," Jeff said, patting his own stomach. "Thanks again for picking it up for me, Doob."

"Yeah. I'm counting the minutes until I get to wear the monkey suit," Doob pouted.

"It'll all be worth it when you see the splash Meagan and I are going to make," Kayla said as she grabbed a bottled water and disappeared up the stairs.

If she only knew how prophetic those words would be.

CHAPTER 9

Thursday, November 7th

AFTER DISCUSSING THE INFORMATION WE OBTAINED FROM EILEEN on Tuesday with Gus at breakfast, it was decided I would have to visit Rusty in prison. I had a sudden flashback to when I'd visited Melanie's father, Vic, in jail before I knew he was her father. Like then, I didn't relish the thought of visiting a complete stranger in the slammer, of all places, but it had to be done.

"I can make a phone call and get you in there whenever you need to," Gus said as he dabbed his napkin at his mouth. Ever the gentleman. It was quite the opposite of watching Doob essentially forklift the entire contents of his plate into his mouth.

I raised an eyebrow at Gus. "And how in the world can you do that?" As I recalled, getting on the approved list at Vic's prison hadn't been that big of a deal, but if Gus was offering to help, I wanted him to feel useful.

An impish smile lit up his features. "Meagan, when you've lived as long as I have, and in a state this small, you get to know everyone. I'll make a phone call and get you all set up. Don't worry about a thing. You'll be a ray of sunshine in that place."

My head fell back against my seat. Ray of sunshine amongst a bunch of felons? Ugh. "Okay, thanks," I mumbled and then glanced at my friends hopefully.

"I'm out," Kayla quipped. "Those prisoners would take one look at me and have all sorts of lewd and filthy thoughts about me later when they do their business. I told you your job sucks."

I watched all three men's faces turn scarlet. Kayla simply didn't believe in tact. Or decorum. Or modesty. Or a host of other things.

"I didn't invite you anyway," I retorted and turned toward Jeff and Doob.

"Yeah, uh…I've got, um, some stuff going on back in…uh…well, here and there, over the next few days, and weeks, or whenever, so I can't make it, either, Meagan. Sorry about that," Jeff said while his face turned one shade deeper.

"Don't look at me," Doob chimed in with a mouthful of scrambled eggs. "I'd curl into the fetal position the minute we entered the property. You're better off without having to worry about me getting my ass kicked, Meg. You'd have to rescue me, and you might get hurt. Truly, I'm just thinking of you."

Kayla cocked her head. "Don't kid yourself, Doob. Some of those beefcakes would work you into their fantasies as well." Doob blanched and set his fork down.

Staring at each of them for a long moment, I snarled, "You all stink, but I can manage myself, thank you very much. Gus, I'll take you up on your offer and look forward to my prison visit once we figure out what day makes sense."

Gus smiled and said, "Consider it done, m'lady." Adorable.

Kayla pulled a face. "When are we leaving, Doob?"

That thought perked Doob right up, and he said, "Whenever you're ready."

"Soon," she replied. "I've got some stuff to do at the office, and you have your appointment to get *measured*." She pointed at his midsection.

Doob flushed anew.

"Leave him alone," I said. "He's stressed out enough about this tux as it is." I turned to him. "Doob, you were doing a little digging around on Les for Kayla. We want to let his girlfriend know he's dangerous, but we need to do it anonymously. Can you tell us what you found out about this guy?"

Doob picked up his fork and starting shifting some of his eggs around, a stall tactic I'd come to know well. The only thing that ever kept him from shoveling food in his mouth was a topic he'd just as soon avoid. Doob and uncomfortable conversations—not so much.

"Doob?" I prodded and gave him a confused look.

"Well…uh…I just think, or rather, I'm kinda wondering if maybe, possibly, not that I'm doubting Kayla, mind you—"

"Doob!" Kayla shrieked. "Spit it out. Do *not* tell me you're waffling on this guy. I know what I know, so if you think you've found something redeeming about him, you haven't. It's a trick. He's gonna kill another kid if we don't stop him."

Gus very deliberately set his eating utensils down and scanned each of our faces. "This sounds serious, people. Is there anything you want to tell me? Or better yet, is there something you need to tell the authorities?"

Kayla screwed up her face, and I could only imagine the colorful language that would be forthcoming if I let her tell the story. So I filled Gus in, and he stroked his chin as I spoke. He didn't interrupt or ask any questions until I was done.

"And you all think sending this woman an anonymous package of information will cause her to get this Les character out of her life?"

"We're hoping," I said. "Unless you have a better idea. We can't really go to the police on a hunch."

Gus nodded. "Please be careful. If Kayla's suspicions are correct—"

"They *are* correct," she interrupted, and I glared at her. Ma always taught me to respect my elders, and I didn't like her butting in on Gus.

"Don't snarl at me, Meagan. You're all acting like I'm a crackpot, but I'm not. I'm right about this son of a bitch." She then turned her attention to Doob. "Swallow your friggin' food, and tell us what you're hemming and hawing about."

Doob slowly swallowed something that looked to be the size of a softball and then cleared his throat. In the smallest voice I've ever heard from him, he said, "I think he has a dog."

Kayla's face instantly contorted, leaving her looking like she'd just sucked on a lemon. "You think he has a *dog*?" She looked around the table, silently asking all of us if Doob was serious. And then, "Who gives a shit? What does that have to do with anything?"

Doob's face now appeared to be permanently suntanned, and I felt bad for him. "Well, it's just that he has vet bills, and he goes to pet stores, and there's regular grooming, and before I do this, I just want to make sure he's a bad guy. He at least seems to be good to his dog. I don't know if killer-bad-guys are nice to animals, are they?"

Kayla started shaking. "Doob, since you're pretty much the nicest, most naïve person on the planet, I'll not rip your larynx out right now. I wish I had your faith in the goodness in people, and I wish I could think well of someone just because he's nice to man's best friend, but I don't, and I can't. But trust me when I tell you—when I tell *all of you*—this isn't me being cynical. I've met him, I saw the claim, and he's doing it again. She reached across the table and put both her hands on Doob's. "I promise, Doob. You're doing the right thing by getting this woman and her child away from this maniac. I *promise*."

There was a few seconds of silence at the table before I got back to it. "Doob, other than the dog, did you find anything incriminating?"

He shook his head. "Not specifically about Les. On paper, his life looks normal." He glanced at Kayla. "But I also found some articles about that poor little girl, and it sounded really awful. If you want to type up a couple of notes to clip to the articles, we can get them sent to the girlfriend."

"Why do you have to type the notes?" Jeff asked.

"Because they don't want it traced back to them," Gus answered for me, and I gave him a little smile.

Wanting to wrap this up, I stated the game plan. "I'll clip the articles together and type up a few sentences for Alicia. God willing, she'll realize who she's involved with, and we'll hope for the best. Since you guys are headed to Boston this morning, you can do me a favor. I need my mail from the office, so please swing by and grab it. And if I give you Alicia's address, will you give the package to Becca, and ask her to send it out for us?"

"Can do." Doob nodded. "Isn't Becca the ditz you're always complaining about?"

"She is," I admitted. "But Norman gets all put out if I don't give her a few things to do a week. And I haven't given her anything in several days. So this is my assignment for her—enclosing the paperwork in a manila envelope, addressing the envelope, putting postage on the envelope, and placing the envelope in the outgoing mail. That should take her the better part of four hours. Just emphasize that she is to send it *without* a return address, and she's not to enclose a business card. I don't think she'll understand the word anonymous, but you can try. Like Gus said, we don't want this coming back on us."

"Wouldn't be good," Doob said as he shoveled some bacon in his mouth.

Truer words were never said.

CHAPTER 10

ABOUT AN HOUR LATER, KAYLA AND DOOB TOOK OFF in her car, and despite the upcoming tuxedo measurements, I'm not sure I've ever seen Doob happier. I've told him a hundred times she'd suck the heart, soul, money, and life out of him, and then leave him for dead, but that only seems to increase his attraction to her. Men.

Jeff had some errands and work-related things to tend to on his computer, so that left me to start the to-do list I'd compiled the day before. I called Eileen and apologized for bothering her again, but she was very gracious. She hadn't noticed anyone at any of the services who shouldn't have been there but also admitted she wasn't exactly paying close attention. I told her my line of thinking, and she said she'd speak with her children to see if they'd noticed anyone or anything unusual.

I further learned Charlie's personal effects hadn't yet been returned to Eileen, and she'd accidentally left the sign-in book back at the funeral home, so she couldn't help me out on that front, either.

"Eileen, that gives me an idea. I'm wondering if you could do us both a favor?" I asked.

"I'll certainly try, dear. What is it you need?"

"Well, I'd be glad to go by the funeral home and get the sign-in book, but I'm sure they'd need permission from you. Would you be willing to give them a call to see if I could swing by this afternoon to pick it up? I'd also like to ask them a few questions, if you don't mind. I know I'm being a pest, but for your sake, and Jeff's sake, I really want to get to the bottom of this."

"Of course. I understand, dear, and I appreciate it. I'll call them right now. I've got your business card, so I'll call you on that number in a few minutes."

As promised, Eileen called me five minutes later and said I could visit Mr. Rosenthal at the funeral home at three-thirty that afternoon. He had a service at one o'clock but thought he could give me a few minutes in his office afterwards. She said he'd give me the sign-in book as well as do his best to answer any of my questions.

"Such a sweet man," she said matter-of-factly after giving me directions to the funeral home. "He's really been so helpful throughout this entire process."

Wait until you get the bill, I thought cynically and then silently called myself a bitch. "I promise to not take up too much of his time, Eileen. Thank you so much for helping me with this. Would you like me to drop the book off at your house sometime tomorrow?"

"That would be fine, dear. If you'd like to come around noon, I'll make us tea and sandwiches."

For whatever reason, my eyes got misty and a lump formed in my throat. This woman was goodness to the core, and I knew many lonely days were ahead of her.

"I'd love that, Eileen, thank you."

"And bring your pretty friend along, too. She's a pistol, that one."

I smiled. "That she is. I'll see if she can make it," I replied, knowing full well Kayla would never go to Eileen's house again.

"I'll look forward to it. See you then, dear."

"Eileen?"

"Yes?"

"Do you like chocolate?"

She laughed a husky laugh, and I was glad to hear it. "Of course I do. Doesn't everyone?"

"Then dessert is on me. I'll see you tomorrow at noon."

It was right around one o'clock, and I decided baking a cake would pass the time until I needed to get to the funeral home. Since Doob and I are junk-food-aholics, I knew we had chocolate cake mix and chocolate frosting from our grocery store extravaganza the other night. What I didn't know was if Jeff had a cake pan, but after opening several cupboard doors, I was pleased to find a glass baking dish that had a sticky note on the bottom that read: *Use this sometime. Love you, Mom.*

Well, Mrs. Geiger, I would try to do right by your gift and make the most fabulous chocolate cake Newport had ever seen. Had ever tasted, whatever.

By three o'clock, my masterpiece was baked and frosted, and I left a note for Jeff that threatened death if he so much as touched the cake.

But I added there was leftover frosting in the refrigerator if he wanted to glom that. After all, it was his house.

After noticing I had a good deal of chocolate on my person, I decided a change clothes was in order. Call me crazy, but something told me a pink GAP hoodie with brown streaks all over it wouldn't be appropriate for a meeting with a funeral director. But it did smell great.

Donned in appropriate black attire, I pulled into the funeral home just before three-thirty. Trying to be conscientious of Doob's rig, I parked his Mercedes in a spot far away from all the other cars. I don't think Doob really worries about door dings, but I didn't want him getting any on my watch.

As I reached for the handle to hop out of the car, I took a minute before getting out. The last time I was at a funeral home had been last March—to attend the wake of my client's brother, who'd been killed by Melanie. A horrible time in my life. I involuntarily shivered. Even though this was a completely different location—a completely different set of circumstances—my heart raced and everything in me screamed at me to flee. When it comes to the whole "fight or flight" thing, I'm all about the flight. Getting the hell out of bad situations is a policy I try to strictly adhere to.

However, that policy doesn't always work. And besides, this wasn't a scary situation, so I needed to get over it. Taking several deep breaths, I steadied myself and walked across the parking lot and through the double front doors of the funeral home. The sickly sweet smell of flowers and an aura of sadness greeted me. Again, I fought off the urge to turn around and run.

I noticed a sign with some family names on it, and it appeared two services were going to begin at five o'clock. If I was going to do this, I needed to do it now. The sooner I did, the sooner I'd be gone.

Despite my little neurotic episode, the visit with Mr. Rosenthal went quite well. He had a tactful, reserved air about him that suited his profession to a tee. I left his office with the sign-in book in hand but with little information about any potential weirdos at the services. I wasn't too surprised when he reported that most of the attendees were behaving normally for people who were mourning a friend or loved one.

Hey, nothing ventured, nothing gained. If Eileen was up for it tomorrow, we could take a look at the people who attended the wake and see if anything jumped out at her. If she wasn't up for it, then we'd have a nice lunch just the same. I'd quickly grown protective of the old woman and didn't want to upset her any more than absolutely necessary.

Rounding the corner after leaving Mr. Rosenthal's office, I breathed easier, thinking of Doob's fancy SUV waiting in the parking lot, my escape from all things funeral-related. I would get back to Jeff's and have a glass of...something, and all would be right with the world. That was the plan.

At least I thought that was the plan until I saw movement to my right and felt someone tackle my legs, sending me to the floor like a sack of potatoes.

CHAPTER 11

"CECILE! I KNEW YOU'D COME!" A man's voice came from nearby my feet.

I leaned up on one arm and tried to assess the situation. A small old man with a few tufts of gray hair had decided to tackle me for no apparent reason. And it was very clear he had me confused with someone named Cecile.

As I struggled to regain my bearings, a woman who looked to be in her mid-sixties rushed out of one of the viewing rooms and took in the scene. She was plump, wedged into an all-black jacket and skirt, and her eyes were red-rimmed.

"Herman! What have you done?" she scolded while helping him up off the floor. She then turned to me. "I'm so sorry, miss, so very sorry." She hefted me back to my feet and dusted me off with jerky swipes of her hand across my backside.

"It's, uh, okay," I said while rubbing my hip. A dull ache spread over my bones, and I winced. Great. I'd probably be sporting a new bruise as a result of today's events. "Just a little unexpected."

"She came! She came! I told you Cecile would come! And you, with your know-it-all-nose-in-the-air said she wouldn't. Well, I was right, and you were wrong, Marguerite. So go suck on a lemon, you old witch!" Herman hooked his arm in mine and pulled me toward the viewing room.

Oh. My. God.

Fortunately, Herman and I were the only ones in the room, but there was a casket at the far end I surmised had a dead body inside. My crack detective skills at work once again. I prayed to all that is holy Herman didn't drag me toward it. *Assuming* there was a dead body and *knowing* there was a dead body were two very different things. And I believe I've mentioned in the past denial is one of my talents.

The old man steered me to the array of photographs artfully arranged on poster boards, propped up on easels, and it looked like the deceased had been a beautiful woman who'd led a full life. At least I was hoping that was the case, and then I wondered why I was hoping anything at all. I needed to get out of here.

"Cecile, there you are! It's you and Betty at your high school graduation." Herman still had his arm hooked through mine, but he was pointing at a girl in one of the pictures. I leaned in to study it, and damned if I didn't look a whole lot like her. The banner behind the two friends in the picture read 1955.

"And here you are again in this one," he said, dragging me to yet another picture. Again, the resemblance to the girl was uncanny, and I was rapidly developing a soft spot for this old man. Some part of his brain saw me and recognized a face from his past. Some part of him was very happy because he thought he saw a familiar girl from his childhood, and he thought that girl was here to attend Betty's funeral. But sadly, he wasn't coherent enough to understand that if I was eighteen years old in 1955, I would be somewhere around his age right now. Which I clearly wasn't, although some days I sure felt like it.

The plump woman caught up with us and put her hand on Herman's shoulder. "Herman, we need to let this nice lady leave. The service will be starting in less than an hour."

"But she just got here!" Herman wailed like a toddler and tightened his hooked arm on my bicep. "She hasn't seen all the pictures, and she hasn't had a chance to go up and see Betty. You ruin everything!"

The woman gave me a weary, sad look and shook her head slowly. "Betty was our older sister. There's three of us. I'm the youngest, and Herman is in the middle. He was always so protective of Betty and her circle of friends, and he always had a little crush on Cecile, although they never got together."

Herman's face darkened. "Marguerite! Cecile was always a perfect young lady, and I only wanted to take her out for ice cream, but we never got the chance." His lids dropped and his voice softened. "That darn Roger Mooney stole her away from me. But even after she was Roger's girl, Cecile told me she'd always regretted the fact we didn't get that ice cream."

He looked at me for confirmation, and I gave him a tight smile. Sure, *I* was always up for ice cream, but I really didn't feel right speaking for Cecile. However, when in Rome...

Herman suddenly jerked out of his reverie and jutted out his chin. With confidence, he turned toward me. "Cecile, let's go up and see Betty—"

Marguerite interrupted him as she leaned close to me in confidence. "As you've probably surmised, Herman has Alzheimer's, and sometimes it can be very trying. He's been living with it for nearly two years. One day he was Herman, and the next...well, my older brother was no longer my older brother." She shrugged with the fatigue of someone burying one sibling while simultaneously trying to care for the other.

Herman leaned across my body and said in a singsong voice, "Quit your whispering, Marguerite, or I'm going to tell Mom! She said it's not nice to whisper, and Cecile doesn't want to listen to your bull poopy anyway."

Marguerite grabbed Herman's arm and gently tried to pull us apart. Herman started screaming, and Marguerite scolded him to act like a grownup and let me go. I shut my eyes, hoping I was in the midst of a bad dream and would wake up momentarily.

Any minute. ..

Any second now...

I opened my eyes.

No such luck. I was still between two geriatric siblings who were now slapping and yelling and spitting like children. Mother of God.

"We have to meet with Mr. Rosenthal, Herman! Let Cecile go, and we'll see her later." My eyes bulged at Marguerite as she said this, but she shook her head and mouthed, "He won't remember you were here."

For some odd reason, that made me feel guilty. The old Catholic-guilt thing rearing its ugly head.

Herman stamped a foot, continuing his childlike fit. "I hate Mr. Rosenthal. Cecile and I want to go outside for some fresh air. This place smells like a funeral home!"

Ummm.

Still caught between brother and sister, I saw my opportunity. "Marguerite, if you want to meet with Mr. Rosenthal by yourself, that might be best for everyone involved. I can go outside with Herman for a little while, and you can come collect him when your meeting is over." *And I can get the hell out of here.*

Marguerite threw me a grateful look. "Are you sure?"

"No problem," I said. "I'm sorry for what you're going through."

A sheen came to her eyes. "That's very kind of you...uh..."

I held out my free hand. "Meagan. It's a pleasure to meet you."

She shook my hand and leaned into me again. "Herman seems fascinated by that huge fountain out front. If you can keep him somewhere near that, I'll come out after my meeting and distract him, and you can be on your way, Meagan. Thank you."

"You're welcome. I'll see you out there in a little bit."

As she left the room, images of my parents and Uncle Larry flashed through my mind, and I thanked my lucky stars all of them were of sound mind and body. Well, they were actually all nuts in their own unique way, but they weren't at the point where they were a danger to themselves or anyone else.

Still linked to Herman, I turned and faced the confused old man. "Herman, Marguerite said we should avoid the fountain outside, but I was thinking—"

"Let's go!" Herman shouted.

I was proud that my reverse psychology had worked. He nearly ripped my arm out of its socket as he dragged me toward the doorway.

As we exited the building, we stepped onto the massive, circular driveway filled with cars, a hearse at the front of the line. I was a little concerned to see that the procession from the previous service hadn't yet left. The possibility of Herman tackling a mourner before they made their way to the gravesite of their loved one was simply unacceptable. How I'd ended up babysitting someone my parents' age was beyond me, and I really didn't want to be responsible for any additional mayhem on his part. My worry was based on my certainty he wouldn't come across another person today quite as reasonable and understanding as I'd been.

It's tough being such a swell gal sometimes.

Fortunately, other than the driver of the hearse, who stood beside the vehicle having a smoke—*completely* tacky under the circumstances—we were the only ones roaming around outside.

Evidently the people who'd attended the service were, thankfully, tucked away in their cars.

So really, what could go wrong?

CHAPTER 12

AS I SCANNED THE CURVED DRIVEWAY FOR any potential tackling dummies, Herman unhooked his arm from mine and weaved his way between the cars toward the fountain. A vision of him discarding his shoes and socks, rolling up his pants, and frolicking in the middle of the water flashed through my mind. And it made me smile. I wondered how Marguerite would react if she came out and saw us splashing around before Betty's service.

It would be best not to find out.

After one last check for wandering mourners, I also zigzagged my way toward the fountain, determined to keep Herman clothed and dry.

And I would do that just as soon as I found him.

Good grief. I'd looked away for maybe fifteen seconds and had lost a senior citizen with Alzheimer's. How would I ever become a decent parent if I couldn't even keep track of a walking, talking adult?

I circled the fountain, making sure Herman hadn't stumbled in and drowned. Marguerite didn't need a second dead sibling on her plate today.

Satisfied he wasn't in the fountain, I scanned the large parking lot and didn't see him. There wasn't movement by any of the cars. I started jogging around the parking lot, calling to him while trying not to draw attention to myself.

As if.

The main problem was Herman wasn't rationale. He could be in the backseat of a mourner's car, wreaking havoc. He could be hanging out underneath a vehicle, pretending to be a mechanic. He could somehow be off the premises altogether and hitchhiking to God-knew-where.

Heaven help me.

I was spinning around like a top and beginning to panic as the seconds ticked by. As much as I didn't want to, I decided to ask Smokey the Driver if he'd seen Herman, in hopes he was a better babysitter than I was.

I scampered from the parking lot toward the large circular driveway and spotted movement at the front of the long procession of cars. I watched as Smokey the Driver rushed toward the double doors at the entrance and disappeared through one of them, tossing his cigarette aside just before the door shut behind him.

What the hell? Had Herman gone racing into the funeral home, bringing devastation to all who dared get in his way? How had I lost sight of him in such a quick amount of time?

As I scurried by the passenger's side of the hearse, I was startled to hear, "Cecile!" come from inside the vehicle. The passenger side window whirred down, and Herman leaned over from the *driver's side of the hearse.*

"Herman!" I exclaimed. "What the hell are you doing? Get out of there right now!" Glancing at the passenger seat and toward the back of the vehicle, I hoped I'd see someone else accompanying the driver, but nope. Didn't they work in pairs? The driver couldn't be expected to lead an entire procession solo, could he? Wasn't it like an airline pilot who needed a co-pilot in case of emergency?

In the back of the hearse was a shiny casket. And I could bet it wasn't the co-pilot.

Ignoring my tone, Herman made frantic hand gestures. "Cecile, I'm getting ice cream whether you're coming with me or not. So get in, or tell me what kind you want, and I'll bring some back for you."

Mother of God. This couldn't be happening.

I put my hands on the passenger's side window ledge and turned halfway back toward the funeral home doors, willing them to open. They did not.

Focusing on the Alzheimer's-chauffeur, I did my best to sound calm. "Herman, this isn't your car, so you should really give it back to the nice funeral home people."

"They're really not all that nice," Herman retorted. "They've got Betty looking all chalky white, and her hair is all wrong. Those people don't know what they're doing."

"Herman..." I pleaded and kept turning back to the funeral home doors. Couldn't someone behind me see what was going on?

Suddenly the hearse started moving, and I trotted to keep up with it, my arms still firmly on the window ledge. Because *that* would certainly slow down the several-ton vehicle with a dead body in the back.

"Herman! Stop this car right now. This is stealing, and you're going to get in a lot of trouble," I hissed.

Herman giggled like a schoolgirl, and I had to pick up my pace to a jog as he gained speed. "Cecile, you can get in or you can get out of my way, but I'm blowing this Popsicle stand. I'm off to find some ice cream!"

I took a final glance at the funeral home entrance, and no one was coming to the rescue. Life comes down to choices, good or bad. Faced with this mess, I could let the deranged old man drive off with the dead body, or I could jump in the moving vehicle and go down with the ship.

As I yanked on the car door, I realized it wasn't going to open, since it was in motion. Given no other option, I dove through the open passenger window, my legs sticking out as Herman gunned it down the funeral home driveway.

CHAPTER 13

AS I REMOVED MY FACE FROM THE PASSENGER'S SEAT, I twisted my lower half into the car and buckled up immediately. God only knew how this joyride would end. Herman looked so happy and free that I cracked a small smile.

Until that practical voice in my head piped up. I hate that voice sometimes. It told me I was a massive dipshit and predicted Herman and I would be arrested within the hour. It further told me I was jeopardizing my career and my safety by face-planting myself in this hearse.

I told the voice to shove it up its ass. Would that be my own ass? Whatever.

Keeping my tone as steady as possible, I leaned over toward my chauffeur. "Herman, I see you're having a ton of fun, and I think that's great. But I have a really nice truck back in the parking lot. Don't you agree it might be a good idea to return this car, as well as the dearly departed, to the funeral home as soon as possible?"

To his credit, Herman kept his focus firmly on the road but seemed to be thinking about my question. Since we hadn't topped the ten-miles-per-hour barrier, I did my best not to rush his answer and get him all upset.

He nodded. "That may be a good idea, Cecile, because this car is really big. But I'd hate to ruin the parade now that it's started."

Hunh?

Then it hit me. I snapped my head toward the rearview passenger window and looked behind us. Sure as shit, the procession of cars was following us on our impromptu adventure to the ice cream shop.

This couldn't be happening.

"Herman, I agree parades are wonderful, but we probably shouldn't be leading this particular one. Mr. Rosenthal had a nice man picked out to lead the parade route, and we should let him do his job. Maybe we should turn around, nice and easy, and escort these fine people back to the funeral home. I can even drive if you'd like. Then we'll ride in Betty's parade later on today." I simply couldn't be having this conversation.

Herman's knuckles tightened on the wheel, and his face flushed. "But Cecile, we have to get our ice cream. We are less than ten minutes away, and I'm getting my Rocky Road!" He was back in child-mode, wailing like a toddler, and I was starting to panic. Really panic. Shortness-of-breath-I-could-die-in-a-hearse panic. I hate that type of irony. I had to calm down. I decided the best thing to do would be to play along.

"What's the name of the ice cream shop again? I keep forgetting."

"Buster's," he said and beamed. He seemed happier now that I appeared to be on board.

"That's right, what a nice place."

As is my nature when I'm faced with utter hysteria, as well as impending doom, I reached out to my rock—Doob. The fact Doob is my rock will probably one day land me in some type of therapy, but for now, he was the man for the job.

Hoping to avoid anymore outbursts from Herman, texting seemed like the best option in order to keep him in the dark as to what I was planning. As if I even knew what I was planning. Whipping out my cell phone, I texted Doob as fast as my fingers would move. I was momentarily impressed with how succinct I'd been in explaining my circumstances. I quickly got a response from Doob:

D: WTF Meg??? You stole a hearse?! This 1 takes the cake, even for u. Ur mom is going to stroke out. Ur dad...well, God help u. U R SCREWED.

M: Shut up! I know! But I couldn't let the poor guy drive off. U call the cops & have Kayla call the funeral home. But don't let them hurt/arrest Herm. He just wants ice cream.

D: What's the license plate on the car?

M: Like I f-ing know! Didn't exactly check before jumping in & landing on my face. Tell the cops we're on our way to Buster's. Pronto! If I die in this hearse, it's on u.

D: Okay, I'll call the cops & tell them how to do their job & I'm sure K will be very convincing when the funeral director gets upset & K unleashes her tirade of expletives. Stay tuned Meg, ttyl.

M: Doob, don't go!

But I was out of luck. He was gone, and I was still in the hearse with the Alzheimer's patient and the dead body. On the upside, Herman was a pretty good driver and seemed to know exactly where he was going. I definitely considered jumping out every time he hit a red light, but really, where would I go? And now that I'd committed, it didn't seem right to bail on him midway through our ordeal.

As we drove down Thames Street in Newport, Herman started playing tour guide. He pointed out restaurants and artsy boutiques and even showed me the dock where he'd had his first kiss. For the briefest moment, I forgot the disastrous part of this little joyride and smiled at the old man, reliving memories fresh in his fragile mind.

As we turned onto a side street and started down another winding road, Herman's eyes lit up. Down the road a ways, a little ice cream shack appeared on the horizon. And God help me, it was closed.

CHAPTER 14

THIS WAS BEYOND BAD. Herman would lose his composure when he realized there was no ice cream. Not to mention the fact that a funeral procession would be pulling in behind us.

On the bright side, the vehicle would, at least, stop and I'd live to see another day. So I had that going for me. I just needed to get through the next hour or so.

Herman actually used his turn signal before pulling into the parking lot, and as he parked the monstrous vehicle, I glanced in the passenger-side rearview mirror. The line of cars followed suit. The lot was a pretty good size, and everyone pulled in behind us. A vision of wildly screaming mourners flashed through my head. How in the world would I defend Herman while simultaneously not offending a crowd lamenting the loss of a loved one?

Good grief.

As if the scene had jumped out of my head, a huge woman in dark clothing with short, blazing red hair rushed toward the driver's side of the hearse. Before I could tell Herman to stay put, he opened his door, apparently oblivious to the closed shop or the charging redhead.

Double good grief.

I leapt out of the hearse, prepared to defend Herman's honor. After all, I'd known him for less than an hour, so I was the perfect spokesperson, right? Ugh.

While I watched in utter fascination, the large redhead wrapped her arms around Herman, sobbing and laughing at the same time. Herman looked thrilled and hugged her back, as if they were old friends.

"This was a *perfect* idea!" the woman exclaimed. "Rufus loved this shop. How in the world did you know this was his favorite place?" She enveloped Herman in another bear hug, and he started turning an interesting shade of reddish-purple. I worried she might just squeeze him to death, but he was quickly rescued when she released him to let him shake the hands of a few elderly men who'd approached.

Within two minutes, all of the cars emptied, and a group of well dressed funeral goers were treating Herman like a hero. He glowed like a child on Christmas and had, evidently, forgotten our ice cream run.

There have been a few times in my life when I've physically *felt* the presence of God, a higher power, whatever the heck is out there. I'm not a religious nutcase or anything, but sometimes you witness a moment that makes you say, "Yep...someone up there got this one right." And I looked to the heavens and winked, hoping the responsible party saw my gratitude.

My eyes welled up, and I was glad I'd ignored my inner voice. This was something to experience. Somehow a crazy old man had made a bunch of sad people happy, and they'd done the same for him.

My bliss disintegrated on a whoop-whoop siren blip, as a police car turned into the parking lot. I hoped the Big Guy upstairs would somehow get me out of this one as well.

CHAPTER 15

OTHER THAN ME, NO ONE SEEMED TO GIVE A RAT'S PATOOT that a couple of law enforcement types had just shown up for the party. A few funeral-goers glanced their way and then continued on with their conversations, as if none of this was the slightest bit odd. The whole thing was kind of surreal. It wouldn't have surprised me if someone actually pulled in with gallons of ice cream and started serving the impromptu get-together. As long as it wasn't Doob.

Deciding to take the bull by the horns, I approached the officers with a small smile as if to welcome them to the party. Meagan-Maloney-Hostess-of-Mourners-Ice-Cream-Socials-Extraordinaire.

"Are you in charge here?" one of the policemen asked, hitching his belt and kind of getting a little too close to my personal space. He was of the tall, lean, and mean variety, with extremely close-cropped hair, a fair complexion, and light blue eyes that were almost clear. I put his age in the late-twenties, but everything about him was pinched.

I tilted my head to one side. "I'm not sure if I'm *in charge,* per se—"

"So who is?" he interrupted me.

"Well, I don't know if I'd say anyone is in charge. It's just that—"

"You're trespassing."

I guess we'd moved past the issue of who was in charge.

"Officers, here's the thing." I looked to the second policeman for some help, but he might as well been made out of stone for all the reaction I got from him. "I was at Rosenthal's Funeral Home because I had a meeting with the director to discuss a case I'm working on. I'm a private investigator from Boston."

Blank stares from both. Dropping my resume didn't have the desired *she's-one-of-us effect.* Okey dokey.

"After I met with Mr. Rosenthal, that man"—I pointed at Herman—"thought I was a friend from his childhood. As you can see, he's quite old, and sadly he has Alzheimer's. His sister recently died, and she's being buried today."

"Is that her?" Lean-and-Mean hitched his thumb toward the hearse, and I wrinkled my nose at him. The question seemed a little insensitive.

"Ummm, no, I'm not sure who that is," I said.

"This oughta be good," he said, folding his arms over his chest and narrowing his eyes.

I went on to explain the chain of events, and just as I was wrapping up, a dark sedan pulled into the parking lot, and Mr. Rosenthal jumped out before it'd come to a complete stop. He didn't seem nearly as calm or refined as I'd seen him less than an hour before, and his face was the color of eggplant.

As he marched toward the officers and me, his eyes were locked on mine, and he looked furious.

"What is the meaning of this, Miss Maloney? Have you no respect for these people or my business? Are you trying to ruin me by stealing my vehicle and destroying my reputation?"

My face instantly flushed, and I began to stammer. "Of-of course not, sir...uh, Mr. Rosenthal. I-I was trying to leave when—"

"When you went out for a jaunt in my *hearse*?! You are a sick young woman, and you should be ashamed of yourself," he huffed. Then he turned to look at the officers for the first time. "Gentlemen, I would like this lady and the other thief arrested for stealing my vehicle, and I would ask you to assist us as we restart the procession to the cemetery for this other family."

Lean-and-Mean-Cop and Silent-Cop both looked stunned that an uppity funeral director was giving them marching orders, and I was pretty surprised myself. Fortunately, my reaction time—and temper—were quicker than both of theirs. I took a step towards Mr. Rosenthal and lowered my voice.

"Listen to me carefully before you bark out one more comment about anyone getting arrested. *Your* hearse was left unattended in front of *your* facility, which provided the opportunity for *your* customer—a sweet, senile old man who's grieving the loss of his sister—to take the vehicle for a drive. Why did he do this? He wanted ice cream, to get away from the tragedy of the day and have some friggin' Rocky Road. Now, if you're so worried about publicity and the well-being of this family and Herman's family, then I suggest that we all thank our lucky stars this didn't end in a complete disaster. Look around you, all three of you." The trio of men did as I directed. "What do you see? Do any of you want to make this a bigger deal than it really was?"

As I said this, an adolescent boy with black hair that fell over his eyes waddled over and snapped a picture of the four of us with his cell phone. "Awesome! This is going on Facebook right away. Could you guys cuff the girl or something cool like that? Maybe you could Taser her and a boob could pop out?"

I turned to the policemen with a questioning look, and they glanced from me to Mr. Rosenthal. His tense body sagged, and I knew I was in the clear.

"Beat it kid," I snarled. I'd Taser his ass.

Mr. Rosenthal wouldn't let up. "Fine! I won't press charges, but I need to get this procession moving. Everything is on a strict timetable."

"And you'll get Herman back to the funeral home safe and sound?" Lean-And-Mean asked Mr. Rosenthal.

The funeral director's face flushed anew, but he kept his temper in check. "I will take the stolen hearse back to the funeral home, and yes, I will take Herman along with me. But I will not take her!" He pointed at me with a dramatic flourish, as if he was on a witness stand, identifying me as a maniac killer sitting at the defendant's table.

I rolled my eyes. "Save the theatrics. I wouldn't take the ride even if I was the corpse."

With some coordination from the policemen, everyone was on their way in no time, and I soon stood in an empty parking lot with the two officers. Lean-And-Mean wasted a little more time with some mundane questions, but it was clear they weren't going to do anything about the afternoon's events.

"We normally don't do this," Silent-Cop finally spoke directly to me. "But earlier you mentioned your car was at the funeral home. We can give you a lift back there if you'd like." Lean-And-Mean shot him a withering look.

"I'd appreciate that," I said with a small smile. I didn't know the name of any cab companies in Newport, and the long walk back at this chilly hour of the day didn't seem very appealing.

As it turned out, Mr. Rosenthal—henceforth called Mr. Fucking Rosenthal—had managed to get my truck towed in the time I'd been gone. How he'd arranged it was beyond me, but my vehicle—check that, *Doob's Mercedes*—was most definitely gone.

What. An. Asshole.

Silent-Cop said they'd wait for me while I went inside to find out where Doob's truck was, and that was met with another death-stare from Lean-And-Mean. Silent-Cop maybe thought I was cute, or possibly amusing, and that definitely didn't meet with his partner's approval.

"We're not running a taxi service," Lean-And-Mean chirped as I climbed out of their vehicle.

"Thanks for the newsflash," I said, but only after shutting the door behind me. I really didn't need to piss him off any further.

When I went in to pitch my fit, I was told Mr. Rosenthal was shockingly *unavailable*, so I had to deal with a young lady who looked ready to wet her pants. I kept reminding myself not to kill the messenger. It wasn't her fault her boss was a dick.

As with all things in life, timing is everything. And, of course, the impound lot where I could retrieve Doob's SUV was closed. And, of course, it didn't matter anyway. I couldn't pick it up if they'd been open, because it wasn't my vehicle. Doob would be thrilled to know where his Mercedes was spending the evening.

So off I went with the two policemen to Jeff's place in Jamestown. When the cop car reached the end of the long driveway, Jeff stood outside the front door, with Sampson beside him. Sampson barked when he saw Silent-Cop let me out of the backseat of the cruiser, and Jeff looked ready to burst out laughing.

"Really?" he said as I approached them, a loud guffaw finally escaping his mouth.

"Don't even," I responded and bent down to rub Sampson's ears.

"So where's Doob's truck?"

"Impound," I said with a dismissive wave.

"*Impound*?" he repeated.

"Yep."

"And I'm guessing he doesn't know?"

"Nope."

"And I'm guessing he won't be too happy?"

"Cor-rect."

"And when do you plan on telling him?"

I stood up, stretched, and thought about the question. "Never?"

Jeff leaned against the door jamb. "Sounds reasonable. Would you like a drink?"

"I would like several," I said and swept a hand through the doorway to lead Sampson inside.

Before shutting the front door behind me, I glanced back at the police cruiser, which had pulled up behind Jeff's car. Silent-Cop appeared to be writing down the license plate number. What in the world was *that* all about?

As if he somehow heard the question in my head, Jeff said, "He's going to check me out."

"Checking *you* out? Why?" I asked, mortified I'd now involved Jeff in my mess.

"My guess would be he likes you. Most cops don't moonlight as a cab company."

I shrugged. "That's what his partner told me."

"So if he thinks you're with me, and if he can prove I'm a creep or a shyster or an unsavory type, well...maybe he thinks you could be Mrs. Newport Cop someday," he said with a chuckle.

Good grief.

CHAPTER 16

Friday, November 8th

I THINK DOOB HAD BEEN PRAYING FOR ARMAGEDDON all week, but much to his dismay, Friday arrived with all-things-gala in the air. To my relief, he didn't freak when he learned about his Mercedes spending the night in jail. And thankfully, he didn't have any problems retrieving the truck. Maybe because I called Silent-Cop and asked him to meet Doobie at the vehicle holding place, just to make sure things went smoothly.

Hey, if Silent-Cop thought I was cute, I figured I should take advantage and help out a friend. Especially since I was the one responsible for putting the friend's baby in impound in the first place.

I had a wonderful lunch with Eileen. She fussed about the home-baked cake, but none of the names on the guest book had jumped out at her as potential bad guys. Still, it was nice to spend some time with her and listen to her stories.

The day seemed to zip by in record time, and before any of us knew it, we were getting dressed for the big event. The plan was to convene around the kitchen island at six o'clock that evening, and I was the last one to get downstairs. When I came around the corner, the sight that greeted me was fairly adorable, like we were all little kids playing dress-up. Jeff looked dapper; Doob looked uncomfortable, yet presentable, and Kayla was—in a word—spectacular.

I circled the island and greeted each of my friends with a hug and a kind word.

"Jeff, thank you so much for these tickets," was rewarded with a smile.

"Kayla, you are breathtaking," was returned with an *of-course-I-am* look from my modest friend.

"Doob, you look the best I've ever seen you. Thank you for doing this," was met with Doob's complexion turning purple while he stared at the floor.

"I hate this, Meg," he muttered.

I hugged him again and said, "I know. Just think, in six hours or so, this will all be over."

His eyes bulged and his purple pallor turned greenish. "Six hours?"

Whoops. "Five?" He rubbed his face with both hands.

Kayla glanced toward the great room and then gestured at the front door. "All right, people, I just saw headlights. Our chariot awaits."

Since Jeff had sprung for the tickets to the event, Doob took it upon himself to get a limo for the entire evening, which was sweet of him. Not to mention smart. All of us were undoubtedly going to have some cocktails, so having a driver made a whole lot of sense. I only hoped Doob had the guy for the entire night so we wouldn't have to worry about five hours or six hours or whatever.

The driver was a dapper little fellow, at least seventy years old, with an adorable black driver's cap on his head and tufts of gray hair sticking out of the sides. He held the vehicle door open for us with such deference we all felt like royalty. Introducing himself as William, he showed us he'd loaded up the limo with all sorts of goodies, including champagne, bottled water, soda, pretzels, potato chips, and mints. When he pointed out the various buttons and gadgets, Doob had a field day changing the interior lights and zipping the center console window up and down. I was certain a disco ball and confetti would soon follow.

Under the pretense of humoring William, Kayla uncorked the champagne, nearly taking Doob's eye out in the process. The four of us split the bottle on the drive into Newport while enjoying the sparkling lights of the quaint little town with its ocean views. I felt carefree and elegant in my strapless, red evening gown. It all seemed tremendously sophisticated, and I had to remind myself the only reason we were attending the gala was so I could do some sleuthing.

As we wound our way along Ocean Drive, Doob's nose was stuck to the window, and he whistled lightly. "I did a little research online before we left, but those pictures don't do these mansions justice," he said. "I've lived within a couple of hours of here for quite a while and haven't ever checked them out. They are massive."

"You should see them in the daytime. They're amazing," Kayla cooed, like a star-struck teenager. "I've been to every single one that's open for tours. My favorite is The Breakers, which was actually the *summer* home of Cornelius Vanderbilt, the Second. Can you imagine your summer home having seventy rooms and forty-five-foot-high ceilings in the Great Hall?"

"You sound like a mansion groupie," I said with a grin.

Kayla shrugged. "I've been called worse. My second favorite is Rosecliff. It was featured in the movies *The Great Gatsby* and *True Lies*, and it was theeee place to party during the Gilded Age. You can actually still rent it for a wedding or a corporate outing, but I'm sure it costs a fortune."

"I read you can do the Newport Cliff Walk along the Atlantic and see many of the mansions from there," Doob said. "I really need to check it out."

I scoffed. "It's about four miles, Doob. You'd get about a quarter-mile before falling into the ocean."

He raised his eyebrows. "Speaking of, Megs, don't you have—"

I pointed a finger at him. "Not tonight, Doob."

"Fine, but in less than forty-eight hours, you're going to be one hurting puppy."

"Please shut your pie hole," I said and noticed Kayla's and Jeff's quizzical looks. "I'll fill you guys in tomorrow. For now, let's just enjoy how the other half lives."

We sipped our champagne and made some small talk along the way, and long before I was ready to relinquish the lovely limo accommodations, we pulled into the winding driveway to the immense mansion. Soft lights lined the driveway all the way up to the house. Every inch of the beautiful brick façade glowed, and the illumination went so high in the air it was hard to tell where the structure stopped and the twinkling stars began. It was simply stunning.

I reluctantly had to shift from relaxed-cocktail-party-mode to let's-get-to-work-mode. My plan was to somehow get some time with Mr. Malcolm Gage Johnson, Prick Extraordinaire, and see if I could cajole, harass, trick him into saying something that would help me solve why Charlie died in Jeff's house. How exactly I was going to do that remained to be seen. I would have to call an audible once I arrived and hope for the best. Getting an audience with this man would probably be more difficult than getting in to see the Pope.

Stepping out of the limo, I noticed a security checkpoint inside the front door of the magnificent house, like a T.S.A. setup at T.F. Green Airport in Providence. I didn't know if that made me feel safe or sad. Regardless, I made sure no one was looking when I slipped my handgun out of my adorable little clutch and slipped it into one of the handy-dandy storage areas in the limo. No one knew I'd brought it, and it was doubtful I would need it anyway, right?

Brisk air chilled my bare skin as we waited in line to get into the enormous house, but the procession moved along at a quick pace, and Kayla was the first one of our party to walk through the metal detectors.

"Want to frisk me boys?" she asked as she spread her arms wide and waltzed through the framed structure. Batting the fake lashes she'd donned for the evening, she purred, "I promise it'll be fun."

A heavily-muscled, six-foot tall security woman with a gray crew cut walked over to Kayla and said, "I'd be glad to," in a baritone voice. Kayla turned back to us with a *help me* look on her face, but we were all frozen in place. It was all I could do to not burst out laughing while the woman patted Kayla down and another guard rifled through her small, jeweled handbag.

I was next through the metal detector and breezed through without incident. As one guard handed me back my clutch, another touched me gently on my elbow. I looked up to see a handsome black man, wearing a magnificent dark suit and a wire curled in his ear. He looked like Secret Service, and I briefly wondered if the President was at this gala.

"Miss Maloney," he said, "Mr. Johnson would like to see you in his private quarters."

So much for figuring out how to get an audience with him.

CHAPTER 17

AFTER BEING CLEARED THROUGH SECURITY, I noticed all the guests were guided to the right of the sweeping double marble staircase. A sign there indicated the direction to the east ballroom. *East ballroom?* It needed a directional indicator? Did that mean there were also north, south, and west ballrooms as well? Good grief.

The guard who'd spoken to me ushered me off to the left where there were two very large, ornately carved wooden doors, probably imported from some remote corner of the planet where special wood is grown just for extremely rich people. In front of the closed doors were several three-foot metal stands with thick, purple velvet ropes hanging loosely between them.

"This must be the V.I.P. section then?" I asked my escort, trying to calm my nerves as he unhooked one of the ropes. He gave me a tight smile but didn't respond. Rather, he brought his shoulder to his mouth and spoke in low tones into a microphone I hadn't noticed on his immaculate lapel. I couldn't make out what he said, but I was certain he told someone the *subject was in hand* and to prepare the guillotine or the dungeon or whatever they had in store for me.

I took a quick glance back at the security area and saw my three friends. Doob's mouth was agape, Kayla looked concerned, and Jeff was speaking to one of the guards and pointing at me. The guard shook his head at Jeff and motioned for him to move along.

I turned back around to face the music. My guide-slash-captor ushered me down a hallway that would rival any grand hotel at any locale in the world. Like the staircase, the floor was white marble with brushes of a muted feathery silver color throughout. Hanging every ten feet from the high ceilings were crystal chandeliers with multiple layers, and above the wainscoted lower half of the walls was artwork undoubtedly worth beaucoup bucks. Between the priceless paintings, sparkling mirrors brightened the long hallway. The entire area gleamed and glittered, so it would have been easy to miss the tiny cameras mounted throughout, but thankfully I'm a crack detective. The child in me wanted to wave at one of them, just to say, "Hi, I see you watching me," but I restrained myself.

We arrived at another massive double doorway, this one made of some type of white material that looked less like wood and more like ivory. I studied the doors as my escort knocked softly. They'd probably been hand-carved out of elephant tusks from Borneo over the period of twelve years by some poor skeleton-like-figure making two cents an hour.

The whole grandiose place reeked of wealth and omnipotence and was so ostentatious I found myself irritated. I guess going from Eileen's modest home and her sad story to this over-the-top castle with directions to a ballroom burned my ass. Or maybe I was grouchy because I arrived at the gala on offense, and now I was being put in the position of playing defense. I didn't even know how they knew my name. What I did know was that I was ticked off instead of afraid, and that was probably a good thing.

Mr. Fancy Suit opened one of the ivory doors and made a sweep of his hand to guide me into yet another gargantuan room. This one was clearly a library, complete with the dark mahogany wood shelving—undoubtedly stocked with only signed first editions—rising three stories high. Rolling ladders were located throughout the room, and I wished I could zip around on them and snoop to my heart's content.

"Miss Maloney, you've entered Edinburgh," came a booming voice with a southern accent. I spun a quarter-turn and saw a tall man standing behind a large desk holding a lit cigar. I stifled a tremor as I recalled Eileen's story about Malcolm holding a cigar to Patricia's eye.

"Edinburgh is the name of the house?" I asked.

He chuckled and shook his head as if I were an ignorant child. "Edinburgh is the name of this *library*," he said as he spread his arms out and looked up. "It's named after a prestigious library in Scotland, where some of my ancestors lived."

His face was weather-beaten tan, his full head of white hair pomaded back to perfection. The tuxedo he wore probably cost more than what I made in a year, and fit him to perfection. He looked to be in his late sixties, clearly comfortable in his own skin. The smirk on his face indicated he was going to bat me around like a cat with a ball of yarn, and it increased my irritation.

"Do you name all your rooms?" I asked flatly. Were extremely rich people that bored?

He dialed back his fake hospitality a notch. "Whether you realize it or not, Miss Maloney, you are amongst treasures in this library. You should take a moment to savor it. Look around and take it all in." He again spread his arms wide as if he'd just delivered bushels of food to a village full of starving people.

This guy was something else.

"Oh, I'm taking it all in, I assure you, Mr. Johnson. How many elephants died for those two doors out there?"

I held his gaze, and something unfriendly flickered in his eyes. He sat in the chair behind his desk as the guard smoothly moved to stand just off to his side. There was an antique mahogany credenza behind him with all sorts of pictures and mementos of a life clearly well lived.

After tilting his head back and taking a long puff of the cigar, he reached for a large manila envelope resting on his desk. "Your dossier indicated you have a bit of a fresh mouth, Miss Maloney. It's quite unbecoming in a young lady. It's no wonder you're still single."

Really? If he thought my single status was my Achilles heel, he had a lot to learn.

It was then I noticed something inside the massive credenza I couldn't believe. *Was that possible? And if so, that could explain a lot...*

I forced myself to regain my composure so he wouldn't notice me noticing. "My *dossier*? I'm so flattered you went to the trouble, Mr. Johnson. As for my marital status and my mouth, I wasn't raised in the south, so I didn't receive an etiquette handbook for my tenth birthday. I spent my time reading about the War of Northern Aggression," I said with a wink.

His face reddened under his tan, and his little smirk disappeared for good as he pulled out what looked to be some black and white pictures from the envelope. Eileen again came to mind, along with the story about Malcolm having pictures of her family. He seemed to be a one-trick pony with his photos and his implied threats. I willed myself not to show any interest in the pictures.

"So very classy, Miss Maloney. Since we're clearly not going to waste time on pleasantries, you need to explain to me why you're at this event." He held up his free hand. "And don't waste my time by lying."

"Why would I lie?"

"In my experience, people like *you*—in your *profession,* I suppose I'll call it—tend to make up stories."

"Do you have a lot of experience with people in my profession?"

"I'm the one asking questions here, Miss Maloney."

"That's where you're mistaken," I retorted, my temper barely in check. "I understand you're used to getting your way because you're incredibly wealthy, Mr. Johnson. But in my experience with people like *you,* no one really respects you. They may fear you, and they probably kowtow and defer to you, but they definitely don't like you. You wave your inherited money, your cigar, your self-important reputation in people's faces, and you think they should bow down to you because you're rich, which makes you feel powerful. So I'll be happy to have a *discussion* about why I'm here, which will involve *you* answering some of *my* questions, and then you can have your pretty-boy rent-a-cop here take me back to my friends." I glanced at the guard. "He probably hates you, too."

The guard's jaw clenched, but he remained silent, standing with his feet apart and his hands crossed over his private parts.

Malcolm's face tightened, and his already dark eyes turned black. "You are very out of your league here, young lady. Or should I say, young woman. A *lady* you are not. Regardless of how I obtained my wealth, I've retained and built upon it, and part of the way I've done that is by doing my homework. I see things, namely I see *threats,* before they happen so I can stop them from harming me or the people and things I care about.

"That said...I pay attention when there's a last-minute purchase to one of my charity events. I pay attention when four young people whom I've never heard of pay eight thousand dollars to come to my home. I further pay attention when one of those people is a private investigator who's been poking around town, investigating the death of a man I despised."

"So you admit you hated Charlie?"

He waved his cigar in the air. "Oh come now, Miss Maloney, do you think that's some type of confession? Everyone in town knows Charlie and I loathed each other."

"Some people might think that's a motive for murder."

He barked out a laugh. "Murder? Well, that's rich. Even richer than me," he said with a grin intended to piss me off. It succeeded. "From what I've heard, Charlie's fall was ruled an accident. Yet, you've turned it into a murder. I've got to wonder why. So you can bilk your lottery-winning boyfriend for some money?"

"I haven't turned it into anything, Mr. Johnson. My friend asked me to look into the situation, and that's what I'm doing. Your name came up in the course of the investigation, so I'm doing my due diligence as a *professional.*"

"I couldn't care less about your due diligence, Miss Maloney. What I care about is the fact you're prying into my life. So, to level the playing field, I decided to pry into yours." He balanced his cigar on an ashtray and flicked photos all around the desk, as if he were dealing a deck of cards at a blackjack table in Vegas.

Then he started pointing to different snapshots. "Lovely sister and an impressive resume, that Moira. Brains *and* a real beauty, too. She doesn't look a thing like you. Your blue collar parents seem like very hard working folks. Salt of the earth you could say. And your Uncle Larry, we'll he's a man I could probably use on staff," he said conspiratorially. "And then there's—"

"Enough," I said in a commanding voice I didn't even know I had. Handsome-Guard stiffened a bit but didn't go for the gun undoubtedly hidden under his impeccable suit. "Your point is taken. You've investigated me; I'm supposed to be scared. I'm supposed to cower and apologize and beg you to not hurt me or my family. I'm not going to do that, but if you want to continue to review my family tree, I've got all night."

"Miss Maloney, you are right about one thing and one thing only. You *should* be scared. You do not want me as an enemy, I promise you that."

"I'm not looking for an enemy. I'm looking for answers. I came to you directly rather than bringing your name up to the authorities."

"The authorities can certainly manage without *you,*" he sneered, looking at me as if I was a bug he'd just squashed. "You've got thirty more seconds to explain why you've invaded my home. I have many more important guests to attend to."

"Did you, or did anyone in your employ, have anything to do with Charlie O'Neill's death?" I asked, looking him straight in the eye.

"No," he responded levelly.

"Where were you the night he died?"

"My wife and I were with my daughter and her family at their home on Cape Cod," he said, with a twinkle in his eyes. "Lots of witnesses, Miss Maloney. If there's nothing further—"

"Did you blame Charlie for your sister's suicide?"

His face turned crimson and he stood up. "This meeting is over."

"I'll need a way to get in touch with you if we need to speak again."

"That is out of the question." He twisted the cigar over and over into his fancy ashtray, turning it into cinders. I got the message loud and clear.

He could do the same to me.

"Gerard, please escort Miss Maloney back to her friends. And Miss Maloney, I'll be keeping a close eye on you and yours."

"Is this the part where I shudder in fear?"

"It would be prudent of you to have a healthy dose of fear in your everyday life, young woman. It keeps you on your toes, keeps you *safe*. Keeps your family *safe*."

With that, Gerard swept around the desk and led me out of the library and back to the gleaming hallway. As we walked back through the expensive paintings and sparkling walls, my knees started to shake, and I was overcome with a sense of vulnerability. My family had been threatened by a steroid freak involved in Melanie's case earlier in the year, and my reaction had been the same. First anger, and then, scared shitless. I was glad I hadn't let Malcolm see my scared shitless state, but it was here, and it was real. Situations like this were really the only times I second-guessed my job.

If I'd only known.

CHAPTER 18

TRUE TO FORM, DOOB STOOD IN THE ENTRYWAY WHEN the guard and I returned, waiting for me like a loyal dog. He rushed over, gave me a hug, and then held me by the shoulders and studied my face.

"Are you okay?" he asked with concern.

I didn't want to tell him how I was really feeling, so I looked at him quizzically and asked, "I'm sorry, who are you?"

He gently shoved me away and said, "You're a jerk. I was worried they were torturing you back there."

"It wasn't anything I'd care to revisit, but no physical torture was involved."

"Mental torture then?" Doob knows I carefully select my words at times.

"You could say that," I conceded.

"Sometimes I hate your job," Doob said.

"Get in line," I said with an eye-roll.

"Did you find out anything helpful?"

I shook my head. "Yes and no. But I don't think he had anything to do with Charlie's death."

"Why?"

I shrugged. "Just a hunch, I guess. He was more than comfortable telling me about his dislike for Charlie. And he didn't have the least bit of remorse that Charlie died. If he was somehow involved, he might not have been so forthcoming."

"So that's it?"

"Not exactly. I won't completely give up on him if we somehow figure out Charlie was murdered, but it just doesn't feel right. But on a *totally* different note…I do think he has some stolen art back there."

Doob scrunched up his face. "Hunh? You're an art connoisseur now?"

"I know some stuff," I said a little defensively. "You didn't live here then, but do you remember hearing about the art heist at the Isabella Stewart Gardner Museum back in 1990?"

Doob scratched his head. "Vaguely. It was the largest art theft in the world. Thirteen or fourteen pieces taken, something like that?"

"Thirteen. There's still a five million dollar reward out there for information leading to their recovery."

"Nice," Doob said. "Could be a big night for you, Meg. You haven't gotten yourself killed yet, and you might get rich by becoming a stolen art snitch."

"I'd do it for free if it would get that asshole in some hot water."

"What do you think he has? And do you really think he'd have it out in broad daylight?"

"One of the items stolen from the museum theft was a finial shaped like an eagle that was on top of a flag in Napoleon's army."

"And you could pick this particular finial out with no hesitation?" Doob asked, not bothering to hide his skepticism.

"I did a pretty in-depth paper on that theft back in school, and I can still name all of the thirteen missing pieces; I could probably pick out eight or nine of them if I saw them. The theft was fascinating to me; it was so well planned, but it was so basic. The thieves dressed up as cops and went to the side entrance of the museum around 1:30 the morning after St. Patrick's Day."

"Smart move by them," Doob commented. "The whole city would have been swimming in green beer."

"*Erin go Bragh*. Anyway, the robbers subdued the guards without hurting them and eventually ended up with about three hundred million dollars in stolen art, which probably resulted in a pretty penny out on the black market. The simplicity of the whole thing, coupled with the fact that nothing has ever been recovered, is amazing to me."

"Until now."

"Possibly until now, yes. Can you imagine if I found one of the pieces?" I got tingly all over just saying it.

"Which again begs the question, would this rich dude just have it out in the open? Did he have it on a flag, or what? Where was it?"

"It was kind of propped up in his credenza. I could see it as clear as I can see you in front of me. Maybe he puts it away if he has someone important or prestigious back in the library. If it's someone he deems educated or sophisticated enough, he might hide it because they might be smart enough to know the origins of that finial."

Doob nodded. "But you? The lowly, female, private investigator, with no money and seemingly no clue—"

I held up a hand. "That's quite enough, Mr. I-Don't-Even-Have-A-Job, but yes, you get my point. He probably didn't even think about removing the piece in my presence. And he made a point of telling me I was amongst treasures. He had all kinds of stuff in there, it was like—"

And then I was struck with a thought.

I whipped out my cell phone and pushed a number I'd loaded just a couple of days prior.

"This is Officer Hurley," he said on the first ring. Silent-Cop was very prompt with the phone.

"Uh hi, Officer, this is Meagan Maloney. Again."

"Meagan! It's great to hear from you! How is Doob's truck? Everything okay?" His voice was full of far too much enthusiasm, and I winced with discomfort.

"Yes, thanks so much for making sure that went smoothly. Listen, I don't mean to be rude, but I'm kind of pressed for time. I'm sure you were pretty young, but do you remember the big art theft in Boston back in 1990?"

There was a beat of silence. "I think so. Wasn't it on St. Patrick's Day or something like that?"

"You got it. Technically, it was a few hours *after* St. Patrick's Day. Anyway, this is going to sound crazy, but what would it take for you to get a warrant if I thought I had a lead on one of the pieces?"

He paused again before answering. "Well, it would have to be a really solid lead. Do you have a picture or anything? Any corroborating witnesses?"

"No and no," I said with disappointment.

"Well, I'd be glad to do whatever I can, but it sounds pretty weak right now, no offense. If you were an art collector or dealer or something, I could probably—"

"That's okay, Troy, I was just kind of wondering. I'll figure something out."

"It'd be a big feather in my cap if your hunch pans out, so please don't forget about me if you get any more information. Or we could get together—"

"Gotta go, thanks!" I screeched and hung up. Good grief. I couldn't get involved with a cop, simply couldn't.

Doob had watched the entire exchange with his eyebrows knitted together. "Just what are you up to, super sleuth?"

"I need to nail this prick for something," I replied.

Doob exhaled loudly. "Great. We came to try to solve one case and ended up with another one. Can we please at least eat some of Mr. Johnson's food before you have him locked up?"

"His library has a name, for God's sake."

"What?"

"Never mind, no more Malcolm Johnson talk for now. Thanks for waiting for me, by the way, which is more than I can say for my other friends," I said, swiveling my head around. "Where are they? Or did Kayla get thrown out already?"

Doob smiled. "The guards were giving us a bit of a hard time about not moving along to the ballroom, so Kayla and Jeff went on in, but they've been texting me the whole time. They didn't ditch you, Meg. They just didn't want to make a spectacle."

I laughed. "Kayla make a spectacle? God, never."

"Let's go find them and let them know you didn't get chopped up."

We quickly found Kayla and Jeff near the entrance to the *east ballroom*, and I quickly recapped the meeting with Malcolm.

"So he's off the hook on just a hunch?" Kayla asked. "That doesn't seem too…I don't know…scientific or whatever."

"Not off the hook completely," I conceded, "but he doesn't feel right for Charlie's death. I just hope I can nail his ass for the finial. But please keep your mouths shut about it until I can tell someone who can do something about it."

"Finial schminial, I don't give a shit. Can we please go scout out some rich pieces of ass now? I'm pretty sure I saw a few of the New England Patriots earlier," Kayla said in an excited whisper.

Jeff smiled. "Are the cheerleaders here too?" Kayla lightly punched his arm. Evidently she was the only one allowed to be a pig in the group.

"I'd settle for a piece of pie or candy," Doob moaned.

I glanced at my watch. "Dinner is in about forty-five minutes, Doob, but we'll find you plenty of appetizers before that. Let's get some champagne, and then Kayla and Jeff can go out on the celebrity prowl. Just get to our table in time for the dinner, please," I said. Meagan-Maloney-Mother-Responsible-Extraordinaire.

As if on cue, a tuxedo-clad waiter glided by our group, and Kayla grabbed two flutes of the golden liquid. Handing one to Jeff and hooking her arm through his, she said, "Let's go. See you suckers later." Jeff looked back at us with a mock-look that pled for help, but the twinkle in his eyes gave him away. He was getting a kick out of Kayla and seemed happy to go wherever she led him.

Doob and I spent the next forty minutes strolling the open parts of the mansion. There were pillars and marble everywhere, standard equipment. Ice sculptures shaped like dolphins—larger than both Doob and me—were scattered around the home, and they didn't seem to serve any purpose except to add to the shine of the evening. Frescos rivaling those in the Vatican domed many of the rooms, while floor-to-ceiling windows glittered by the light of endless chandeliers. Several sections opened up to outdoor, intricately carved, stone gazebos lit with hundreds of candles and featuring gemstone-crusted waterfalls.

Just before dinner, I went into one of the bathrooms and counted fifteen stalls. I had to remind myself I was in a home and not a grand hotel. The restroom contained black granite, gleaming silver fixtures, and muted rose lighting so the women in front of the sparkling mirrors would see themselves in a lovely pinkish hue. Did this room have a name?

"We're going to have to see the wine cellars after dinner," I said to Doob as we walked toward one of the ballrooms to meet up with Jeff and Kayla for dinner. "What number table are we at again?"

"Twenty-two."

We found our friends already seated at the beautiful table with six other dinner guests. The tablecloth was a delicate white fabric with lace trim, and the silverware twinkled like stars. Our centerpiece, twenty-four white roses surrounding eleven tiered, white pillar candles, brought out the perfect shine in the wine glasses. Above each setting was a thick place card with our names stenciled in elegant silver calligraphy.

No detail had been overlooked. I guess this was what two thousand dollars a plate bought.

I lost count after the fourth of fifth course as we wined and dined on one of the most fabulous meals I've ever eaten. We began the feast with a charming appetizer of tiny Parmesan cheese baskets filled with goat cheese mousse, followed by a shrimp cocktail with a peppery sauce, served in fabulous martini glasses with lemon juice and minced parsley coating their sparkly edges. A fresh grapefruit and mint sorbet came next, and then we moved on to the soup, butternut squash garnished with swirls of crème fraiche. A mesclun salad over stuffed pasta shells had the perfect balance of garlic and onion. By this point, I glanced over at Doob who hadn't moved his head more than three inches from the top of his plate since dinner began. It would be a while before he'd be capable of speaking again.

Then came the entrée, oh sweet entrée. Here in the Ocean State, I should have guessed the main dish. Mouth-watering lobster was paired with creamy twice-baked potatoes. Snow peas and carrots tossed in olive oil and lemon juice, topped with a red tomato flower garnish, finished off the presentation brilliantly. Dessert was a choice between small chocolate round cakes or lemon hazelnut tiramisu. The final course offered luscious lattes. Never before had my caffeine tasted so delectable. The variety of colors, flavors and textures were simply heavenly, and I vowed to enroll in a cooking class as soon as I got back to Boston.

As the servers cleared the lovely china, the evening's speakers were announced, and I admired the smart planning of the organizers: *get to their wallets while they're still orgasmic over the food.* As I pondered the caloric intake just ingested in the massive ballroom, I did my best to listen to the three presenters discuss literacy for underprivileged children. They all did a spectacular job, and I had no doubt the evening would be a huge success for the charity. When we were excused to enjoy the remainder of the evening, I wondered how in the world anyone could possibly move.

Whining, Doob echoed my sentiments. "I can't walk."

"You didn't have to eat everything they put in front of you, Doob," Kayla quipped. "Plus, you could use some meat on those bones. Let's go find some champagne and dance it off." One of the areas with live music was a string quartet, and Kayla had wanted to check it out since we arrived.

This perked Doob up immediately, and we were soon swaying to the music in another magnificent ballroom and enjoying some cocktails a la rich people. It was very pleasant until...

"Oh. My. God," I whispered as I spotted Gina Giovanni. She looked absolutely friggin' gorgeous, strutting our way like a model on a catwalk. Her long jet-black hair was tied back in a severe ponytail, and she had on a sequined gold dress with a neckline that plunged down nearly to her belly button, coupled with a hemline almost as high as her belly button. Somehow she pulled it off.

Gina was my arch nemesis and everything I disliked in another human being. We'd met at Suffolk University when I was toiling to get my master's degree, while she was there just for the heck of it because *her daddy* wanted her to get a graduate degree. God has less money than her family. She'd never finished Suffolk. She'd never worked a day in her pampered priss-ass life. I'm sure that hadn't changed since I'd last seen her.

Doob saw her coming, blanched, and took Jeff by the arm to stealthily guide him away. Doob is usually up for a catfight, but he knows there's *meow* and then there's *MEOW*. He tends to avoid the latter.

Kayla turned, and her jaw dropped as Gina approached. Several other jaws in the vicinity had already hit the floor, and Gina ate up every second of the attention.

"Meagan Maloney, as I live and breathe. I had to come see for myself if it was actually you, because I couldn't imagine *you* attending an event like *this*," she said in a voice that was way too loud for the occasion. She waved her arm around, gesturing at the room in general. "Are you part of the wait staff or doing the coat-check or something?"

"Where's the rest of your dress, bitch?" Kayla snarled. She'd never met my rival, but given the fact Gina was garnering a lot of attention from the men, not to mention insulting me in the process, was enough for Kayla to release her claws.

Gina looked at Kayla as if she'd just passed gas and then turned back to me. "And I see you brought a foul-mouthed little friend along with you. How nice they let you work in pairs; that way you two can ride together and save on gas money or whatever it is you people do."

"Gina, there you are!" A handsome older man in a tuxedo swooped into our little threesome and cupped one of Gina's elbows while giving her a kiss on each side of her cheek. His slicked-back salt-and-pepper hair was perfectly groomed, and his tan was very dark for this time of year. It was also kind of orange. Gross.

"Gina, darling, I want you to meet the senator from Connecticut. He's been asking after you," the man said with a conspiratorial wink. As he steered Gina toward the senator, he flashed a dazzling smile our way, his overly-bleached teeth nearly blinding us.

Gina couldn't resist a barb over her shoulder as they walked off. "Keep up the good work, ladies. The bathrooms look spectacular."

Kayla started to lunge after Gina, and I had to physically restrain her, which was no small feat. She is amazingly strong for such a skinny thing.

"*That* was fucking Gina Giovanni?" Kayla snarled.

I nodded and took a deep breath. "The one and only."

"We can't let the bitch get away with that! Who the fuck does she think she is?" Kayla barked, her volume increasing with each word.

I hooked my arm through hers. "I didn't even get a word in edgewise," I said, steering Kayla away from Gina's general direction. "Don't let her wreck our night. Let's go find the boys."

"Hey, no broken bones that I see," Doob said with a smile as we found them in a different section of the ballroom, this one with a lady playing a beautiful, wooden harp that looked to be about six feet tall.

"Not yet," Kayla growled.

Jeff gestured toward the harpist. "She used to play in the Boston Symphony. We've been ka-bitzing with the locals," he said, a playful note in his voice, as he smiled over at two elderly women sitting at a small table near the music. They looked like Queen Elizabeth and Princess Anne, with ridiculously large hats atop their gray heads. One waved coquettishly when we looked over, and both of the boys waved back in similar fashion.

"Are you *serious*? They're a hundred," Kayla quipped. "You two have lost your touch."

"Eunice has a house in Tuscany we can visit anytime, and Mildred is donating two hundred fifty thousand dollars to the cause tonight," Doob said indignantly. "I could do worse."

Laughing, I motioned to a waiter walking by and grabbed two glasses of champagne for Kayla and myself. The four of us continued to enjoy the music and actually had some very interesting conversation with Eunice and Mildred. I definitely wanted to be as cool as them when I was a hundred—minus the hats—and I was sad when they left for the evening.

The effects of the Gina-sighting had just about worn off when the priss re-entered our space, a huge smile on her face I could see from across the ballroom. Once again, Doob darted like a scared rabbit and took Jeff with him.

"Good grief," I said and grabbed Kayla's arm. "Let's go check out the pool pavilion, shall we?"

"The wha—"

Steering her toward the pool area, I leaned in to whisper to her. "I had a Gina sighting. Hopefully I misread her stupid clown face, and she's zeroing in on someone else."

We arrived at one of the many sets of French doors that opened to the pool pavilion, a term the very rich evidently use for a grandiose pool area. If Eunice's Tuscany home had this setup, I was in.

The pool itself was long and narrow, and looked to be about one hundred feet long. The floor surrounding it was all beige marble, and dotted throughout were oversized plants, chaise lounges and elegant chairs in warm brown, orange and neutral colors. The walls had some type of golden hue—probably paint dipped in actual gold—and the ceiling was mostly glass so the guests could look up at the stars. Like the rest of the mansion, there was no shortage of multi-tiered chandeliers and candelabras. The view from any of the multiple sets of French doors overlooked the Atlantic Ocean.

I was soon going to be on sensory overload.

"Ladies!" I heard Gina squeal as she stalked us, and I groaned loudly. Didn't she have her own pavilion to go play in?

Kayla and I turned, and Kayla's hand went immediately to her hip. She was looking forward to Round 2, and from the look on Gina's face, she was also relishing the opportunity.

"What now, Gina?" I asked, impatience lacing my voice. "Done with the senator so soon?"

She ignored my tone and kept the mega-watt smile on her face. "Oh no, Meagan. I'm certainly not done with him. But men like him will wait for girls like me. They know quality when they see it."

"He's clearly drunk off his ass," Kayla said. "You totally look like a hooker, and your whoo-ha is hanging out of your dress."

To her credit, Gina didn't look down to see if her crotch was, in fact, hanging out. She just kept smiling, and I sensed the insult-train coming, but I didn't know how quickly or how hard it was going to slam into me.

"That's exactly why I came over to see you two ragamuffins again," she said in a sing-song tone. I thought she might actually reach out and ruffle our hair.

"Listen, you sequined Amazon—"

I put a hand on Kayla's arm to shut her up because I felt—*knew*—something huge was coming, and every part of my brain was trying to figure out what it was.

Gina kept prattling on, her giddiness and enormous smile growing by the second. "See, Bab's daughter, Coco, is a great friend of mine. And yes, she's named after *the* Coco, a dear friend of Bab's. High society tends to stick together, you know." She sniffed and looked us over. "Actually, you two probably don't know. Just take my word for it."

I felt Kayla stiffen beside me, and both my fists reflexively balled up, but Gina didn't even take a breath before she plowed on.

"Anyway, Coco and I were sorority sisters. I've been in this house hundreds of times, so I don't look like a gaping little schoolgirl like you both do. You could really at least *pretend* to blend in. My heavens." She shook her head as if we were a lost cause.

I'd had it. "Gina, that's enough. If you know what's good for you, you'll shut your over-painted mou—"

But she cut me off by holding up a perfectly manicured finger. "Oh shush, Meagan. I'm just getting to the best part. As I was saying, Coco and I were chatting it up with the politicos earlier when she noticed her dress from across the room!" Gina exclaimed and pointed at me. "She said it's a little too loose in your chest area, but she was so glad a less fortunate girl was able to use it. After all, that's why she drops things off at those consignment-type shops." She stared at me in triumph, with that ridiculous huge smile still plastered to her perfect face.

Can. Not. Be. Happening.

I barely felt Kayla take my champagne glass and set it on a small nearby table. Then she touched my arm lightly and hitched her head toward her right. I nodded in agreement.

As smooth as if we'd choreographed it, we each grabbed Gina under one arm and herded her the two remaining steps and plopped her in the shimmering pool. She screamed as she hit the water, and Kayla and I took off running as fast as our second-hand shoes and dresses would allow.

CHAPTER 19

THE LIMO RIDE HOME PROVED TO BE EXTREMELY JOVIAL as Kayla recounted the dumping-of-Gina into the pool several times over for the gentlemen. The champagne made Kayla even more animated than usual, and Jeff and Doob were both engrossed with the recap, but Doob was upset he'd missed it.

"You were the one who scampered off both times she came around," I pointed out.

"I know," Doob whined. "That's because I don't want to be collateral damage. But with her in the pool, she wouldn't have been able to catch me. I'd have *loved* to have seen that catfight."

"It really wasn't much of a fight," Kayla countered. "That snippy bitch flung some insults, and we shoved her in. I wonder what that senator thinks of her now. Hopefully her hair extensions got caught in the pool drain and wrapped around her throat—"

"Kayla!" I exclaimed. "That's bad karma. I definitely hope she *looks* like a drowned rat, but I find myself wondering if she can swim," I mused.

Kayla batted a hand my way. "Oh, fuck her! I'm sure some muscle-bound rich guy got her out of the pool, and there are probably lowly servants fawning all over her as we speak. She's fine. Uppity bitch."

I looked at Jeff and Doob for confirmation, and they both shrugged as to say *who cares*? And they were right. Gina wasn't going to drown at some shee-shee-foo-foo event in Newport. It would be bad press, and God knows the elite of Newport don't want bad press.

"Well Jeff, thanks again for getting us those tickets, although I don't think we'll be invited back to a gala anytime soon. I hope we haven't ruined your reputation this early into your residency."

He smiled. "Oh, I really couldn't care less about all that. It's not like I attend those events regularly."

Suddenly Kayla put her hand over her mouth. "You gonna be sick?" I asked. She was a legendary puker if she had more than three glasses of anything other than light beer. She nodded vigorously and started reaching for the door.

"William, please pull over for a moment!" I yelled. "Otherwise you're gonna have a mess all over the inside of your car."

Fortunately Kayla jumped out of the limo before regurgitating all her drinks and eight-course meal. She stumbled back into the vehicle relatively intact, and Doob handed her a couple of napkins he'd dabbed in bottled water.

From there on, the ride was quiet. As we closed in on Jeff's house, I remembered my cell phone, the ringer dutifully shut off. Resting in my sequined clutch all night. I had half a mind to leave it in there, but I'm nothing if not a modern girl. So I fished it out of my clutch to see if I'd missed anything.

And I had.

There were six missed calls from Moira. They'd started at ten o'clock, and like clockwork, she'd redialed every fifteen minutes thereafter. 10:00, 10:15, 10:30, 10:45, 11:00, and 11:15. But she hadn't left a single message, which was very odd. There was no way she'd butt-dialed me that many times at those exact intervals.

I glanced at my watch; it was only 11:22, and I didn't have the patience to see if she'd call back at 11:30. Given the pattern, that was almost a certainty, but given the weird circumstances, I wasn't going to wait. I told my limo-mates what was up, punched the speed-dial for her number and heard someone pick up immediately. "Moira?" Worry crept under my skin when I received no reply.

"Hello? Sis? Can you hear me?" I pulled the phone away from my ear and studied it, wondering if something was wrong with our connection. I hung up and immediately redialed.

Again, someone picked up right away. But this time, I heard Moira's voice in the background, and she yelled. "Meagan, don't—"

I heard a whap and Moira cry out in pain. Then silence.

"Hello?!" I screamed at the top of my lungs. "Who is this? Who's there? Put Moira back on the phone!"

A menacing voice growled in a whisper. "Get home, you fucking bitch. Or your sister isn't gonna be pretty much longer."

What the hell? "Who is this?!" I demanded. "What the fuck is going on? Put Moira on the phone right now!"

I heard an evil, deep-throated chuckle on the other end of the phone. And the world stopped spinning for a moment.

My God.

Melanie.

There was no one else who would be sadistic enough to do this. There was no one else who would want to hurt me by hurting my family.

My voice came out in a whimper, but I couldn't help it. My baby sister. The air left my lungs. "Melanie, don't do this," I begged. "You've done enough already. Don't add to the list of bodies. Don't do this to Moira. She's done nothing to you. Your beef is with me."

Silence.

I was becoming hysterical. "Melanie, what is oh or ho or whatever you're trying to tell me? I'll do whatever you want, but don't you hurt her. I'll kill you; I swear to God, I will *kill you*!" I was shaking and sobbing and screaming as we pulled down the long driveway and wound our way toward Jeff's home.

I heard the menacing whisper again. "Get home quickly, Meagan. And if you call the cops, she's dead." The line disconnected.

In a stupor, I explained the situation to my friends and watched as the men sprang into action. Watching them was like observing people in fast-forward. Jeff was at the driver's door, asking the man how much it would take to keep the vehicle for the night. As Jeff handed over a wad of bills, Kayla touched me lightly.

"I'm sorry I got sick, girlfriend. I'll stay here with Sampson and bring him back when everything is okay." She paused and looked at me imploringly. "And everything *will* be okay, Meagan."

"Melanie..." was all I could say.

"Are you positive, Meg? Is there any chance you misunderstood what was going on there?"

"I know what I heard, Kayla!" I screamed. "Moira's in danger, and it's my fault. If anything happens to her—"

"It's not going to," Kayla said firmly. Then she squeezed me hard. "We shut one bitch up tonight; there's always room for more. Call me when you take care of business." Then she was gone.

Jeff leaned in and hugged me tightly. "Be careful, Meagan."

Too terrified to speak again, I nodded. Doob gave the driver the address to our apartment on Commonwealth Avenue. I couldn't imagine what we would find when we arrived.

CHAPTER 20

I DON'T REMEMBER MUCH ABOUT THE DRIVE TO BOSTON. I recall Doob shoved another wad of money toward the driver and told him to get us to my condo as quickly, and safely, as possible. I remember dialing Norman, but I reached his voicemail and did my best to coherently explain the situation.

I considered phoning my parents, but I banished the thought as quickly as it came. If something happened to Moira...well, I couldn't quite process the possibility. But our family would never, ever recover. I would never forgive myself, and my parents would never forgive me, of that I was sure.

The drive to Massachusetts passed mostly in a fog, and before I knew it, the bright city lights were in my sights. As the limo maneuvered through the mostly-deserted, complicated streets of Boston, adrenaline kicked in. This psycho bitch would not hurt my sister. This was between Melanie and me, and I think even Melanie knew that. She was just using Moira to call me out.

Well, here I was. And this time I wasn't leaving anyone behind.

Three blocks from our condo building, I turned to Doob and demanded, "You stay in the limo, Doob. I don't know what we're going to find up there, and I can't have you getting hurt. Norman will be here any minute, and we'll handle it. Don't challenge me on this. Promise me you'll stay here."

His eyes were huge when he nodded solemnly. "I promise, Meg," he whispered, his voice shaking.

A million thoughts rushed through my mind, mostly about Moira, my parents, and Sampson. But right here, in this moment? Here was my little Iowa friend, and I knew he was so worried about me he could barely function. I grabbed him in a bear hug and squeezed as hard as I could. Then I clamped my hands on his shoulders and put my face very close to his. "You are my very best friend, Doob. Don't ever forget that."

And then the limo was suddenly at my address, and I rushed outside and into the building. I burst out of the stairwell into the hallway on the floor one level below Moira's and mine, gasping for breath. I'd sprinted up the stairs in high heels and barely noticed; being on auto-pilot tends to do that to a person. I hadn't wanted to take the time to change at Jeff's house, so now I would be fighting the devil in my second-hand evening gown.

Before blazing up the final set of stairs, I decided to make one more call to the apartment, just to have the tiniest gauge about what I'd be walking into. If Melanie didn't let me speak with Moira, then Moira could already be gone. And then my life may as well be over, too.

I dialed the apartment number, and Moira answered right away, her voice shaking like leaves in a windstorm. "There's a gun to my head, Meagan. If anyone besides you walks through our door, I'm dead." She clicked off.

As I listened to her terrified voice, something—some fissure, something tiny—cracked within my psyche. My brain wasn't totally keeping up with the situation, but I was aware enough to know that a part of me was shutting down and abandoning me for good. I wasn't sure I was going to survive this.

I took a deep breath and said a quick prayer. Time to go upstairs to get my sister.

CHAPTER 21

JUST AS I PUT MY HAND ON THE DOORKNOB TO THE STAIRWELL, my phone blared out its melodic tune. Norman. I answered and quickly told him what I was doing, and he was livid, insisting I wait. I explained there wasn't time, and I asked if he could get a shooter lined up directly across the street from our apartment.

"I've already done that," he said in his baritone voice. "I called in a few favors. Meagan, I'm telling you, do *not* go in that apartment. The shooter can get her without you putting yourself in danger. He'll be set up in less than five minutes—"

"Norman, *Moira* is in danger, and I'm not waiting one more second. Get that shooter ready to go, and I'll do my best to get Melanie in front of the window. And when you get here, be quiet about it. She said no cops."

"Goddamn it Meagan—"

"Conference in your shooter on this call, and then push the mute button on your phone. I'm going to leave my phone on so you guys can hear what goes down, but I don't want Melanie hearing you."

He did as I asked, and when we confirmed the shooter was on the line and almost set up across the street, I told Norman I was going upstairs.

"You're a stubborn little shit. Don't get yourself killed," he muttered, and then his phone went quiet. I put the volume up as loud as it would go and put my phone in the clutch I'd been so proud of just hours before. How silly the whole stupid night seemed at this point.

I hustled up the stairs toward the upper floor. I noticed every crack in the wall of the stairwell; every nick of chipped paint seemed larger, and the already-annoying fluorescent light burned my eyes. I smelled the food odor from the Carmichaels' apartment at the end of the hallway even before I opened the steel door to our floor.

With my back close to the wall, I side-stepped my way down the corridor. I didn't plan to announce myself before going into the apartment. Assuming it was unlocked, I would simply walk in and hope to God I could execute the game plan. The fly in that ointment was neither Moira nor Melanie knew their roles in said game plan. The potential variations on that theme ranged somewhere in the billions. But I wouldn't dwell on it; it wouldn't change anything anyway.

My breath came in quick bursts as I neared the apartment, and my heart seemed ready to leap out of my chest. And then I was at the door.

Taking a gulp of air, I reached out, turned the knob and found it unlocked as I'd anticipated. I forced myself to quickly turn it the rest of the way and was then inside, shutting the door behind me in less than a second.

It took a moment for my eyes to adjust from the stark brightness out in the hallway to the low lamplight in the family room. When I took in the scene, I couldn't quite process it. Bags of groceries lay all over the floor of the entryway, some with contents strewn about. Moira huddled on the couch, and her mouth had dried blood on one side. A gun was held to her head as she'd told me.

But the person holding it was a man.

CHAPTER 22

I TRIED TO COMPREHEND WHAT I WAS SEEING, but it was like trying to run at top speed underwater. Where was Melanie? This *had* to be about Melanie. It was time. I was ready.

Well...I was ready for *that.* This? For this I was completely unprepared.

"Fuckin' bitch, good of ya to show up. Took yer sweet fuckin' time, dint ya?" the man snarled at me. "Drop the purse and put yer hands in the air where I can see 'em. Nice 'n high, getem up there."

Hearing his backwoods-rapper-wannabe-voice helped clear my internal fog just the tiniest amount, and I did as instructed, twisting the clasp on my clutch open as I set it down. Studying the wiry young man, I hoped the phone would pick up every word for Norman and the shooter.

"Ya happy? Are ya happy with what ya done?!" he demanded and jabbed the gun at Moira's head to emphasize his point.

That's when I fully took in her appearance. Beautiful Moira, who'd aged ten years while sitting on the couch. Whose porcelain face was mottled with splotches and whose red nose betrayed how much she'd been crying. The blood around her mouth was the icing on the cake. How had this happened?

She wouldn't make eye contact with me. Instead, she stared straight ahead. It didn't look like she was in shock, and she wasn't whimpering or cowering. She might have been before, but now? She just looked...angry.

Somehow I knew, simply from looking at her, she would do nothing to get us out of this situation. Her glazed stare told me, *You got us into this, you get us out.*

And she was right. I needed to fix this, and I needed to fix it now.

Sadly, I'd been in a similar situation before, and I'd done almost everything wrong. The one thing I knew I wouldn't do was go sit by Moira on the couch. I wasn't going to give this madman any advantage.

Well, yeah, other than the gun at Moira's head. I wasn't going to give him any *additional* advantage.

The other thing I absolutely would not do is run. I ran last time, and I'll regret it for the rest of my life. So here we were, all three of us, sequestered in this apartment. Someone would win, someone would lose.

My decision was either I would leave with my sister on my arm, or I'd leave in a body bag. That decision would mean the same outcome would go for her. Since Moira leaving in a body bag was unacceptable, it was time to outsmart this asshole.

I cleared my throat and found my voice. "So, uh...sir, what's your name?"

He guffawed. "Cut the act, bitch! Sent my girl a bunch o' shit 'bout me, and you're gonna play stupid? Fuckin' bitch."

His *girl?* "You have a daughter?"

His face pinched as he snarled at me. "Ya *know* I don't have a fuckin' kid! That's what this is all about, ain't it? Meagan fucking Maloney tryin' to be a goddamn hero, sending shit to the house. To my girl's fuckin' house! Who the *fuck* ya think ya are?"

Holy shit. This was the guy Kayla told me about. This was Les. We sent the anonymous package to his girlfriend. Is that who he meant by his *girl*? How in the hell had he found us?

And then it hit me like a ton of bricks. Doobie had given it to *Becca* to mail. Stupid, inept, always-on-Facebook, forever-putting-on-lip-gloss Becca. And moron that I am, I asked him to give it to her. I knew her limited capabilities when I did it. She *is* capable of Facebook and lip gloss. She *isn't* capable of anything else. So really, who was the idiot in this situation?

Becca clearly hadn't sent the information anonymously. The sweet young thing had probably enclosed business cards, a pamphlet, our Yellow Pages ad, our website, and maybe a couple of close-up head shots of Norman and me for good measure. Then she'd probably called to ensure they received the package and offered our services for any of their future needs.

If I got out of this alive, I was going to strangle and then fire Becca.

"Sinkin' in, bitch?" He was taunting me and still jabbing the gun at Moira's head. "The light bulb done gone off in that there noggin'? You went and fucked up, and now we're all in a helluva bind. This is all yer fault."

And just that fast, I became utterly *pissed*. I am so tired of people, of society—of whoever—blaming their bad decisions on someone else. This man, who was holding a gun to my sister's head, believed it was *my fault* because I dared to warn someone that he's a psycho.

I could hear it all now. I'm sure his mommy smacked him around, and I'm sure his daddy left when he was two years old, and I'm sure he had to drink milk past the due date. I'm sure he had acne and Santa gypped him, and some pretty girl called him a loser at some point. I'm sure he played violent video games, and looked at porn, and I'm completely sure his little boo-boo pee-pee had been letting him down for years. I'm sure everyone in the *entire blessed world* was to blame for his issues. Everyone, but him.

So, no. This guy wasn't getting the better of me. Moira and I wouldn't go down tonight because of anything I did or didn't do. This was on *him*. I wouldn't let the newscasters announce our demise at the hands of this creep and use his full name—first, middle, last—like they always did with these sickos and tell the world of how he was wronged as a child.

And then I remembered a key fact about Les. *Thank you, Doob.*

I nodded. "It *is* sinking in; I'm with you now. Your name is Les, and you're pissed at me for sending a package to your girlfriend. But that doesn't have anything to do with Moira. So she needs to leave right now, and I'll take her place on the couch."

"Ya ain't in charge bitch!" he exploded. "I say what the fuck is gonna happen, and no one leaves 'til I fuckin' say so." Spittle flew out of his mouth, and his complexion had turned an interesting shade of purple.

"Les, please think about this for a minute. We're definitely in a bad place. But it's really between you and me. You seem like a smart guy—" I almost threw up in my mouth a little, "—and I know you can see Moira had nothing to do with this. None of this is her fault; it's mine."

His eyes darted around as I was talking, and it was obvious he was on some type of drug. His mannerisms were nervous and jerky, and that couldn't be good. I needed to get Moira out of here.

"And Les, not only is it not Moira's fault, it certainly isn't our dog's fault, either."

His dilated eyes stopped darting and fixed completely on me. Good.

"The fuck ya talking about? Ain't no dog around here," he said as he scanned the room. His movements had slowed a fraction, and he genuinely seemed to be looking for a dog.

My hands still in the air, I motioned toward an end table with my chin. "There is a dog. His name is Sampson, and he's in the picture there with Moira and me. He's a Springer Spaniel, and he loves to run and jump. A great hunting dog, you know?" Yeah, if hunting included homemade dog-treats from an overpriced delicatessen on Cambridge Street.

Les didn't move away from the couch, but he strained his head to glance at the picture. "Well, I don't see no dog here now," he said with a little less aggression.

"I know. That's what I've been trying to tell you. He's outside. He's probably been outside for hours."

Les narrowed his eyes, and Moira kept staring straight ahead.

I kept up the bullshit. "See, I think I know what happened. Moira was grocery shopping tonight; she's a creature of habit is how I know this." I knew no such thing. "And she always takes Sampson with her because he loves to be outside. Isn't that right Moira?"

She nodded her head just enough to show she agreed with me, but she didn't join in the conversation.

"So, she always ties him up to this cute little doggie post outside the store, and he waits for her when she's inside." Sampson so wouldn't do that. "He's such a good boy. People come by and pet him and talk to him. There's really nothing better than a dog, is there?"

He scowled. "I din't hurt no dog, if that's what yer gettin' at."

My arms ached, and I lowered them to ear-level as I shook my head. "No, no, I'm sure you didn't. You wouldn't hurt a good dog like Sampson, a great hunting dog like him. Anyway, my thinking is Moira tied him up outside our building when she got home because they were going to go on a longer walk. But she needed to come up and put these groceries away before some things melted. Does that sound right Moira?"

She nodded a little more vigorously this time, like she was catching on to my angle. Still no words.

I rambled on. "I saw Sampson when I pulled up. He's outside, and he looked really cold. But I was so scared for Moira that I just ran right by him. So here's where I need some help putting this together. Les, did you pull the gun on Moira as she was at the door?"

"Yeah, only 'cuz I thought the bitch was you. I dint know you had no dog or a fuckin' sister til she told me she ain't you. She dint tell me about the darn dog."

"I understand," I said softly. "You pushed Moira inside, and she couldn't go back outside to get Sampson. She's been up here for a long time, and he's out there getting colder and colder by the minute. So could you just let Moira go? She can go down and get Sampson, and then it'll just be you and me."

"Shee-it bitch! How dumb ya think I am? This here Myra, whatever-her-fucking-name-is will call the cops the minute she gets outside."

"But what about Sampson?" I pleaded. "If you look out that middle window, you can see him. He's tied to a hydrant, and he's shivering like crazy." There was no hydrant, no Sampson, no shivering.

I prayed to God that Norman could hear all this. I prayed his shooter across the street was getting this as well. *Middle window*! I prayed I'd picked the right window, the one without the tree blocking it. I prayed if there was a tree that its leaves were all down and there'd be a clear shot. I said a lot of prayers in a one-second span.

Les hesitated, thinking about it. "I don't need to see no cold dog. Those kinda dogs got fur, he'll be okay. Yer fuckin' fault if he ain't," he said with a shrug.

There it was again. My fault. "Well, I'm just thinking someone will look at his tags and come up here to find out what's going on. Someone may even call the police. A lot of people know Sampson and will be worried if he's out there all night. I'm surprised someone hasn't stopped by already."

Les's eyes started getting shifty again. "Well, I ain't lettin' her go get him," he said defiantly, back in charge.

"Okay," I said. "Maybe we can all go and get him. You can put the gun on me, and we'll all go down together and come right back up."

"I ain't stupid!" he screamed. "No tricks, we ain't all goin' together."

"Okay," I said, feigning defeat. "Can you at least tell me if he's still out there? If he's not, then someone took him, and that someone may be calling or coming over here any minute. If he's still there, you probably still have some time to decide what you're going to do."

It was odd watching the nuances of Les's face as he thought this through. According to Kayla, he'd killed a beautiful, young girl. And he was most likely planning on killing another child. He now had a gun held on Moira, and he seemed pretty much drugged up and out of his mind. But he also genuinely seemed like he wanted to check on Sampson. Like Doob had mentioned days before, weren't these nutcases supposed to torture small animals at some point in their sick lives? Was a pretend-Sampson really going to entice this lunatic?

Norman, please have your guy ready.

In a flash, Les shifted the gun, aiming at my head, and started backing toward the wall of windows. "Keep yer fuckin' arms up or I'll shoot yer fuckin' head off. And don't you move a muscle either, Myra, whatever the fuck yer name is."

I'd never been so glad to have a gun pointed at me. Because that meant it was off Moira. I snuck a quick glance at her, and she trembled but still refused to look at me.

"That middle window, you might have to angle just a little bit to see him," I instructed.

"I heard ya the first fuckin' time, bitch," he muttered. The gun stayed trained in his right hand, his arm outstretched toward me. He continued to slowly back up, never turning his head away from me. He finally inched his way to a small space of wall between two of the windows, and he quickly glanced toward the shade on the middle window. In that split-second, I lowered my hands a few more inches. They were now level with my chest.

Les glanced back at me but apparently only saw my hands still in the air. "Bitch, I'm gonna reach for this here blind and sneak a look out. If I see or hear or even fuckin' smell one of you bitches doing something cute, I pull the trigger. And it's aimed right at yer purty face. I ain't gonna miss."

With his back firmly planted against the wall space between the large windows, he reached his left hand toward the shade, not taking his eyes off me. His extended gun arm didn't waver, didn't flinch. He would undoubtedly pull the trigger if he sensed we were up to something.

Given the angle, and the fact his body stayed against the wall, it would be very difficult for a sniper to get a good shot at him. And if they got a shot off, it would probably just nick his arm. Les was slightly smarter than I gave him credit for. He wasn't going to stick his face in the window. I'd hoped the asshole would stand directly in front of it, let the shade roll up to the top, making himself a huge target. He wasn't cooperating.

When Les finally took his eyes off me, he slowly turned his head to the left and reached out to move the shade. Craning his neck a bit to look outside, his right arm was still perfectly extended, still aimed at me. As I'd thought, he didn't expose himself to the front of the glass pane, but his head was turned all the way to the left.

Looking at his profile, all I could think was, *I ain't gonna miss, either.*

Whipping out the gun from the top of my dress, I shot him directly in the stomach and watched him hit the floor like a rag doll.

CHAPTER 23

MOIRA LAUNCHED OFF THE COUCH INTO A BALL ON THE FLOOR while Norman and several men burst through the door to our apartment. As if frozen in place, I still had my gun aimed at the wall where Les had just been standing. He writhed in pain, and I fleetingly wondered if he would live. He'd dropped the gun when he'd collapsed to the floor, but it was still within his reach. One of Norman's men obviously saw the same potential problem and ran over to kick the gun away from Les before checking on him. I had to turn away. I didn't want to watch anyone help that son of a bitch.

Norman gingerly pressed my arm down and pried my gun from me. With his face inches from mine, his mouth moved, but I swear I couldn't hear him. There was that weird underwater feeling in my head again, and I could only process one thought. *Get to Moira.*

I broke away from my partner and raced to the couch where my sister was curled in a fetal position on our floor. A couple of the men stood near her while she openly sobbed. She had her face toward the floor, shutting out the world. My stomach turned. I didn't want her pretty face rubbing up against the gunk that lived in our carpet. I irrationally thought back to a time when we'd discussed getting hardwoods and wished we had.

The men parted when they saw me, and I scooched in and rolled up by my sister. My stupid dress was bunching up all over the place, and I snuggled into her as close as I possibly could, vowing I would remain there for decades if that's what it took.

I reached out and touched her soft, blonde hair and told her everything was okay in my best maternal voice. Moira jerked as if she'd been electrocuted.

And then she slapped my hand away.

"Get away from me, Meagan," she said in the quietest, most hollow voice I'd ever heard.

CHAPTER 24

Saturday, November 9th

I WOKE UP THE NEXT MORNING AND WISHED FOR NOTHING other than to bury my head back into my pillow and sleep for about a year. Or two. Two years would be good. Everything would blow over by then. My sister had been terrorized by a killer because of me, and now she hated me.

The night before had been one of the worst of my life. After hours of questioning by the police, my parents came to get Moira to take her to their home. I wasn't invited. Their looks of disgust and disappointment were ones that would stay with me forever.

As always, Doob waited in the background throughout the whole ordeal, and since my apartment was a crime scene, he'd invited me to stay with him. I thought *why not*? For all the time I'd lived on the same floor as Doob, I'd never seen his apartment, but I figured I deserved to stay at the roach motel.

So I was amazed when we walked across the hall at four o'clock in the morning, and the entire place looked like something out of an extravagant magazine. I'd have never guessed. I'd passed out in his guest room, still in my second-hand gown.

I sat up in the comfy guest bed and tried to erase last night's memories. Mustering up some courage, I reached for my cell phone as if it were radioactive. I punched the speed-dial for my parents' house with bile rising in my throat. Ma answered on the first ring and curtly told me Moira was still resting and they'd do their best to call me later in the day. *Don't-call-us-we'll-call-you* came through loud and clear, and my stomach pitched. Eyes welling with tears, I barely choked out a good-bye to my mother before she hung up.

I tossed the phone on the bed and stared down at my hands. There was no evidence of the horrible thing that had happened the previous night. I didn't even know if Les was dead or alive. After a two-second reflection, I realized I didn't care. Guilt would eventually rear its ugly head—*you shot a human being, Meagan*—but for now, I was glad I did.

Moira was alive because I stopped that lunatic in his tracks. So fuck him and fuck the little voice in my head.

Yep, it would eventually have me on a therapist's couch.

Sitting on the bed and staring at the wall, self-pity overwhelmed me until my cell's ring tone bleated. A spark of hope flickered, and I clung to the tiniest delusion it might be Moira or Ma, who'd decided to forgive me and called to extend an invite for coffee cake. Or just coffee. Either would be good by me.

I reached for the phone and looked at the display before answering. It wasn't Moira or Ma, but the number was familiar. I wracked my brain for a second and then decided to just answer the damn thing before it went to voicemail. I mean really, isn't that what phones are for?

"Meagan, hi. It's David Fontana."

Oh. My. God. This was just friggin' perfect. I associated David with the most guilt-ridden event in my entire life, and now that I had a silver-medalist-guiltiest-moment, thanks to last night's horror story, I couldn't believe David Fontana was calling me. Was the universe really this cruel?

"Meagan?"

In the past, *tongue-tied* was an understatement to describe how I'd behave around David, mostly because he's this perfect specimen of human being, and I, very simply, am not. There was a time when I'd hoped my schoolgirl crush would evolve into something wonderful between us.

But when I'd managed to leave his brother in an abandoned house with Melanie-the-psychopath—who ultimately murdered him—that abruptly ended my little fantasy. David and I run into each other at our mutual coffee shop on Boylston Street occasionally, but I've basically changed my entire routine since that horrible period in my life. I wish David nothing but the best, and the best is very much not me.

Sigh.

"David, hi. I'm sorry. I'm just surprised to hear from you. Is everything okay?"

"Everything's fine, thanks. How's it going with you?"

God. Certainly he wasn't calling just for chit-chat? Because today wasn't exactly the day I could pretend to be all things sunshine and light. And David calling *today* goes to show that sometimes timing in life just plain sucks ass. How many times had I hoped David Fontana would call me, for any reason whatsoever? And now that it had happened, I only wanted to hang up.

But I forced myself to play along. It was, after all, David Fontana.

So. Now I had to answer his question as to how things were going. Let's see...*because of me, my sister nearly got shot in the head last night, and I might have killed a guy, I'm not totally sure. Moira hates me, my parents are barely speaking to me, Sampson is on vacation in Newport, and Doob's apartment—which I've been terrified to see for years—is a majestic, fairytale palace. How's it going with you?*

That would probably be a wee bit too much information for the time being, so I opted for a little less drama. "Things have been kinda crazy, but I'm plugging away," I said, wincing at my poor attempt at cheeriness. "How are you doing?"

"Things are going really well, thanks."

Enter the awkward pause.

Most times in life, I feel obligated—compelled, really—to fill that void, but today I didn't. I would have sat in silence for the entire morning and been just fine with it. For the time being, small talk was not in my repertoire.

Thankfully, David cleared his throat and went on. "Okay, so I won't keep you long Meagan, but I'm making some calls today, reminding everyone about Darrin and Bobby's scholarship run tomorrow. We've got more sponsors than I could have hoped for, and I think it's going to be a really great day."

Good grief. Well over a month ago, I'd received an invite in the mail, announcing the first annual 5K run in Darrin's, and his friend Bobby's, honor. Bobby had left Darrin a lump sum of cash after his death, which ended up being just shortly before Darrin's murder. That money, combined with the monies to be raised from the approaching fundraiser, would go toward a scholarship for a college-bound high school senior each year. I wasn't sure of all the criteria for the scholarship; David was in charge of that, but I was certain it would go to someone very deserving.

"Meagan?"

"Sorry...again." Why in hell couldn't I form sentences around this man? In person was one thing, but we were on the phone, for goodness sake. "Yes, of course I'll be there. I'm sure I'll be *walking* four point nine of the five kilometers, but I wouldn't miss it for the world. I've gotten a bunch of people to donate online, and I've got quite a bit of cash for you, too."

"That's great to hear. Thanks Meagan. Will Moira and Doobie be joining you?"

"Here's the thing. I openly admit I'm totally out of shape, but I will attempt—and somehow survive—the walk. However, Doob gets exhausted coming across the hall, so he elected to make a very nice donation, and he's also volunteering. I think his motivation is so he can be close by to make fun of me, but at least he'll be helping. Moira also donated, and she was very impressed when she saw your mailer. This is a really good thing you're doing, David." My words trailed off because of the lump in my throat.

This time, the silence held all kinds of innuendo, sadness, and hurt; I could physically *feel* the wave of emotion coming through the phone. If only it could carry me off somewhere, preferably to a place free of guilt. To a land of *happy*, where Darrin was alive and Moira wasn't forever damaged. Tom being there would be icing on the cake, but that was just selfish.

David cleared his throat again and said, "Well, it will be great to see you, Meagan, and thanks for your support."

"It's the least I can do," I said in all sincerity. As I said that, I noticed another call coming in. Norman. "David, I've got to run. I'll see you tomorrow."

I clicked over and Norman told me Les had died of his injuries. I don't know what else he said after that. I don't know what I said to him. I don't know if I said anything. I don't remember hanging up.

I sat on the bed and returned to staring at the wall for a while. Eventually, the phone slipped out of my hand and settled on the lovely bedspread. I lowered my head on a pillow while memories swirled in my mind.

Meeting David, finding Darrin in California, my family threatened by a steroid freak, a gun smashed in my face by Melanie, Darrin's bleeding body, Darrin in a coffin, telling his mother I was sorry, a gun at Moira's head, and...shooting a man last night.

I *killed* a man last night.

My God. What type of life had I created? I buried my face in the pillow and sobbed.

A soft knock interrupted my pity party, and a black and white tornado burst onto the bed. Sampson whimpered and licked and pranced and jumped and acted like a very happy dog.

"Jeff and Kayla dropped him off this morning. I didn't want to wake you, but they said to tell you they're both so sorry about what happened." Doob walked into the room and sat on the edge of the bed, trying to pull Sampson off the ceiling.

I nodded. "Yeah, me too. We'll have to get back to Jamestown once all this—"

Putting his hand on my arm, he said, "No one cares about Jamestown right now. We'll get back there when it makes sense. Jeff is staying at his place in Boston for the time being."

I nodded. "Doob, I killed a guy last night," I murmured, focusing at a spot on the floor.

He wrapped me in a hug and, after releasing me, held me by the shoulders, forcing me to look right at him. "You shot a man in self-defense last night, Meg. He was going to kill you and your sister. I can't change what happened, but I'm not letting you start the guilt parade." He pulled me off the bed and steered me into the bathroom. Handing me the bag I'd packed, he ordered me to get cleaned up.

"What for?" I mumbled.

"I've got an idea. Have you ever served at a soup kitchen?"

"No. Why?"

"It's getting to be that time of year. I've gone down there and dished out food to some homeless people on occasion." His face colored, but he kept talking. "And I dunno...I just always feel better afterwards. No matter how bad or lonely I might feel, that always makes me realize how lucky I am."

Thinking of Doob being lonely made me sad. I didn't know he ever felt that way. But heck, he hardly ever saw his family. And if I was his best friend, then my God...

"Sounds like a plan," I said and faced my weary self in the mirror.

CHAPTER 25

Sunday, November 10th

DESPITE THE FACT I'D ENDED SOMEONE'S LIFE, my day at the soup kitchen had gone a long ways to restoring my soul. Doob and I met some wonderful people—both working at the facility and those we served—and we vowed we'd do it again on Thanksgiving. Despite the strained relations with my family, yesterday made me realize I had a lot of reasons to be thankful. At some point, I was going to have to deal with the fact I'd shot and killed a human being, but for now, I relied on that denial thing to get me through another day.

One thing I couldn't deny was the fact that it was about fifteen degrees today, well below the average low for this time of year. I had done some good yesterday, so I thought karma might help me out with the weather, but evidently karma was still paying me back for a lot of other shit. It was one thing to do the 5K, quite another to freeze my fanny off while doing it.

Nonetheless, I reminded myself of today's cause—and the role I'd played in Darrin's death—and decided whining about the weather wasn't the way to go. After coming to terms with the cold, I bundled up in a few light layers, a Patriots winter hat, and stuffed a few more clothes and some mittens in a backpack for later. I even remembered to throw a couple of protein bars in the bag, and okay, I threw in a Diet Coke as well. The weather would keep it cold, and I was thinking I might need a jolt of caffeine at the midway point. Or some oxygen. Maybe a stretcher. An ambulance wasn't out of the realm of possibility, either.

I was eating a bowl of cereal over the sink when Doob's bedroom door opened. Right on schedule. Doob was rarely one second early or one second late for anything. He was the human form of the national atomic clock.

When he came into the kitchen, I nearly choked. He was in some type of dark purple, nearly black, unitard. It looked like a wetsuit a person would wear when doing the Polar Plunge in Boston in the middle of the winter. It was a full-body get-up that left nothing—*nothing*—to the imagination. I shuddered.

To be kind, I'll say Doob's not exactly a physical specimen. He's far too skinny for the amount of food he eats, something that's always been a mystery to me. And in this particular outfit? I didn't know if there was a physical specimen alive who could pull this off, but it certainly wasn't Doob.

Doob beamed and spread out his arms in true *ta-da* fashion. "I'm wearing it, Meg. Not a thing you can do about it." His smile doubled, daring me to try to talk him out of it.

"You're going to freeze your ass off and possibly get arrested for indecent exposure."

"You wish. Besides, you're just jealous. You'll haul along fifty pounds of clothing and probably keel over one minute into the walk. While I, on the other hand, will be light on my feet and feeling very warm the entire day."

"You're not even walking," I argued. "Why in the world would you wear that? Don't the volunteers have to wear some type of designated sweatshirt or hat or something?"

"I have my volunteer button on my coat."

"The big bubble coat that makes you look like the Michelin Man?"

Doob pointed at me. "Nope, I've got a new one. It's freezing out there, and standing around handing out water and what-not will make me colder than if I was walking. Besides that, I *donated*, so I think I can wear whatever I want. We're going to see all kinds of crazy clothes, so I'll fit in just fine."

"Yeah, you're big with fitting in," I said with an eye roll.

But *donated* he had. I would venture his donation had been the largest received for the foundation, and I couldn't help but smile as I watched this generous human-seal prance around his living room.

"So where's the new coat?"

"So glad you asked." He headed for the front closet.

For the second time, I almost choked on my cereal when he pulled out a brown, full-length, faux mink coat.

"Absolutely not, Doob." But I knew it was pointless.

"I got it at the Salvation Army a couple of weeks ago, and I love it," Doob countered. "I figure I'll give it to someone in need today, or I'll wrap your comatose body in it and bring you home when you collapse just after the starting gate."

I had to admit, it wasn't a half-bad idea.

"When did you start shopping at the Salvation Army?"

"I like it there. I usually go to drop things off—mostly computer-related stuff—but sometimes I find some cool, vintage clothes."

"Doob, all your clothes are from the fifth grade. It doesn't get more vintage than that." I paused. "And for the record, I will make it past the starting gate."

Doob arched his eyebrows. "We'll see."

CHAPTER 26

WHEN DOOB AND I ARRIVED OUTSIDE THE BOSTON PUBLIC LIBRARY, I was thrilled to see tons of people milling around. An electric feeling surrounded the building that was established in the late-19th century, with its arched windows and numerous flags flapping in the wind. Everyone's breath plumed in the cold air and, as Doob had predicted, there were all sorts of get-ups. One guy had a unitard similar to Doob's, but this guy's looked like an American flag. Another lady had face-paint with black and white stripes and wore what looked to be old-time prison garb to match her face. I'm sure there was some story to go along with her outfit, but I didn't stop to ask.

In group fashion, one lady had three teenage children with her, and they all had Thanksgiving turkey-hats on their heads. A young couple was duct-taped together at her left ankle and his right ankle, and at the waist; that was going to make bathroom visits interesting, I mused. Along those same lines, two men in tuxedos with purple boas were handcuffed to each other, and one was singing Anne Murray songs at the top of his lungs for no apparent reason. A cluster of ladies represented friends with breast cancer, and they all looked lovely in their pink outfits and ribbon pins. An assembly of younger kids—maybe eleven or twelve-year-olds—dressed in navy, sported Red Sox foam fingers on each hand.

And finally, there were tee shirts embossed with a photo of Darrin and Bobby together—Darrin in a baseball hat and Bobby in sunglasses—and they looked young and vibrant and happy. It was wonderful to see the support for these two men amongst all these people. Yet, I found myself looking away every time one of those tee shirts got in my line of sight. Each time I saw their smiling faces, it was a punch to my gut.

Doob went in one direction to check in as a volunteer, and I headed off in the opposite to get myself checked in as a participant.

From the corner of my eye, I noticed someone watching me, but it was one of those things my subconscious realized before I was completely aware. When I made eye contact, she took off her sunglasses and did a little finger wave. The black baseball hat and blonde ponytail made for a good disguise, but with her glasses off, there was no doubt.

I was fifteen yards away from Melanie.

CHAPTER 27

THIS WASN'T ONE OF THOSE *I think I saw her in a supermarket aisle* moments I shunned aside. This was a *she is fucking here, right now* moment. This was a *maybe I can do something this time around* moment. I'd suspected it before, but the ho clue she'd sent me must have meant she was coming home.

People milled around us, and my brain screamed at me to react while my feet struggled to get out of the cement boots they'd suddenly become encased in. A large group of walkers crossed between Melanie and me, laughing and chatting it up, unaware of their proximity to the monster. They wore the Darrin/Bobby tee shirts and had balloons bearing the same photo—and here was the girl who murdered both of them right in the middle of it all.

As if straight from a movie, once that group of people passed, Melanie was gone. Like she'd evaporated into thin air. Like I had imagined her. But I hadn't.

I swiveled around three or four times, trying to get a bead on her, but it was pointless. There were too many people, and the balloons, being handed out at a nearby table, seemed to multiply as they clustered and blocked my line of sight.

What to do? I needed to call the cops, but I had to let Doob know, and—God help me—I had to let David know as well. I needed to prioritize. I needed to act.

First things first. I whipped out my cell phone and speed-dialed Colin Burns, the detective I'd worked closely with when Melanie had fled the scene of Darrin's murder. I liked Colin, a short, stocky, red-headed detective who always looked disheveled. He always appears to be running late for whatever event he's going to and arrives with bread crumbs on his jacket and ketchup on his mouth. It's easy to underestimate guys like that, and that works to his advantage. He's got a sharp mind, a quick wit, and he definitely doesn't like to see bad guys get away. Melanie's vanishing act had really bothered him, and he contacted me regularly. I appreciated his tenacity and his follow-up, and I knew he'd be like a dog on a bone if he heard she was back in town.

"Burns," he answered brusquely. I pictured him cradling the phone between his ear and shoulder like he does, with a toothpick hanging out of his mouth.

"Colin, it's Meagan. I'm at the charity walk we talked about last week, and I just saw Melanie. It's her, there's not a doubt in my mind. She waved at me, taunting me, then I lost her in the crowd. You've got to get down here right now."

"Okay, tell me exactly where you're at," he said with an immediate sense of urgency. I loved that he didn't ask any questions, didn't doubt me. He was at-the-ready and headed my way.

Now we just needed to find her again.

CHAPTER 28

I SPEED-DIALED DOOB, AND IT WENT STRAIGHT TO VOICEMAIL. *Damn!* He was probably heading toward his volunteer post. Would Melanie mess with him? I had no idea.

I'd keep dialing Doob every five minutes and find David in the meantime. David, whose step-brother was dead, in part, because of my shortcomings. David—of the huge heart and huge brown eyes—who was organizing an event in an attempt to bring something positive out of such a tragedy. And now I needed to tell him Darrin and Bobby's murderer was here, roaming around the festivities.

The walk was scheduled to start in about thirty minutes, so I didn't have a ton of time to find and warn him. I assumed his step-mother would be in the area as well, and I wanted to get her to safety.

And then I thought of Vic, Melanie's intended final victim in her family murder spree. Weaving around the people and looking for David, I speed-dialed the geriatric frat house and willed someone to pick up.

Thankfully Vic himself picked up on the third ring. "Hi Meagan," he said cheerfully, evidently seeing my number on their Caller ID.

"Vic, listen to me," I urged. "Melanie is here in Boston. I'm at the charity walk for Darrin and Bobby, and she's here. I've lost sight of her, and I've called Colin Burns to get down here to help me, but I need you to be very careful today. Warn the guys at the house, and get the hell out of town if you need to. I don't want anything happening to any of you." I paused for a beat. "Obviously, you're her target, so don't go getting killed on me."

There was silence for a moment, and Vic's voice was ragged when he spoke. "Okay. The guys and I have planned for this. Six of the eight of us are home right now, and I know how to get in touch with the other two. Your uncle has some friends who said they'd be willing to help guard the house when this happened, so we'll put our plan into motion."

He sounded a little bit mechanical. I guess that was a good thing. "Vic, I'll call you once Colin gets here and we form a plan. In the meantime, I've got to call my folks and a few other people. Are you okay?"

"I'm fine, Meagan. We're ready for her."

I felt a pang of hurt for him. The *her* he referred to was his psychopathic daughter. That couldn't be easy even though he'd never been a part of her life.

As I jumped up on a park bench to scan the crowd, I made a similar phone call to my parents, and it was extremely brief. Given the already fragile state of affairs with my family, the news I relayed to Pop did nothing to help, but I didn't care. I only wanted them safe.

When Norman picked up his phone, he stopped just short of telling me he thought I was seeing things. I knew what he was thinking—*Meagan has been feeling guilty since Darrin's death in March, Meagan is emotional because she's at the walk today, Meagan recently stole a hearse, Meagan shot and killed a man, and now poor Meagan has officially lost her mind.*

"Norman, it's her." I was losing my patience. "I'm positive."

"Kiddo, you've been through so much this year. I'm not saying I don't believe you—"

I hung up on him and blurted a few expletives. I was the one who'd walked into that apartment to save Moira, and I was the one who'd gone face-to-face with Melanie on that snowy night earlier in the year. Yeah, I wasn't perfect, but I wasn't an idiot, either. And I didn't appreciate Norman implying I was unhinged.

As my eyes scanned the area, I finally saw David in front of a long table with brochures and pens scattered about. He was shaking hands, doling out balloons, and posing for pictures. It almost seemed like a political rally, and for a few precious seconds, I let myself get lost in it. I just stood and stared and appreciated everything about him.

And then—out of nowhere—a certain girl with a dark hat, sunglasses, and a long, newly-blonde ponytail shook his hand and received a balloon. She quickly pulled out her cell phone, leaned in toward David and snapped a picture of the two of them, their heads almost touching and both grinning. They appeared to be the best of buddies; they could have even been a couple.

He had no idea.

She looked through the crowd right at me, blew a kiss, and once again, disappeared into the swarm of walkers.

CHAPTER 29

I PLOWED THROUGH PEOPLE WITH NO REGARD FOR COURTESY, grabbed David by the arm, and pulled him behind the table, just to have a barrier between us and the growing crowd.

"Hey there, Meagan. I'd be glad to talk sometime, but I'm a little busy right now," he said with a grin.

I put both of my hands on his shoulders. "Sorry for the dramatics, but it was necessary. This is going to be hard to digest, but that girl you just took a picture with?" I softened my voice and tried for a sympathetic look. "David, that was Melanie. She's *here*."

His face drained of color, and he aged twenty years in an instant.

"My God, no," he whispered and whipped around in all directions.

"I need you to keep your cool. Keep doing your thing, keep smiling. I have Burns coming down here, and he'll come with at least one other guy, probably more. I need to know if your step-mom and your dad are here. I don't know if they're targets, but I don't want to find out the hard way."

David rubbed his face with his hand, and once again, I felt like the worst person on earth for bringing more trouble into his world.

"She came down with some type of flu bug yesterday. She spent all day trying to shake it off but still felt like crap last night. She was devastated she wasn't up to coming this morning, but now I guess it's a good thing."

"And your dad?"

"He stayed at home with her, didn't want her to be alone. I'll call them right now." He paused. "You're sure about this? Positive?"

Anger sparked up inside me, but I squashed it hard. David deserved a smidge of slack, all things considered. "I'm positive, David. Call your folks, and stay alert. We're going to find her."

His voice cracked as he put his hand on his head. "Do we need to call this off?"

Hell if I knew. But if we did, wouldn't that mean Melanie had won? Again? "I don't think so," I said. "Colin will be here any second, and we'll see what he says." I stared at him, helpless, for a minute. "I'm so sorry."

He nodded. "I know." And he pulled out his cell phone and turned his back on me.

CHAPTER 30

THE NEXT COUPLE HOURS PASSED BY WITHOUT INCIDENT, and to my immense frustration, without any more appearances from Melanie. The only solace I had was that two newspapers had coincidentally snapped the shot of David and Melanie posing together—probably thinking they made a dashing couple—so at least I had a small degree of proof the Melanie-sighting wasn't just a figment of my imagination. Colin's people down at the station determined her face was a match in their facial recognition system, despite the sunglasses and baseball cap.

So friggin' what? We still had no idea where she was.

At Colin's insistence, I'd actually finished the walk, scanning for Melanie the entire way. Colin, another detective, and two Boston policemen staggered themselves along the route as well, but she had disappeared.

I finally reached Doob just after the walk began, and he was on the lookout for her at the final kilometer, although I wasn't sure how Doob would hold up if he saw her. He'd probably crap his purple unitard.

The Green Line and the Orange Line were along the walk, which was part of the reason David had selected that route. He thought it would be an easy way for people to get in and out of Copley Square. Now it seemed it might have been convenient for Melanie as well. And one thing I knew about her—she always had an escape plan. Melanie was meticulous and conniving, and she'd leave nothing to chance.

That said, something told me she was still in town. She didn't fly in from overseas to wave at me, pose for a picture, and disappear. She had some unfinished business with Vic, and she wasn't going to get this close and just leave.

So...where was she?

Time to think. Did she come back under her own name or under an alias? What mode of transportation did she use to get back to the States? How long had she been here? When did she change her hair color? Was someone helping her with money or housing? If not, how was she supporting herself? What was her next move?

I had zero to go on and felt my blood pressure shooting through the stratosphere. I took a few deep breaths through my nose and let them out in slow puffs through my mouth. I saw that on some Zen television show, but it wasn't doing shit for me right now. Fucking serene yoga people anyway.

With no crystal ball at the ready, I went through some *what-if* scenarios. Such as...Melanie never had a formal education; she'd learned only from the school of hard knocks. So, *if* she'd been in Boston a while, and *if* she was working, she wouldn't be at any type of professional job. And I didn't think she'd take a job with a set schedule. She wouldn't want to get into a predictable routine.

But who could say how long she'd been here? Or if she had a job at all? She'd need money, but she'd proven herself resourceful in the past. She could have killed, stolen, gambled, sold her body, or God-knew-what to get her hands on some real cash. Trying to pin her down with a place of employment probably wasn't my best play.

So fine. She had to be staying somewhere, didn't she? Maybe she shacked up at a hotel somewhere? But again, did she have that type of money? Maybe at an extended stay type-of-place, or an apartment? But apartments required paperwork—leases, security deposits, references—and that was something Melanie would definitely not risk. I was leaning toward the extended stay type-of-place. Unless she'd really landed a jackpot and holed up at the Ritz or Marriott Copley Plaza. Or maybe she was just jumping around from hotel to hotel, which would make it much harder to find her.

Colin, the other officers, Doob, David, and I tossed all this around once the walk had wound down. The event had been a tremendous success, and David should have been somewhere celebrating, instead of brainstorming the whereabouts of a sadistic killer. Would the guilt I felt in relation to this man never end?

As we were forming our game plan for the coming hours, my cell vibrated. Uncle Larry. My heart shot to my throat, and I wondered if she'd somehow penetrated the geriatric frat house.

CHAPTER 31

"TALK TO ME, LARRY," I URGED, ALTHOUGH I WASN'T SURE I wanted to hear what he had to say.

"Talk to *me*," he retorted, sounding as anxious as I felt. "Are you all right?"

"Physically, I'm fine, but I'm totally freaked out. How are you guys doing?"

"We're holed up like Fort Knox, kiddo. There's nothing to worry about here. If we even smell that bitch, she's dead."

Ummm, great. I'd been denying the Uncle-Larry-as-a-bad-guy rumors that had circulated around me for years, but hearing him now? It made me shiver. But my disappointment in him would be hypocritical, considering I hoped he'd blow her away at the first opportunity. And yeah…there was that matter of me killing a man a couple nights before.

I guess you realize what you're really capable of when your family and friends are threatened. Sometimes I wished I still lived in the naïve snow-bubble I'd grown up in. That was a much easier time.

"Larry, if you think you smell her, see her, hear her—whatever—please call the cops. That's the right way to handle this. I don't need you getting thrown in the clink because you got trigger-happy and accidentally shot some innocent young girl."

"You handle things your way, I'll handle things mine. And you got some of your old uncle's blood running through your veins, missy. When this bitch is out of our hair, you and me are gonna talk about that guy you killed."

Oh, lovely. "Larry—"

"Not now. Another time. Right now, tell me what you know about her whereabouts."

"Exactly nothing. I spotted her a couple of times and then lost her in the crowd. She's still stick-thin, and her hair is long, but it's blonde now. She was arrogant enough to pose for a picture with David—"

"*What?*"

"Yep. She had a hat and sunglasses on, so he didn't recognize her. He's never seen her in person anyway, so it's not like he could have known. I've seen her several times and couldn't quite process I was seeing her, especially with the drastic change in hair color. Anyway, I saw her pose for the picture with him, but I couldn't get to them before she scampered off. No one's spotted her since.

"I'm with Colin and some of his cop buddies, and we're circulating her picture among the remaining people right now. So far, nothing, but I'll keep you posted. If we get really lucky, maybe someone will have seen her grab a cab or go into the subway."

"Okay, stay on it. We're gonna get her this time, I can feel it."

"I'm on it, don't worry about that. And you guys be careful. I highly doubt she'll come strolling up to the house and ring the bell, but be on alert. She's smart. She's a planner, and she's on a mission."

"So am I. Locked and loaded."

I paused a beat. Nothing I said would get him off his vigilante train of thought. "Larry?"

"Yeah?"

"How's Vic holding up?"

"He did twenty-five years in the joint, Meg. It's gotta be eating him up, but he's got his game-face on. He'll be okay."

I doubted it, but there was nothing I could do. There was nothing anyone could do. It had to be odd for Vic to be hunkered down with a bunch of old men prepared to kill his daughter.

Motion to my right caught my eye, and I noticed Colin waving me over.

"Larry, I gotta go. Colin might be on to something. Be safe, and stay in touch."

"I'll text you," Larry replied and disconnected. Despite the circumstances, I smiled. Larry prided himself on keeping up with the times, and I could only imagine his big, weathered, Irish fingers fumbling to send me a text. Good grief.

I jogged over to where Colin and the others stood. His cell phone was wedged between his ear and shoulder, eyebrows knitted in concentration on what was being said on the other end. I waited impatiently until he concluded the call, his chin jutted out in determination.

"We've got a lead."

CHAPTER 32

HE THRUST HIS PHONE IN MY FACE AND SAID, "See that mark on her hand?"

I squinted. Someone back at the department had enlarged the grainy image of Melanie's hand to zoom in on some type of black blob.

"The black thing?" I asked.

"Yeah. One of the techs noticed it when they were combing over the picture. We're pretty sure it's a stamp from The Cat's Meow, which means she was likely there recently. Probably last night."

"Is that the bar on Tremont? I haven't been there in a few years; it's kind of a college hangout, I think." Was Melanie actually bar-hopping in Boston? Living her life like a normal twenty-something?

"Yep, exactly. Once we confirm it's the right place, we'll head over there and question every person who worked last night. It was a Saturday night, so the place was probably packed. If they have security videos, we'll get a warrant and study them until we spot her. She might be nuts, but she's also attractive, and the more people we can find who interacted with her, the better."

The excitement in his voice was contagious. I couldn't help but get a little tingly at the possibility of catching Melanie once and for all.

CHAPTER 33

WITHIN A FEW SECONDS OF COLIN GETTING ME UP TO DATE, his cell rang. "Burns." While he listened, his face didn't give anything away, and I wanted to shake the shit out of him. "Okay, good. Get somebody working on the warrant. There's probably no judge working on a Sunday, so if not, find one at home. Find one at his country club, the shopping mall, on the toilet for all I care. Just find someone. We can't sit on this." He hung up and his eyes danced when he looked at me.

"I guess we're headed to the bar?"

"Don't get too excited, Maloney. I can't expense your booze. But yeah, I think you gotta be in on this if you can keep your mouth shut and let us do our job."

"*Moi*?" I held my hand to my chest in mock surprise.

Colin rolled his eyes. "Your about as French as I am." He looked me up and down. "I'm going right now. Do you have something to change into?"

Even though Doob had mocked my overstuffed backpack, I was now grateful for it. "Give me two minutes," I said and scampered over to one of the porta-johns to change. I hate those things. Holding my breath, I began whipping off my layers. Leggings, sweatpants, tee shirts, sweatshirt. I replaced them with black yoga pants, a gray turtleneck and a different pair of running shoes. It wasn't runway-model material, but it was better than what I'd worn on the walk.

A sudden banging shook the flimsy porta-potty door. "Tick-tock, Maloney. You've been in there three minutes."

I opened the door and gasped for some clean air. "Let's go find this bitch."

CHAPTER 34

THE CAT'S MEOW IS LOCATED IN A BLOCK OF BUILDINGS OFF Tremont Street, and it's a place where college students from Harvard, MIT, Boston College, Boston University, Suffolk University, and countless other schools hang out. That mixture generally results in some testosterone-induced fights on occasion, but the place has a good reputation for the most part.

Colin essentially parked right on the sidewalk and put his little "I'm a cop" emblem on the front dash before we got out of the car. I instantly wanted one of those things; it would be an immense help with parking in this city.

A few steps from the door, Colin stopped and put his hand on my shoulder. "This is *my* interrogation, Maloney. I mean it. The other guys are back at the station, ready to do whatever we need. But this needs to go well, so please keep your mouth shut and your eyes open. If you screw this up, I'll cuff you and book you myself."

I glared at him. "We're on the same side here, Burns. I'm not going to mess it up. You won't hear a peep out of me." I twisted an imaginary lock over my mouth.

He smirked. "That'll be the day."

It was about two o'clock when we arrived at The Cat's Meow, and the door was locked when Colin went to open it. We cupped our hands on the windows in the wooden doors and saw a bartender wiping the inside of a glass with a towel. He waved us off, yelling something we couldn't quite understand, and Colin pressed his badge to the window.

"You can open for us, bub," he shouted.

After the man unlocked the door to let us in, we let our eyes adjust to the low lighting within the large space. Empty, it had an almost reverent feel. The calm before the storm. The barkeep locked the door behind us as we continued to take in our surroundings.

It was a long, narrow establishment with Boston sports memorabilia lining the walls. Televisions were everywhere, and a huge mirror spanned the length of the dark wooden bar that looked to be older than the city itself. Bottles of liquor stood several rows deep along the mirror, and the bar stools were all turned perfectly at forty-five degree angles. Booths rimmed the outer perimeter, and dozens of circular tables ringed the center. An aged pool table and some dartboards waited in the back, and it was easy to picture a bunch of college kids blowing off steam in a place like this.

What was extra-cool about this establishment was a walled-in staircase that ran along one of the inside brick walls. I peered up the stairs and couldn't see the top, partially because of the low lighting, but also because the stairs seemed to go straight up to the heavens.

The man who'd let us in looked to be in his mid-fifties. As he settled in again behind the bar, he looked up, but didn't say a word. Previous experience with the cops? Who knew? But he didn't seem flustered or anxious. He seemed like a man content to stay silent for the remainder of the day.

As Colin continued to take in our surroundings, the man polished a glass and glanced occasionally at a television mounted in one of the corners.

After taking in a few more sports pictures, Colin approached the bar, introduced himself, and again showed his ID, giving the man a close-up look at it so he'd know it was the real deal. Colin went on to say he appreciated the man opening up for us. Like the guy really had a choice.

"If you've got a few minutes before you open, I'd like to ask you a couple questions. And if the owner is available, we'd like to speak with him, too. We need some help finding a person we believe was in here either last night or possibly the night before."

The bartender put down the glass and rubbed his chin with his hand. Finally, he said, "Her."

Colin's eyebrows narrowed. "Excuse me?"

"The owner is a *her*. You said *him*."

Colin flushed a million shades of red and said, "Oh, sure. Sorry about that. I shouldn't have assumed..."

"I guess women can own businesses, too," I chirped and gave Colin a thousand-watt smile.

Colin glowered at me and turned back to the bartender. "Your name, sir?"

"The name is Liam Connery," he responded with a bit of drama. "I've been bartending across this city since I was old enough to serve a drink. You need information, I'm your man."

Colin nodded appreciatively. "That's good to know. And the owner's name? Miss, uh, Mrs..?" He was starting to flush again.

"Meow."

"Excuse me?" Colin and I asked simultaneously.

The man smiled broadly. "I've seen her signature, and her name is actually spelled M-i-a-o, which is pronounced Mewo, I believe. But everyone just calls her Meow, and she doesn't seem to mind. Meow Wong."

"Meow it is," Colin said with a shake of his head as he wrote down the name in his little spiral notebook. "Can you give me a little background on Miss Wong, please?"

"I sure can," he said. "I haven't known her very long, but it's quite a story, that one," Liam said with admiration in his tone. "From what I understand, she traveled to the United States by herself as a young Vietnamese girl. She'd come here to live with a grandmother and cousin in Chinatown, but it didn't go well."

"How so?"

Liam shook his head in disgust. "The cousin viewed her as chattel. It was a shady scene, with drugs and what-not, and he treated her like something to be passed off to his scumbag friends. She turned into a drunk herself, a druggie, too."

I couldn't hold my tongue. "Didn't the grandma see what was going on?" Colin glared at me for talking, but it was a legitimate question.

Liam nodded. "It took a while, but the old coot finally couldn't ignore the fact her granddaughter was becoming a junkie right in front of her. When Meow was forced to become *engaged* at the ripe old age of seventeen, she rebelled, and the grandmother intervened and sent her to a different set of relatives somewhere in the southwest."

Good grief.

"Her behavior didn't improve once she moved, but those folks got her some help. She smartened up and got some type of degree; now she's on her way to becoming quite a business lady. She's owned this place for about four months."

Colin jotted in his little notebook. "I'm surprised she came back to Boston, given what you just told us."

Liam shrugged. "The cousin eventually met his maker when he put too much white stuff up his nose one night. That tends to happen when you lead the lifestyle he did. So Meow came back to help with the grandmother; she's still alive and kicking, but she's very frail. Evidently they've made amends and put the past behind them."

"Sounds like a real after-school-special," Colin remarked. "If you would, Liam, does this girl look familiar?" He thrust an enlarged picture of Melanie from the charity walk in Liam's face, and the bartender looked at it and frowned.

"It's difficult to say, Detective. I mean, with the hat and glasses, this could be almost anyone."

I felt my blood pressure spike for the billionth time today. She wasn't just anyone; she was a stone cold killer who seemed to be slipping away. Again. I couldn't take it.

"She's got long, blondish hair, is probably about five-seven´or—"

Colin shot me a look, which shut my mouth quicker than if he'd put a clamp on it. But then he finished my sentence. "—or five-eight, slender, in her late twenties, with fair skin and blue eyes. We're working on getting a better picture of her as we speak."

Liam shook his head. "I can't say I have or haven't seen her, I'm sorry. That description could be about half the young ladies here on any given night. If you get a different picture, I can probably give you a better idea."

"Not without a warrant you won't," came a voice from behind me.

CHAPTER 35

I TURNED TO SEE A LOVELY, YOUNG ASIAN WOMAN AT THE BOTTOM of the stairwell who I quickly surmised to be Meow Wong. Her jet-black hair fanned around her heart-shaped face, stopping just above her shoulders. Her skin was porcelain, and her tiny body was lean and toned. If she'd had some hard knocks along the way, she certainly didn't look the part. The lady was stunning.

Colin introduced himself, showing his badge in the process, and brought Meow up to speed on the purpose of our visit.

She spoke in a clear and precise manner, but her speech was a bit stilted. "Detective Burns, I do not want trouble. I hire good people to keep this place an upstanding business, and I pay my taxes. I know my rights. If you want information from me, you must present to me a warrant."

"Ms. Wong, I can and will do that, but it's going to take a bit of time. I don't think it's much to ask for you to simply look at a picture?" Colin held up Melanie's photo, and she studied it but made no move to take it. Usually when people look at a picture, they hold it and analyze it. Meow just looked at it, her face a perfect mask.

"Is the woman in danger?" she asked, and I immediately wondered how Colin would answer. Given the brief history we had on Meow, I thought it would be prudent to indicate Melanie was in some sort of peril. She definitely would be if Larry or I ever got hold of her. Maybe Meow would feel some type of kindred pull toward Melanie if she thought this young woman was vulnerable.

"I don't know that for sure," Colin replied brusquely. "But she's a person of interest in a couple of open cases, and it's imperative we speak with her. If you could just let me know about the picture..?" he prompted.

"I cannot say if I have or have not seen this woman," Meow said. "She is all covered." She moved her focus away from the photo and then looked at Colin evenly. It was clear she wouldn't offer up anything further.

Colin glanced up at the corners of the walls. "You have video surveillance," he stated.

She nodded and continued on in her stilted speech. "I do. My business has video. They are kept on file in weekly increments. As I said, you will need a warrant if you want to see the videos." With that, she turned and walked back up the endless staircase, presumably to her office area.

"It's never easy," Colin muttered, whipping out his cell phone and poking a speed-dial button. He paced the length of the entire place while waiting for the other party to respond. I heard only snippets of what he said, but it was clear he wanted the warrant he'd ordered less than an hour ago, and he wanted it yesterday. His side of the conversation became clearer as he came closer to the bar. "...get the self-satisfied prick of a judge who plays golf with McClellan's dad to quit feeding his fat face and sign one. Or try to find Stevie and see if his wife can get ahold of her sister who's married to that guy who became a judge last year. Just pull in some type of favor, for God's sake. We're running out of time here, and it's your ass if we lose this girl." He clicked his phone off and ran his hand down his face.

I proceeded with caution. "Should I even ask?"

"I'm not leaving until we get that warrant," Colin insisted. "She was that friggin' close..." he said, holding his thumb and forefinger together. "That close."

"You folks want a drink?" Liam asked good-naturedly.

"Seems like a good idea to me," I chirped and sensed the steam coming off Colin before I could finish the sentence. "What? I walked five entire kilometers today."

Colin rolled his eyes and settled on a stool beside me. "Ginger ale for me, Liam."

"And for the lady?"

"Diet Coke," I muttered and curled my lip at Colin.

Halfway through my caffeinated drink, Colin's phone chirped and he squinted at the screen. "Hot damn! Joey and McClellan came through for us. It looks like it's for the video equipment only."

"Not enough evidence to search the entire place?" I asked.

"Exactly. But the video's a start." He punched keys on his fossilized phone. "Shit! I can't read the attachment at all. It's too small."

I looked at Liam. "Does Meow have a fax machine up there?"

"That she does, but I don't know the number."

Colin hopped off his bar stool and sauntered over to the staircase where Meow had disappeared earlier. Better him than me. No way would I make it up the endless number of stairs now that my legs were locking up after my morning trek.

After a few moments, I heard Colin pound on a door upstairs, announcing to Meow he needed the fax number for her office. After a few more moments, Colin's footsteps thundered back down the staircase.

"She wouldn't let me in," he said, irritation coloring his voice. "She gave me the number through her closed door. She's doing something up there, and it better not be destroying evidence."

CHAPTER 36

I WATCHED HIM STEW. "SO WHAT NOW?"

"Well, I can't force my way into her office, but when that fax arrives, she's the only one who can retrieve it. So that's an issue. Also, I'm not the best with all the techy stuff involved with the video surveillance. I've asked for one of the guys from downtown to get over here, but it's going to be a while. You probably suck with electronic equipment and computers, yes?"

"I do my bills online and can manage email just fine," I said. "That's the extent of my computer prowess. But I've got a whiz-like-no-other who can be here in less than ten."

"Is he expensive?" Colin asked. "I don't know if I can get it approved—"

"I pay him in Frito's," I said with a smile and speed-dialed Doob's number while watching confusion cross Colin's face.

While I spoke with Doob, a few workers shuffled in. The bar would be opening soon, unless Burns decided to shut it down. Colin ended a phone call of his own, and I watched as he corralled three of the employees.

He turned to me. "Is your guy on the way?"

"As it so happens, he was on his way over here anyway. He knew I would need a ride home at some point, and he'll be here in about two minutes. What's going on with these guys?" I gestured my chin to the assembled workers.

"I'm going to talk to each of them separately," he replied. "And I just got word the fax is being sent. I need you to go up and get it as well as tell Meow we're going to start reviewing the videos and will be speaking with her employees. She can stay up there; I'd actually prefer it. But I'll extend her the courtesy of observing the video review if she wants to."

A slight smirk formed on Colin's lips.

"Something amusing you, Detective?"

"Yeah. I just realized you can't make it up and down those stairs on a good day, Maloney. Ten bucks says we'll need to install an escalator to get you back down; or maybe I could have a chopper land on the roof to pick you up."

I couldn't really argue but wrinkled my nose at him anyway. "I'll be just fine." No, I absolutely wouldn't.

Doob walked in at that particular moment, and we brought him up to speed.

"You wouldn't want to go up there for me, would you?" I asked, batting my lashes in exaggerated fashion.

"Not a chance." He chuckled. "That lady doesn't even know me. If you'd been doing the treadmill religiously, this wouldn't be a problem. Text me when you get halfway and let me know if you need oxygen." He glanced at his phone. "I'll expect to hear from you in about two hours," he said and walked away, giggling as he left.

I slowly shuffled to the stairwell and then looked back to see Burns already questioning one of the workers and Doob getting a soda from Liam. "If I die of exhaustion, it's on you two jackasses," I muttered under my breath.

CHAPTER 37

GAZING UP THE ENDLESS STAIRWELL, MY LEGS SCREAMED UP TO my brain not to do it, and my brain couldn't think of a good reason to turn them down. I couldn't help but think of Charlie's body that Jeff had walked in on earlier in the month. Shuddering, I dismissed it; thoughts like that wouldn't help the situation.

Looking at what I estimated to be about forty stairs, I viewed it as follows: sometimes the anticipation of a dreaded event ends up worse than the event itself. For example, I hate bridal and baby showers. I know that makes me the devil as well as a tremendous asshole; I further know that makes me almost a man, but they're a time-consuming pain in the ass. The only people who truly want to be there are the people who are getting the gifts. I've been to enough of those events that I know of what I speak. But to be fair, I've attended one or two showers that actually ended up being okay. We didn't have to play stupid games, the gifts didn't take two hours, and the mimosas made everything right with the world.

So I just needed to treat the staircase as such. This would be the mimosa staircase as opposed to the let's-build-a-wedding-dress-out-of-fucking-toilet-paper staircase. That was my attitude when I lifted my leg to start the upward trek.

Sadly, the motivation from my little internal pep talk lasted for only the first three steps. This dreaded event created a whole new category of dreaded events. I hadn't considered how locked up my hamstrings would be by the time I got about one-third of the way up. Nor had I realized it would be about seven hundred degrees, causing sweat to run down my butt crack before the halfway point. At the two-thirds point, I gave up and sat on a step to catch my breath. A bar full of liquid downstairs, and I hadn't thought to grab a water or a soda.

After using the banister to pull myself up, I did the last segment of my journey at a snail's pace and almost kissed the top step when I finally made it.

I would need that chopper to get back down after all.

After I gathered myself and caught my breath, I decided to enter with the element of surprise. To cover my ass, I knocked quietly and then quickly entered the dark room. From what I could make out, it looked to be some type of apartment that had been transformed into an office space. A dim light came from somewhere toward the back, and I assumed Meow was in there. "Meow?" Flipping on the tiny flashlight app in my phone, I tiptoed in the direction of the faint glow.

I nearly jumped through my skin when I heard the fax machine ring in an adjacent room. Knowing I needed the arriving document, I pointed my beam of light toward the sound of the ring. Just as I got to the machine, I sensed movement to my left and assumed Meow was coming to get the fax as well.

I pointed my light in that direction and found myself face-to-face with Melanie.

CHAPTER 38

I SAW HER RIGHT LEG WIND UP AND JUMPED BACK JUST in time to avoid getting kicked in the stomach. Her foot connected with the fax machine, and she yelped. I doused my cell phone light, assuming she'd be less effective in the dark. Any weapon she had would also be less effective in the dark. I hoped.

Where the hell was Meow? Was she going to just let me get attacked?

And then I thought of Doobie and the others downstairs. If Melanie hurt or killed me and then got to them...well, that was something I wasn't prepared to deal with. Swinging blindly where she'd just been, I hoped to connect with some part of her, but she'd obviously moved. Whirling and spinning like a crazy person, all I kept finding was air.

Get to the stairwell. I heard that voice in my head as clearly as if someone had announced it over a PA system. As evidenced in prior situations, I don't always listen to the voice, but in this case I was in total agreement.

From the room I was in, I could see the light coming through the slightly open stairwell door and started racing to it, thankful the rooms were sparse so nothing would trip me.

But that's when I felt it. The snap to the back of my left calf. The falling to the ground in disbelief. The instant, searing pain.

I'd been shot.

Adrenaline kicked in, and I tried to stand up, but my leg wouldn't support me. Losing my balance, I toppled in a heap on the floor and wanted to whimper in pain, but that wasn't an option. Knowing I had to get out, I started crawling toward the door, using my forearms and good leg to scuttle along. I couldn't die up here with this maniac. I just couldn't.

I knew Melanie was on my tail. In the darkness, she wouldn't know I was flat on the ground, so I swung out wildly with my right arm. Jackpot. I connected with her leg and pulled on it until she fell over. Then I latched onto both her feet as if my life depended on it.

Because it probably did.

She kicked furiously, but my arms worked their way up her legs and wrapped around her waist. I was outmatched because of my leg, but I wasn't going down without a fight. For once in my life, I was grateful to not be a dainty little thing. The height advantage went to her, but I had more pounds and more upper-body strength.

Game on, bitch.

I launched the loudest, longest scream I've ever let go in my life while I dragged her toward the stairwell. Bright spots danced in my field of vision as the pain seared through my leg, but I was going to tug her with me until my body gave out. Sensing where I was trying to pull her, she changed her tactic, and instead of resisting me, she went with it and dove over me with her upper body. We turned into a rolling, fighting, kicking, screaming ball, and before I knew it, the stairwell door was wide open and we were teetering at the top of the steps.

Lying on my side, I now had a great grip on her ponytail with one hand and my other arm had her in a pseudo-headlock. My Herculean strength had to be coming from sheer adrenaline, and there was no doubt I was going to run out of gas any second.

Not that she was going quietly. She reached back and clawed at my face, biting at whatever body part of mine she could get to. I wondered how much blood I was losing and started to panic, thinking I might pass out soon.

As Melanie and I see-sawed on the top landing, I got a quick glance down the stairwell and saw Doob appear at the bottom of the stairs. His mouth was in a perfect O, disbelief written all over his face. Doob to the rescue? Good God. Where the hell was Colin? Not that it mattered. If he'd been there, he wouldn't have been able to shoot at us because he'd have a very good chance of hitting me instead of Melanie.

With my strength waning, it was decision time. I didn't want to end up like poor Charlie in a heap at the bottom of the stairwell, but I had no choice.

"Doob, get Colin and get outta the way!" I yelled as I launched Melanie and myself down the steps. We stayed together in a ball for the first part of the fall, and then at some point, we disentangled. My head and neck banged into the wall and edges of several steps, and my body twisted in ways it wasn't met to twist.

We gained momentum as we plummeted toward the lower level. The trip up might have been a doozy, but the descent was the true definition of "going to hell in a handbasket." Every part of my body was mercilessly battered and bruised. A nail or something sharp in the wall sliced my arm during one of my somersaults, and I howled in agony.

Melanie hit the ground before me, the back of her head smacking the floor with a sickening thud. I landed on her lower body a split-second later, my face planted in her lap. Aware I was losing consciousness, I rolled off her and briefly caught a glimpse of Doob and Colin's horrified expressions.

And then it all went black.

CHAPTER 39

Monday, November 11th

THE EVENING BEFORE WAS A GROGGY BLUR OF BLUE and red flashing lights, police, sirens, ambulances and EMTs. Just before I'd gone down for the count, I'd evidently murmured that Melanie had shot me in the leg. Colin had then frantically tried to find a gunshot, to no avail. Relieved I wasn't bleeding to death, they just assumed I'd lost my marbles in the fall.

I'd come to as they were taking Melanie out on a stretcher and putting me on a stretcher of my own. Seeing the dark pool of liquid at the bottom of the stairs, I'd asked if she was dead and learned that she wasn't. I'd then inquired if it was her blood or mine, and the EMT looked at me quizzically and responded I hadn't lost any blood.

"But I was shot!" I'd insisted and had been rewarded with a smirk.

In the hospital a couple of hours later, I learned my Achilles had ruptured.

"I wasn't shot? No bullet? No blood?" I asked, completely stunned.

The handsome doctor smiled at me. He had gelled, brown hair with some gray flecks on the side, and a set of killer olive-green eyes. He appeared to be built like a brick shithouse under that white coat as well. I've watched my share of "Grey's Anatomy" and I know all about McDreamy and McSteamy. I immediately dubbed this fine-looking physician McGreeny. Yum.

"You seem a little upset about that," he commented with some amusement in those eyes.

"Of...of course I'm not," I stammered defensively, simultaneously flustered by his comment and his green-ness. "I don't exactly want that on my résumé. But I can tell you *something* hit me in the back of the leg, and it took me down like a sack of potatoes. I didn't imagine it."

He nodded agreeably. "I've been in sports medicine for about eight years, and almost every time I've seen this injury, the patient said it felt like they'd been shot. Given the circumstances you were in, it sounds like you had legitimate reason to think so. It was an honest mistake."

Embarrassment washed over me. God. "So this was what again? A tendon or something?"

He looked up at the ceiling for a second and then looked back down at me. "Your Achilles, yes."

"My *heel*? Are you kidding me? I wasn't jumping off a house or kicking a cement pole; I was just running for a door."

McGreeny pursed his lips. "Do you happen to be a Red Sox fan?"

What in the world? I raised an eyebrow at him. "Uh...yes. And I'll have no problem requesting a new doctor if you're a Yankees lover."

He smiled to reveal some perfect white teeth, and it made the corner of his dark green eyes crinkle. *Oh my.* Eight years in sports medicine? *Is that what he said?* So how old did that make him? *Too old or too young?* Or just right. *Get a grip, Meagan.* You've seen hotties before, no big deal.

"I asked if you were a Sox fan, because there was a player several years back named Gabe Kapler. You remember him?"

"Of course! Gabe the Babe. He was another hottie."

Oh fuck!

"I mean, uh...he was a hottie. Because if he was *another* hottie, then that would mean that there was a first hottie, and ummm..."

McGreeny let my sentence fade, so the word awkward doesn't adequately cover the weird quiet that suddenly blanketed the room. I willed myself invisible.

Finally, he spoke. "Yes, I believe the ladies were fond of Mr. Kapler. He was rounding second base in a game, and he sort of tripped and went down just as you described. He was an athlete in peak physical condition, and this thing took him down hard. Ended his season in 2005. I don't think he was back until the following June."

"I remember that!" I said excitedly. "Tony Graffanino hit a home run, and he was running behind Kapler when he went down. They weren't sure what to do since Kapler couldn't finish running the bases."

McGreeny's face lit up, and I couldn't have been happier if he'd come over and ruffled my hair. "Exactly right, you *are* a fan. All kinds of major athletes have had this injury, so you're in good company, and you definitely didn't imagine it."

We grinned at each other for a second, but then a thought struck me. "This trip down Sox memory lane is great, but what I heard you say loud and clear is that Gabe didn't get back to baseball until the following *June*. I believe his injury happened in September or thereabouts?"

McGreeny nodded as his mouth formed a thin line. "That's correct. So let's get down to it. This is *not* a quick or easy recovery, Meagan. There are two routes you can take, and they're both a long process. One is surgical, and the other is not."

I found myself not looking at the doc as he described what the next few months of my life were going to be like because I couldn't concentrate when I was looking at those green eyes. They were like a vortex sucking my brain cells right out of my head, and I really needed to pay attention if I was going to opt for a major surgical procedure.

When he was done telling me about the risks and recovery times of my options, I didn't hesitate. "Surgery," I said with finality, and he studied me for a moment.

"You're positive?"

"Completely. The thought of *not* having surgery and just letting scar tissue fuse me back together isn't an option." I shuddered.

The doc nodded, said he'd be in touch with an orthopedic surgeon and get back to me with a couple of options. Then he and his olive eyes left the room. After just a few seconds, he popped his head back in the door, and I was hoping he'd mention that he happened to be a Sox season ticket holder, and that maybe next spring, if I was interested...

Instead, "You've got a couple of guys out here who are chomping at the bit to see you. Are you up for visitors?"

I looked at my watch. 3:00 AM. "That's okay with you?"

He shook his head. "Not really, but one of them is completely prepared to arrest me, and the other one looks ready to cry. I'm willing to make an exception."

I beamed. "Yes, please send them in."

Seconds later, Doob rushed into the room and practically knocked me out of my hospital bed as he enveloped me in a hug. Colin shuffled in behind him, looking sullen and tired.

"You've taken years off my life, dear neighbor. I'm glad you're okay." He hugged me harder, and I thought he might crawl into the hospital bed with me.

"Watch the leg, Doob," I said laughing.

He jumped back about a foot, hands in the air. "Which one? Is it broken? I didn't listen to a word the doctor said after he told us you were going to be all right."

"Left leg. It's not broken, no. But it's an Achilles rupture, and it sounds like the recovery period is close to ten thousand years."

"See what happens when you try to do a charity walk with no preparation?"

"The doctor said it happens to *major* athletes, and that I'm in good company. It could have happened to anyone."

Doob rolled his eyes. "Okay, Miss *Major Athlete*, I stand corrected. You gonna need surgery?"

"Yep, very soon. So you'll have the enviable job of waiting on me for the next ten thousand years."

"Like that's anything new," he said without missing a beat. His eyes then traveled to my arm with the zig-zag of stitches. He tentatively walked back over to the bed and peered at it as if studying a freakish zoo animal. "That's awesome! How many?"

"Twelve, I think," I replied, pulling a face as I examined it. I'm not particularly vain, but I wasn't too thrilled about the scar that bad boy was going to leave.

Doob beamed and scanned the rest of my body. "Anything else?"

I scoffed. "Not enough battle wounds for you?"

He rocked his head from side to side. "It'll do. I just wish I could have videoed it. The number of hits on YouTube would be epic."

"YouTube? Are you serious? Doob, I could have been killed."

"Well, duh. I wouldn't have posted it if you'd been killed. But it was awesome. We'd have called it the Catfight-in-Flight. Very impressive, Meg. And she definitely got the worst of it."

"I thought the bitch shot me."

"You're lucky I didn't," Colin grumbled, finally speaking up from his chair in the corner.

I grimaced as I took in his five o'clock shadow and the dark circles under his eyes.

"I'm sorry, Colin. I really am. But what the hell was I supposed to do? You'd just been up there yourself—"

"But I didn't walk in without permission. Save me your sob story, Maloney. You'll make it up to me, I promise."

"I'm having surgery. Give a girl a break," I whined.

"I could break your neck," he suggested.

McGreeny to the rescue, as he knocked and then entered without waiting for a response. There was an available orthopedic surgeon for late the following morning—rather, later *this* morning— so I signed a few sheets saying I understood the risks involved in the surgery, and soon I'd be under the knife.

CHAPTER 40

Saturday, November 16th

"DOOB, YOU READY?" I LOOKED AT MY FRIEND WHO WAS stuffing as many Fritos into his mouth as humanly possible.

Doob saluted. "Aye aye, Captain Maloney, at your service. Here to serve. Happy to help. Whatever you need. Will work for Fritos but generally work for free—"

"We got it, Doob," I said dryly. Then I yelled toward the phone, which we'd put on speaker a minute before. "Colin, are you there?"

Colin's Boston accent chimed through the phone. "You should demand Abe & Louie's or The Capital Grille at the very least," Colin responded. "It's the least she can do. Especially at friggin' midnight."

"From your lips to God's ears to my mouth," Doob replied.

"Would it be possible to get some work done? Or do you two need a nappy?" I asked, wondering how I'd afford either of those steakhouses if Doob started making ultimatums.

"I'm fine. I never sleep. But are you sure *you're* up for it?" Doob asked me.

"What else am I gonna do?" My leg was in a cast up to my knee, the size and weight of a submarine, and propped up on Doob's couch with three pillows because Dr. McGreeny said I needed to keep it elevated.

Sampson and I had been staying at Doob's apartment since my surgery. Doob insisted it would be easier to wait on me that way, plus, with Moira gone, I wasn't too keen on staying at our place anyway. It was just too quiet.

Before surgery, I'd given Doob and Colin a laundry list of things we'd need to go over once I was coherent. I'd spent the first four days after surgery in a pain-killer-induced-fog and finally took myself off them after getting quite sick. Pain or no pain, I was done with the drugs.

While I was laid up in my semi-conscious state, Colin had been calling me faithfully with daily updates, and every day I remained surprised to hear that Melanie was still in the hospital. This was quite curious. Our tumble didn't merit five days in the hospital in my humble opinion, but that was one of the reasons I'd gathered this little meeting.

"Okay, I'm going to go through my list of items one at a time—" and then stopped and pointed a finger at Doob. "You realize I can see you, correct? Rolling your eyes isn't going to get you out of this."

He rolled them some more. "Sorry. But do we really need a checklist? We're grown men."

"That's up for debate," I retorted. "I'm doing it as much for me as for you guys. I want to make sure we don't miss anything." Then I looked down at my yellow legal pad with scribbles everywhere and turned to the phone. "We'll start with the small stuff and then work up to the psychopathic stuff. Burns, what do you have for us on Meow? How did they meet? And where the hell was she when I was getting attacked up in that office?" I asked briskly.

Colin dove in from the speakerphone. "All right, we're starting with Meow." Doob and I heard some papers shuffling. "From what she told me, the girls met when they were both at the, uh, boarding school—or whatever you call those places—in the southwest. That was probably about seven or eight years ago."

"Boarding school?" I scoffed. "Don't you mean they met at the cuckoo farm for troubled teens that I told you about?"

"You're very politically incorrect," he said with phony admonition in his voice.

"Sue me," I retorted.

"It was a pain in the ass to get the information because they were juvies. I had to call in a favor from a guy who knows a guy. I'm just glad you remembered Melanie had spent some time there."

"Sadly, I can recite a lot of the events in her life."

"Obsess much?"

"How can I not? It haunts me. Like you don't do the same thing with your cases?"

"I do. Anyway, Melanie was already there when Meow arrived, and Meow was some type of mess. Melanie kinda took her under her wing, became friendly with her when she learned Meow had lived in Boston."

"There's probably some psychology to that. Melanie saw a broken girl from Boston; it was probably like looking at herself in some warped way."

"I'll leave the psycho-babble crap to you, Maloney," Burns said through the phone. "So Melanie got out of the home about six months before Meow—"

I knew what he was going to say before he said it. "Any chance her release coincided with the cousin's overdose? That's been Melanie's MO throughout."

"Way ahead of you, kid. I remember you telling me she'd drugged people in the past. As it turns out, Melanie had been out just under three weeks when the cousin OD'd. We can't prove anything, of course, but months later, she showed up at the facility the day Meow was released and gave her a manila envelope with nearly twenty thousand dollars in it."

Doob whistled lightly.

"Where in the heck did she get that?" I wondered.

"Well, Meow had told Melanie at one point that the cousin was a dope dealer. Probably had a lot of cash at his place. It's pure speculation, but if Melanie killed him, she probably took the time to find the cash."

"That sounds reasonable," I agreed. "I'm surprised she didn't keep it."

"Yeah, I thought of that, too, and I've got a couple theories. Number one, we don't know she didn't. There could have been forty grand, and she kept half. Number two, Meow said Melanie gave her the money and said she'd collect on the favor someday. They agreed to keep in touch, which they did via email, and Meow didn't see Melanie again until about a week ago when she showed up at the bar, said she was running from a guy and needed a place to lay low for a while."

"Playing on Meow's sympathy," I said.

"Yep. Meow said Melanie was ecstatic when she learned about the little apartment area above the bar. Meow offered to let her stay at her place, but Melanie claimed she didn't want to disrupt things with the grandma and she'd just use the bar for the time being."

"I'm going a little off the grid, here," I said. "But it's got to take a lot of capital to buy a bar in Boston. Even if Melanie's seed money helped Meow out, how in the heck did she manage to buy The Cat's Meow?"

Colin chuckled. "Good old Gram."

"The grandmother?"

"Yep. She's ten billion years old, and her place has been paid for forever. She put up a lot of the money and is also on the paperwork."

"Cool," Doob said.

I nodded. "Okay, sorry, I need to get back on track. So where the hell was Meow when I was fighting Melanie up in that office, or apartment, or whatever?"

"Meow internally freaked out when we came to the bar with Melanie's picture, especially since she knew Melanie was upstairs. Then when I pounded up to her office to ask for the fax number, she thought she was going to be arrested. After I went downstairs, they argued. Melanie tried to convince her they should slip out via the fire escape, but Meow wanted Melanie to turn herself in. They had a little tussle, and true to form—"

"Melanie drugged her," I finished.

"You got it," he said. "Not enough to kill her, but enough to knock her out. We think Melanie was about to take off out the fire escape, when you walked in."

"And the rest, as they say, is history," Doob chimed in.

I mulled all this over. "So, I hate to say it, but it seems like Meow didn't intentionally do anything wrong. It sounds like she crossed paths with a psycho at a rough point in her life, and the psycho recently tried to call in a chit."

"I tend to agree with you there," Colin said. "She answered all our questions and didn't lawyer up, even though she probably should have. She just got scared when we showed up with that picture, and by demanding a warrant, it bought her some time to speak with Melanie."

"Come to think of it," I said, "Melanie fed her that bullshit story about being scared of a guy. Because of her past, Meow is probably not a trusting person; she may have suspected *us* of being in cahoots with the mysterious boogeyman Melanie was supposedly running from."

"Yep, could be. Regardless, I don't think Meow is going to get into too much hot water over this."

I scribbled some notes on my pad. "Okay, on to the murdering bitch. Why is she still in the hospital?"

I heard a big sigh and envisioned Colin rubbing his forehead with his hand.

"Burns?"

"Yeah...I'm here. I wasn't exactly sure when to tell you."

Wasn't exactly sure when to tell me? "Tell me what? What's going on? What are you guys hiding from me now?"

"Listen, don't bust my balls. You've been doped up on pain pills and—"

"Cut the shit, Burns. I'm fine, I'm awake, I'm alert, I ditched the pain pills. And my leg got hurt, not my head, so don't protect my fragile psyche. Why is she still in the hospital? If she's even in the hospital! If she isn't there, I swear to God—"

"Hold your horses there, tough girl," he responded. "I don't want you to come after me with your crutch."

"You're just full of compassion, caveman. *Talk to me*. Why is she still there? And the cops have had to have questioned her by now. What's she saying?"

His voice sounded muffled as if he was rubbing his face again. "According to reports, she's not doing too great, so she's not saying a lot." He paused for a beat. "But her lawyer certainly is."

"Her *what*?" I exploded. "Tell me I heard that incorrectly."

"Maloney, you're smarter than that. Every scumbag, drug dealer, murderer, and terrorist we've ever seen in this city has ended up with a lawyer. Think about the bombing at the Marathon and all the idiots who came to the defense of those animals. Melanie's no different."

"Who'd she get?" I asked, hoping it was a pimply-faced twenty-something who'd flunked the bar exam a few times before squeaking by on the final attempt.

"Bragginini," Colin replied, aggravation in his voice.

"Are you fucking kidding me?" I wailed, as my world started spinning. Maybe I would need those pain pills again after all. "Arturo-two-g's-Bragginini. How in the hell did she manage that?"

"I don't know, and believe me, I'm as disgusted as you are. That publicity-hound is licking his chops at this story. Artie will have her decked out in a wheelchair and a slinky dress to show the casts on both her legs, as well as a little T and A. Not to mention she's getting tested for whatever's wrong with her head."

"*Excuse me*? Because of our fall down the stairs? I saw all the blood. Does she have brain damage?"

"I'm not sure, but something is up. Melanie's biological brother—"

"Bobby?"

"Yeah, Bobby. He had a terminal—"

"I'm well aware of the brain tumor he had."

"You gonna keep interrupting me?"

"As often as I need to, yeah."

"Try to shut it until I'm done; we'll do Q&A later."

"I'll ask questions when I feel like it. I don't work for you."

"Thank God. Anyway, Bobby had a terminal brain tumor, but as we both know, he was murdered before it killed him."

"By Melanie."

"Well, supposedly over the past few months while she's been gone—"

"While she's been running from the law—"

"Her lawyer is claiming she's been having headaches for quite some time—"

"Could be the guilt from murdering a number of people."

"The lawyer is further saying she was treated at that juvie home just before her release. They told her she had some type of mysterious mass in her head—"

"That mass is her psychotic brain—"

"And they would have treated her before letting her go, but she just up and—"

"She's making all of this up. She sold her lawyer a bill of goods. Or he's making it up, it doesn't matter! This is what she *does*, Burns. She's taking her brother's horrible illness and trying to use it to her advantage. She was in that home eight years ago. Wouldn't a mysterious mass have somehow manifested itself by now, and—"

"Maloney, enough. The doctors are pissing in their pants over Bragginini's claims, and everyone is running scared. So they're taking every possible precaution to make sure she doesn't have some type of health issue that might keep her from facing an arraignment and eventual trial—"

"*What?* Are you fucking kidding me?"

"Not at all. Outside of the fact she may have a hereditary problem, she did take a vicious blow to the head."

"She's not sick. They're buying time."

"Nothing Bragginini does would surprise me. But he's claiming she's entitled to any required medical care before her clerk's hearing, however long that may take."

I scoffed. "She's *entitled*? Are you kidding me?"

"Everyone's entitled," Doob piped up from the peanut gallery. "God bless America. The taxpayers will be footing the bill for those tests of hers until the end of time."

I rubbed my temples. "We're not getting into a political discussion right now, Doob." As if by divine intervention, his cell phone rang, and his face lit up.

"It's my mom."

"At this hour?" I asked.

He shrugged and headed toward his bedroom. "I think they're in France or somewhere."

"So Burns, how long can her attorney keep up this crap? Do they really want to be under this type of scrutiny?"

"Of course they do. That weasel loves the attention. He's telling the world how she was viciously attacked the other day and unjustly accused many months back. They're turning her into the victim."

That took a minute to sink in, and when it did, I thought I might vomit. "The victim?"

"Yeah," he mumbled.

"Viciously attacked? Unjustly accused? By me? He's going to tell the world what *I* did to *her*? *Me*? To *her*?"

He didn't respond, just cleared his throat like people do when they're tremendously uncomfortable.

"Burns, tell me this is a really bad joke. Tell me this is you just being a dick because I screwed up in that office, and we can go laugh about it over a beer when I'm back on my feet."

"I wish I could, kid. It's kind of looking bad; I'm not gonna bullshit you."

"Bad for *me*?" I squeaked. I was feeling tremendously self-absorbed at the moment, but the situation merited it.

"Yeah."

"I can't believe this."

"Trust me when I say that telling you this is the last thing I want to be doing right now, but you need to be ready for the shit-storm that's likely headed your way." Another pause. "And since you brought it up, yes, I'm doing this despite the fact you royally screwed things up by going in that office."

"She'd have bolted if I hadn't gone in there, so I'm done apologizing." Looking down at my cast, I said, "I'm gonna be paying for it for months, too."

"Rationalize all you want. Once you're out of this mess and walking again, I'm going to whip your skinny ass and put you back on crutches."

Out of this mess? Had the world gone crazy?

Colin's voice softened. "I'm just kidding, Maloney. I wish I'd been the one who found her. I've got quite a few pounds on you; I would have shut her down quickly. That damn fall down the stairs is getting her all kinds of sympathy."

"That's great. She gets sympathy, and I'm suddenly the bad guy. So tell me what I'm up against," I said, hating the sound of resignation in my own voice.

"Okay, it's not me saying it, and it's not—"

"I *got* it," I said impatiently. "Your disclaimer is duly noted. Tell me what the horrible bad *other* people who most certainly aren't you are saying about me."

He sighed heavily. "Okay…if you just go with the facts, you killed a guy recently."

I felt like he'd sucker-punched me in the stomach, and I couldn't catch my breath. *My* reputation was suddenly on trial. *My* credibility was in question. "Burns, the cops all know what happened—"

"With your sister as the only eyewitness," he interrupted.

That stung. "My sister is an attorney, an officer of the court, *Detective*. She wouldn't lie for anyone, especially me. She hates me right now."

"I'm just saying...to some people, that looks pretty bad."

"Well, some people can go fuck themselves."

"Responses like that aren't going to get you any brownie points." He plowed on. "So then you've got to look at the facts with you and Melanie. You were with her earlier in the year when all that shit went down at the abandoned house. But it was just you and her—"

"My word against hers is what you're telling me," I interrupted, not wanting to hear his long, drawn-out, blathering explanation.

He hesitated. "Exactly that, yes. And you didn't see her kill Darrin, did you?"

I remained silent. I simply could not process this.

"And you didn't see her kill that homeless woman." He didn't ask me this time; he just stated what we both knew. "You weren't an eyewitness. There were no eyewitnesses to any of the claims you've brought against her."

"Burns, she *told* me all the shit she did. She almost bragged about the people she'd killed, all the planning she'd done—"

"Did you have a recorder going at the time?"

He was pissing me off. "When I had the gun to my head? When I was being held hostage in a truck that wasn't mine? No, Colin! I didn't whip out a fucking recorder. For someone who claims to be my friend, you sound an awful lot like a cop right now."

"I am *both* your friend and a cop. I know you're shocked, but believe me, I'm putting this lightly compared to what some others are saying."

"She *told* me," I whispered. "She murdered those people. And she's coming after Vic."

"Yep, according to you, kid."

My anger flared again. "Yeah, according to me! I'm not the murderer here. I'm not the psychopath who's killed countless people. What about her mom who she burned up? What about the guy she dumped in Boston Harbor? What about poor Bobby? She shot him in bed, for God's sake." I couldn't help the hysteria in my voice.

Colin remained nonplussed. "Again, you've got evidence for all of those? Heck, do you have evidence for even *one* of those?"

"Whose side are you on?" I pleaded. "Colin, she can't be the victim here. She would have killed me. She's killed people in cold blood. She pre-meditated for *years* while her sick brain rotted away. She's a monster. She killed people, and then she ran away."

"She claims she ran because she was scared of you."

That was it. My brain shut down.

"Colin, stop talking. My mind is too full to process one more miniscule grain of this crap." I reached over and rang the little bell that was propped on the end table beside my perch.

"Tell me I didn't just hear what I thought I heard," Burns chirped.

"It wasn't my idea," I insisted as Doob rushed into the room, still on the phone. "Diet Coke, please," I mouthed at him, and he dutifully delivered one and then went back to his bedroom.

"Maloney—"

"We'll call you back in a little bit," I said and disconnected.

CHAPTER 41

AFTER I HUNG UP ON COLIN, I STARED AT THE WALL FOR quite some time. Literally stared at the wall. I'm not usually a fan of wallpaper, but Doob's brownish-gold ornate curlicue design had me staring at it like an infant in a crib mesmerized by a mobile toy dangling over her head.

What in the hell was this world coming to if Melanie was viewed as the victim and me the aggressor, the criminal?

Doob resurfaced about twenty minutes later. He looked at me and then at the wall—trying to see what I was so fascinated with—then back at me. "You look like hell, Meg. Do you want me to make you something?"

I shook my head.

In one hand he held his laptop; he perched his free hand on his hip.

"Did you finish your Diet Coke?"

I nodded.

"You want another one?"

"Please." He went into the kitchen and came back with a two-liter and a glass full of ice. "It saves me time if I hydrate you in bulk."

I gave him a weak smile. "Well, time is of the essence. We're supposed to call Burns back."

"True dat," Doob said and then did some weird hand gesture. "That's me being gangsta. Did it scare you?"

"I'm shaking in my cast," I sighed. "Let's call Burns and get this over with. I guarantee we'll be waking him."

"Sissy," Doob said and then quickly held up a hand. "Don't tell him I said that."

I smiled. "Before we call, let me switch gears for a second. Did you find out when Ava's house was paid off?"

Doob cracked his knuckles. "Through no small feat of brilliance, I was able to determine Ava's house was paid off in one large sum three months after Rusty was locked up. She also made a bank deposit of ten thousand dollars each year on the anniversary date of his incarceration. Might make for some nice kitchen renovations," he mused.

"Hunh. Seems Mr. Malcolm Gage Johnson was paying hush money. The bad guys seem to be winning the wars at this point," I said miserably.

"Meg, I don't know what all Colin told you, but Melanie's not going to get away with anything. She and her lawyer are grasping at straws."

I shrugged. "What's incomprehensible is she's trying to turn the tables on me, but that's not my main concern. I'm just worried there's going to be enough *reasonable doubt* in the case against Melanie. Our society is a little bit nuts right now. She could get away with everything."

Doob's face fell. "That would be bad."

"Understatement of the year."

My ring tone blared, and I was surprised when I saw it was Burns. Putting him on speakerphone, I asked, "Did you miss us, Detective?"

"Melanie's been shot."

CHAPTER 42

"WHAT?" I SCREAMED AS DOOB COUGHED UP HIS mouthful of potato chips.

"I can't believe it, either. My phone started blowing up twenty minutes ago. She got shot. She's in surgery right now."

"She's in a hospital, Burns! She has a policeman outside her door. How could someone just walk in and shoot her?"

"They didn't. Someone shot her right through her hospital window from the parking garage across the street. It hit her in the stomach, and the nurses came in and found her when her monitors started going nuts."

"The window didn't break? The cop didn't hear anything?"

"Did you pay *any* attention in physics, Maloney?"

"Hey, I knew about the fermentation in the tank that caused the great molasses flood."

"The what? Don't answer that, I don't have time. Anyway, it wasn't a machine gun that would have blown out the window. I don't have all the particulars, but it must have been almost like a sniper shot. I'm heading over there now; I just wanted to let you know. And Doob?"

"Yeah?"

"If you have to tie her up and gag her; if you have to pour pain pills down her throat; if you have to lock her in a room; if you have to rupture her other Achilles, keep that one-legged snoop at your apartment. Do not, I repeat, do *not* let her come down here. I will keep you guys updated as I can."

"I'm right here, and I don't appreciate—," I said, but he was already gone. I looked at Doob. "If you even try to tie me up, you will have a crutch so far up your—"

"Like I'd try," Doob interrupted. "I don't have a death wish. But he's right about us not going down there. You aren't exactly coordinated on those crutches *here*, let alone getting around at a hospital crime scene. Why don't you try to get a little sleep? He'll call us later." Doob grabbed my cell phone and put it in his pocket. "Sleep," he ordered and pointed toward my temporary bedroom.

"You suck," I said as I stood with the help of my crutches and shambled away.

"You're welcome," he called after me.

Going to bed was a crap idea. *Doob's a bully.* Instead of staring at the wallpaper, I now stared at the ceiling. *As if sleep would come.* Melanie had been shot. *How did I feel about that?* I couldn't deny I thought the world would be a better place without her, but I always pictured myself as the one bringing her down. *But would I kill her?* Could I kill her? *Was it better this way?* Was it better I wasn't the one pulling the trigger? *I didn't know if I wanted her to live or die.*

So what type of person did that make me?

Despite my conviction I wouldn't sleep, Doob knocked on my door at about five o'clock in the morning. "Rise and shine, my pissy patient. Burns has some news. Should I bring your phone in so you don't have to get up?"

I flipped on the bedside lamp and waved him in. "Yeah, thanks," I said with a raspy voice.

We learned Melanie was in critical condition after surgery. Burns had been right. A sniper shot from the parking garage across the street. The police assumed the shooter went for her mid-section because he or she didn't have a clear shot at Melanie's head or upper body due to hospital monitors blocking her. Both her legs were in casts and under the covers, and a leg wound probably wouldn't have been as severe as a shot to the stomach, so they concluded that was the logic in the shooter's head. They were now trying to gather evidence at the parking garage, but so far they'd come up with nothing other than the thought the sniper left on foot because no cars had exited the garage within the hour window after the time of the shooting. They didn't have cameras at all of the pedestrian exits, so someone could have easily gone down the stairwell and vanished into the dark, cold night.

"Are the blinds usually open in a hospital?" I asked.

"I dunno. Why?"

"I'm just wondering if they're typically open, or if someone at the hospital made *sure* they were open. If that's the case, you could have an accomplice right there in the hospital. Or it could have been a visitor, if she had any."

"Good point, Maloney. I didn't ask, but I'll look into it. You now know all I know at this point, kids. Including the fact that Bragginnini is going nuts, claiming he's going to sue everyone from the Boston PD to the owner of the parking garage to Santa Claus."

I rolled my eyes. "I can only imagine. If she was getting some sympathy votes before, it'll get even worse now."

"Tru dat," Doob said.

"Enough with the gangsta," I replied.

"I'll call you guys later. Take care of that leg, Maloney." Burns disconnected and left us to our thoughts.

Doob looked at me. "Time to get ready for prison, princess."

CHAPTER 43

LATER THAT DAY, I FOUND MYSELF OUTSIDE THE STATE PRISON located in Cranston, Rhode Island. Doob, my dutiful chauffeur, helped me to the entrance but then retreated to the car as previously agreed upon. Doob and prisons don't exactly mesh. Plus, he wanted to stay in the car with Sampson.

True to his word, Gus had expedited the requisite channels, but that didn't get me out of the rigamarole one has to go through in order to get through the door. It was extra-fun while on crutches, and evidently they thought I'd smuggled a blow torch in under my cast. The guard who frisked me was the size of a baby whale, with red hair, ruddy skin, and foul breath. Fairly certain I was supposed to have a woman handle me, I wanted to tell him to fuck off and go find himself a mint, but I didn't want to give him the satisfaction of knowing he'd pissed me off. He seemed to get a little too familiar when searching certain parts of my person, but I managed to stay mum. After all, I was on this man's turf, and he easily had a hundred pounds on me, along with an attitude that was begging me to try something. I reluctantly remained docile, and told myself a perverted guard would be a small price to pay if I solved this case once and for all. The man instructed me to sign a form, and I couldn't resist a little jab before moving on to the visitor's room.

"I should have at least gotten dinner for that," I quipped. To my surprise, the guard smiled menacingly, and I noticed one of his front teeth had a huge gold cap on it. His breath had probably eaten away all of the enamel on the original tooth. One day he'd have an entire mouth of glimmering gold teeth. Gross.

"I'm on vacation next week. Maybe we can arrange that, Miss Maloney."

A shiver ran down my spine. This dude was something straight out of *Deliverance*, and I actually looked forward to meeting a criminal after dealing with Big Red.

When I visited Vic in prison the previous March, I drove home in silence, thinking about our discussion the entire time. I found myself doing that again today. Evidently prison visits put me in a reflective mood. I replayed the visit as if watching it on television.

Rusty McGraw was a downtrodden, sad man, who looked to be in his mid-seventies instead of in his forties. He said—rather *mouthed*—exactly one word during my visit, but this was an issue of quality over quantity.

I'd introduced myself as a friend of the new owner of the home, and when I told Rusty Jeff was concerned about the way Charlie had died, Rusty seemed intrigued. That is to say his mouth twitched. However, the only thing Rusty would confirm was that Charlie had visited him the day before he died. He did this by nodding when I questioned him about it.

I went on to ask him if he knew the name Malcolm Gage Johnson, and again, he nodded slightly and his mouth twitched. But this time it was like he made a full circle with his closed lips, which was the most emotion I'd seen from him to that point.

"If Malcolm had anything to do with you being in here, you could have said something. You could still say something," I gently prodded. He cast his eyes downward, and I made out just a barely perceptible shake of his head. There was something more there, but I wasn't going to get it out of him in one visit when it had been buried in him for a couple of decades.

So I moved on. Through my inquiries and Rusty's nodding or shaking his head, I managed to learn quite a bit. It was kind of refreshing I could glean so much from a completely one-sided conversation. Rusty had learned of Charlie's death from the newspaper and nodded that Charlie didn't deserve what happened. Agreeing with him, I then suggested Charlie might have been looking for something, but I didn't mention the coins. I knew the guards were listening and didn't want to get thrown out. When Rusty cocked his head at my comment, I shrugged and explained Charlie might have been looking for something important that needed to be retrieved before the new owner took occupancy. I raised my eyebrows to heights previously unscaled, in my own non-verbal plea for some information, but Rusty didn't budge.

Thinking he might want to know about the new owner of the home, I told this stranger everything I knew about Jeff: he grew up with a single mom who'd always worked two jobs to make rent, his love for books that developed his passion for school even as a kid, his college years and his sports prowess, his lottery winnings, his success with his security company, anything and everything I could think of to show this man Jeff was a sincere person trying to figure out what had happened in his home. As I babbled on, I realized my speech would have been more effective if Jeff had actually come along with me. Maybe next time.

During my ramblings, Big Red had come over and gruffly told me to wrap it up. Wasn't he supposed to be working the entrance of the prison? Was he following me? Creepy.

Rusty had stared at Big Red with loathing, and I realized this man might never have a visitor again in his lifetime. Knowing my time was up and I'd accomplished jack shit, I heaved a sigh and put my head down. But if I felt defeated, I could only imagine Rusty's life. Compelled to say something reassuring to him, I looked back up.

"You and your aunt had a beautiful home, and I know Jeff will take care of it to the best of his ability. I truly don't want to bother or upset you; I'm just trying to get to the bottom of Charlie's death. If something bad happened to your friend, I intend to find out what that was, and if you have any information that might help me, I'd be really grateful."

He stared at me but didn't flinch. As I'd gained nothing to this point, I played my trump card.

"And if someone I've previously mentioned bought your silence by paying off your aunt's house and sending her money regularly, then that someone is a really bad person. And that someone may still be up to no good."

Rusty's jaw dropped a little bit, but he still didn't speak. I wanted to bust Malcolm Gage Johnson so bad I could taste it, and all I needed was for Rusty to give me an inch. If I could get some more information, maybe we could get Officer Hurley that warrant.

I gave him my best sad eyes. "I will help you."

Big Red mocked us. "You gonna get him out of here, Miss Detective? And what exactly would he do? Apply all his *talents* out there in a world he couldn't even function in a few decades ago?" He scoffed and shook his head. "My man Rusty is a lifer. He doesn't want to get out of here. He wouldn't survive it. The best thing he did for his aunt was staying in this place."

I hated Big Red for spewing his hurtful words in his superior manner, but the basis of what he said was true. Rusty was exactly where he wanted to be, where he was comfortable, the place he now considered home. It made my heart hurt.

I looked at Rusty. "I'm sorry," I murmured. I didn't have any more speeches or energy or earnest looks in me. But then I remembered something. "By the way, Jeff has three boxes of your aunt's things. Charlie had packed them away for you. When you get out of here, Jeff said to tell you he'd have them in a safe place."

Rusty's brown eyes softened and then they flicked to Big Red. Flicking back to me, Rusty barely mouthed the word, "Attic." My own eyes grew wide, and I almost repeated the word out loud.

How stupid would that have been?

Now back in the car, I wondered if Rusty had actually given me a clue. Had I imagined it? There were cameras everywhere in that place. Would Rusty really have risked saying something revealing? If so, I had some hope, and hope's a good thing in my book.

After replaying the visit in my mind while Doob drove, I synced my phone up with Doob's truck and called Jeff's cell to relay the whole story. He sounded like a kid at Christmas and said he was out running some errands, but would wait for us to go to the attic if he arrived home before we did.

I then called Gus, who didn't sound nearly as excited as Jeff when he learned the details of my visit; he told me to call him once Jeff and Doob were finished poking around the attic. When he said that, it made me realize I wouldn't physically be able to go snooping with them. I'd have given up a month of coffee to do so, but with my friggin' cast, I'd just have to sit and wait. When I asked Gus why he wasn't more enthusiastic, he said if Charlie *had* found the coins and *had* been killed for them, then the killer likely had them in his or her possession. They may have even been sold on the black market by now.

While I knew he was right, I found myself irritated with Gus as I disconnected the phone. Too much shit had gone down lately, and I wanted a happy ending. I wanted Jeff to find some treasure in the attic floorboards, and I wanted Charlie's death to be an accidental fall. I wanted something good to happen for a change.

"He's right," Doob crooned. "I can tell you're pissed, but he's right. Those coins may be long gone."

"I know he's right," I said while rubbing my temples. "And obviously the coins aren't rightfully Rusty's or Ava's, or even Jeff's for that matter, but to think someone got away with them and killed Charlie...well, it just plain sucks."

Doob motioned toward the navigation unit with his head. "We'll know in about a half hour. Patience, Meg, patience."

I knocked on my cast. "Yeah, yeah, I know. Everything is testing my patience as of late."

"The poor patient has no patience," Doob said with a big grin, pleased with himself.

"Just drive, funny man."

As it turned out, we pulled into the long lane on Jeff's property at the exact same time he arrived. The sky had turned dark and ominous, and I wondered if we'd get rain or maybe some snow later this evening.

A stout, brown-haired woman waited at Jeff's doorstep. She had items in both arms and turned around to face us as the vehicles approached the house. Jeff got out of his Porsche and went to greet the woman while Doob walked around to my side of the car to help me with my crutches. Working my way toward the front door, I noticed the woman smiling at Jeff and heard their exchange.

"Hi neighbor," she said cheerily. "Margie Watson, I live next door." Her head motioned toward the house south of Jeff's about a half mile.

"Well, hello Margie. My name is Jeff Geiger. It's a pleasure to meet you. I'd shake your hand, but you're loaded down. May I help?"

Margie nodded and handed Jeff a basket full of homemade chocolate chip cookies. She also held up a large salad bowl covered in Saran Wrap, full to the brim with lettuce, tomatoes, cucumbers, onions and all sorts of other goodies.

"I didn't know if you were a health food person or not, so I opted to bring both sweets and a salad. A lot of the stuff in the salad is from your garden; I can the veggies and use them all year long. So I guess the salad isn't really a gift. I'm just returning it in a different format." Her cheery laughter easily reached us as Doob and I made our way to the steps, and I was an instant fan of Margie Watson. From the look on Jeff's face, he was as well. And Doob...well, she'd brought food, so she could have been a serial killer and Doob would have given her two thumbs up.

Jeff took the salad bowl from her and smiled. "This is incredibly thoughtful. Thank you. Meet my friends, Meagan and Doobie. And that maniac tearing around"—he pointed with his chin—"is Meagan's dog, Sampson."

"Those Springers have some energy, no doubt about that. It's nice to meet you both. What happened here?" She gestured to my leg.

"Nice to meet you, too," I replied. "Ruptured Achilles."

She gritted her teeth. "Oooh, that's a nasty one; I'm sorry to hear it. My niece had that a few years back; she ran hurdles in high school until the same injury got her. Ruined her chance at a college scholarship because she tried to rush the healing process. If you don't mind some advice from an old goat, you need to listen to your doctor and don't skimp on the physical therapy. It's not a quick recovery."

I nodded. "That seems to be the recommendation I'm getting from everyone. I'm being as patient as I can with it, but I'll be really glad when I'm better."

Ever the host, Jeff said, "Well, let's get Meagan off her one good foot, and Margie, please come in and see the house. I can offer you coffee, lemonade, water, a variety of sodas, wine, or straight scotch."

Margie chortled again, and her brown eyes crinkled so much they almost disappeared in her jovial face. My guess was she was in her early fifties, but she had a manner about her that would keep her looking young for a long time.

"I'll take a raincheck on all of the above, but especially on the scotch," she said with a wink. "I'm going into Providence this evening, and I wanted to drop these off before leaving. It's been over a week, and I've just been busier than all get-out. But I didn't want you to think I'm a snooty neighbor or anything."

"No chance of that. I've been flat out myself. But thank you so much. You can *borrow* things from the garden anytime you like. It's far too big for me to use all on my own."

She blushed. "I took care of the garden for Ava for the past few years. She was well into her eighties, and I just couldn't stand seeing her out there. If you'd like, we can strike up the same deal."

"Done. I could definitely use some guidance in all things planted, so consider my garden your garden."

She grinned and shook his hand. "You've got yourself a deal, Mr. Geiger. Now I've got to get going. Nice to meet you, uh, Doobie and Meagan. Take care of that leg."

She started to turn away, and Jeff looked after her curiously. "Margie, before you go, can I ask you something?"

"Sure."

"Did you see anything or anyone weird around here before I moved in?"

"Are you asking because of what happened to Charlie?"

He nodded. "I'm not trying to be an alarmist, but it was pretty shocking to walk in and see that. I guess I just want to make sure it was an accident."

She patted his arm. "Bart and I were in our house for over two decades, and then I lost him to cancer. I've been on my own in the house for the last three years."

Jeff's mouth turned down in sympathy. "I'm sorry to hear it."

She waved it off. "It was a blessing at the end. Anyway, the reason I bring it up is because I can count the times we locked our doors on one hand. I still don't lock them, even being alone. I've kept an eye on Ava, this house, and this garden for that entire time, and she never had any problems, either. I think it was just a horrible situation you walked in on, so don't let your imagination get the best of you."

"You're probably right, I'm sorry to bring it up."

"Not at all, you let me know if you have any trouble. I'll bring the dogs and the shotgun down and take care of things for you."

He threw back his head and laughed. "I can't wait to meet them. Thanks for stopping by, and have a great trip into Providence."

She started walking away, and he called after her.

"Margie?"

"Do you need any help with the dogs while you're gone?"

"Thank you, but they're coming with me. We're visiting my sister overnight, and she's a dog-person, so they're welcomed guests." She cocked her head. "I think they're more welcome than me, truth be told." And then she cackled that infectious laugh of hers.

"Okay, have a great time. And don't let those dogs eat at the dinner table."

Margie smiled and started walking away but then turned back to us. "Talking about the dogs reminded me of something. Sometimes I swear I'm having senior moments, which is impossible, me being twenty-five and all." She winked at him but then grew serious in the next breath.

"What's that?"

"A day or two before you showed up, I was winterizing Ava's garden —sorry, *your* garden—and the dogs were with me, and they started barking. They're both German shorthairs, nine years old, so they're usually pretty docile. But they were making a ruckus like I've haven't heard in a long time. So I quit what I was doing and went to find them."

She gestured toward the lane. "The dogs were on your driveway here, and there was a man walking away from them, back towards some junker car parked on the side of the road. I yelled after him, and he stopped and said he'd heard the McGraw house was for sale. Well, the darn sign that said SOLD was right in front of his face, so I pointed at it and said it'd been sold. Duh. He said he hadn't seen the sign until he got closer to the house. Do you think that could have been anything significant?"

Jeff shrugged. "I don't know. Seems like a logical explanation to me."

She wrinkled her nose a little. "Yeah, I guess so. I was glad the dogs were with me, though. Maybe I'm the one imagining things now, but the guy was creepy."

My senses went on full alert. Margie was believable, and something in her tone had me worried.

"How so?" Jeff asked.

"He was a real big sucker with red hair. He had a gold tooth right smack in the middle of his mouth, and he didn't seem to like that I was questioning him. Anyway, he drove off, and that's the last I saw of him. I hadn't really thought about it since."

My heart began to race. Big Red, the prison guard. He must have heard Charlie's and Rusty's conversation the day Charlie had visited the prison. Had Rusty told Charlie about the attic? Had Big Red come to try to find the coins? Had he killed Charlie?

"Did you happen to tell this to the police?" I asked her, trying not to sound alarmed.

She shook her head. "I've been gone so much I haven't talked to the police. Do you think I should call them?"

Jeff reassured her the best he could. "I'm sure everything's fine Margie, but thanks for telling me. I don't want to hold you up any longer. Have a great time in Providence."

"Okay, but if you think I should tell the cops, just let me know. I'll stop by in a few days to talk about it."

The minute she was out of earshot, I whirled on my crutches. "Holy shit, you guys! I know who did this," I squealed out a whisper.

Jeff looked confused. "How could you possibly know—"

Doob started herding me inside. "That's great if you've figured it out, Meg, and I know better than to doubt you. But let's get you inside before the sky opens up."

We moved inside, and I plopped down on the couch while Jeff took Margie's gifts into the kitchen and Doob retrieved beverages for everyone, including Sampson. Once they joined me on the couch, I relayed everything.

"Creepy guard from the prison, I didn't see that one coming," Jeff mused.

I pointed at the stairwell. "You two need to get your asses up to that attic right now," I insisted. "I'm going to get myself upstairs and wait for you. I want to know every single thing you're seeing every second you're up there."

Doob chugged the remainder of his soda in one gulp and nodded toward the staircase. "All right Jeff, you go up first, and I'll follow her. That way if she falls *up* the stairs or falls *down* the stairs, we'll be able to catch her either way."

Jeff nodded. "Yeah, one dead body at the bottom of those stairs is enough for my lifetime."

I scowled at both of them and stood on my crutches. "I'm not going to fall up or down. Actually, I'm getting around pretty good on these things and could probably still outrun you, Doob."

He rolled his eyes. "Like that's a big accomplishment. Are we going to go find some coins or what?"

"Let's do this," Jeff said.

CHAPTER 44

SAMPSON LED THE WAY, AND I REALIZED WHEN WE GOT UPSTAIRS the attic had a door with another set of stairs leading up.

"This is great," I said. "I thought it was a pull-down staircase I wouldn't be able to climb. I should be able to get up these just fine."

Doob, peering up the attic stairwell, shook his head while Jeff laid down the law. "This is an old house, Meagan. I don't know when they started making those pull-downs, but it was well after this house was built. And as steep as those stairs are, there is *no way* you're heading up there." He handed Doob a hammer he'd stuck in his back pocket and pulled out an even bigger one for himself. "Besides, there isn't much up there at all. After we go through the boxes I've already been through once, I guess we'll start pulling up floorboards."

"I second that," Doob chirped. "There's nothing you can do up there that will help."

I blew out a breath in exasperation. This sucked. "Fine, but we're leaving that door open, and I want you guys to yell down to me the minute you find anything." I turned to Jeff. "Are you sure you want to start ripping up your floors?"

He shrugged. "Not really, but what else are we supposed to do?"

I felt a twinge of guilt, but I know what I saw, and Rusty definitely mouthed the word, "Attic."

Sampson and the boys headed upstairs while I went into the closest guest bedroom and plopped down in an oversized nautical-looking chair that swallowed me up. It was very cushiony and cozy and bigger than my car.

"Anything yet?" I yelled toward the ceiling.

"We've been up here fifty-two seconds, Meg," Doob yelled back. "We'll work faster if you quit bugging us."

The nerve.

I decided to call Gus with an update, and he was extremely interested in all the details about the prison guard. Maybe with Gus's connections, he could look into the red-headed jerk. Gus told me he was going to make a few calls and to let him know if we found anything.

Over the next half hour or so, I yelled up to the boys a couple more times only to get barked at in return, and not by Sampson. Jeff didn't seem too thrilled about ripping up his floors, and Doob becomes completely disagreeable when it comes to manual labor in any sense. Deciding to leave them alone for a bit, I played solitaire on my phone.

I must have dozed off for a spell because I woke up with a start, my senses on alert. Glancing at the clock, I noticed an hour had passed, and it was now completely dark outside, rain pattering on the window panes.

I could hear Jeff and Doob's efforts from above. But something besides their previous irritation kept me from yelling up to them. My body tingled, and my heart thumped hard in my chest. The voice in my head told me to stay extremely quiet.

And then I heard it; a squeak from the stairwell below. I remembered the sound from my previous trips up the stairs. If memory served me, it was the second step.

What in the world? *Who* in the world?

My mind raced back to when we came inside from speaking with Margie, and I couldn't remember if we'd locked the door behind us. Reaching for my crutches, I slid off the chair and hobbled as quickly and quietly as I could toward the doorway. I scanned the dark room for a weapon even though I knew it was fruitless. My gun had been confiscated after the shooting, and I didn't see anything in the bedroom that would do any damage. And that's assuming I had two good legs. Even with a weapon, I was far from one hundred percent.

Hiding behind the open door, I peeked out the crack into the hallway. My breath came out at Darth Vader volume, and I hoped whoever was coming after us was frightened of *Star Wars* villains.

A tiny circle of light dotted the wall at the top of the stairs and then disappeared. Whoever it was had a flashlight and probably focused the beam up the steps to gauge his or her progress. If I could trip him or her up somehow, I'd scream for Doob and Jeff, and then...

Yes, then what? The boys would come down with their combined weight of three hundred pounds brandishing their hammers? And then Doob could mess his pants while Jeff fainted?

I needed to call 911.

As the thought crossed my mind, I cursed myself because I'd evidently dropped my phone in the enormous chair when I'd fallen asleep. On two good legs, I could get it in a flash. On crutches, I could possibly get it before Christmas.

But maybe I could scramble over to it on my hands and knees.

Using the crutches to steady me, I got to my knees and told myself I'd transformed into a three-foot superhero. Laying the crutches on the floor, I tried to stay as low as possible and then wondered if I had the upper body strength to lay flat and use my forearms to drag me to the chair. I instantly dismissed that as delusional.

Taking one last peek through the crack in the door before starting my trek, I saw a large form emerge and creep down the hallway toward the bedrooms, alternating the beam of light between them and the open doorway that led to the attic. I wasn't going to make it to the phone and probably had a maximum of five seconds to figure out what to do.

When I'd sat down in the chair earlier, I hadn't planned on falling asleep, so I still had a shoe on my working foot. Since I didn't have time to form a good plan, I decided on a bad one. I scrambled to a sitting position and yanked the shoe off. Watching the beam of light and the dark form, I grabbed for a crutch.

Crutch versus possible gun or knife or Taser or God-knew-what. I was fucked.

When the giant form got to the bottom of the attic doorway, I knew I had one shot at this. I threw the shoe at the wall as hard as I could from a sitting position and waited for the thunk. When it came, the large form whipped around and charged toward my room.

CHAPTER 45

ADRENALINE COURSED THROUGH ME. I'd wanted his attention, and I had it. Go-time.

If I do say so myself, I positioned and timed the next move pretty well because when Big Red came into the room, I swung the crutch at his mid-section and connected squarely with his sizable gut. He doubled over and dropped the flashlight while he cursed and howled like a wounded animal. I crab-walked away from him while I yelled at the top of my lungs for Doob and Jeff to call 911.

Despite his obvious pain, Big Red flailed out and got hold of my good leg. He pulled me toward him, and I kicked at him with my casted leg, but I had no power. His two arms against my one leg were like quicksand dragging me under, and I wondered what he had for a weapon. Heck, he could just sit on me, and it would be all over. His disgusting breath would probably be the last thing I smelled as he crushed the life out of me.

It sounded like thunder as Jeff, Doob and Sampson pounded down the steps. By the time they got to the room and switched on the light, Big Red and I were sitting side-by-side on the floor, he with a handful of my hair and a gun to my temple.

"I told you I'd pay you a visit," he sneered.

"What the hell are you doing in my house?" Jeff demanded, and I was surprised at the strength of his voice. As I would have expected, Doob looked ready to cry, but he had a firm grip on Sampson's collar, who was growling and straining to get free.

Big Red snarled. "Same thing you're doing. Looking for something that doesn't belong to me."

Jeff's face contorted with rage. "You heard Rusty tell Charlie where to look. You killed him. And now you're threatening us?" He then gestured to the attic. "Be my guest. There's nothing up there."

Big Red smirked. "I have friends on the police force around here. I heard that Charlie thing was an unfortunate accident."

"Don't you think *two* accidents and four dead bodies might just draw some attention to this place?" Jeff asked, not backing down.

Big Red ignored him. "I did get a kick out of the fact Rusty told this bimbo about the attic. The idiot doesn't know that we see everything."

Bimbo?

Jeff was relentless. "You won't get away with this. We've already called the cops. Plus, I'm telling you, there's nothing to find. Go dig around for yourself. Put the gun on me, and we'll go up together. There's nothing."

"Yeah, like I'm gonna leave these other two down here while we go upstairs. I work around criminals all day; I know all the tricks people try to pull. Don't think I'm going to fall for any crap from you amateurs."

"All I'm saying is there's nothing up there."

Big Red jerked hard on my hair. "I heard this one tell Rusty there were some boxes of stuff. I want to see them. Obviously the old lady hid the coins somewhere. I've heard all the rumors about them. And they're here; we've just got to keep looking. There's a shed outside, and I know there's a basement, too."

"And we'll search all those areas before the police arrive?" Jeff asked, incredulous.

"Of course not. But you three will be getting acquainted with Charlie by the time they get here, and I'll be long gone with the boxes."

While Jeff and Big Red had been arguing, I noticed Doob had inched back ever so slightly into the hallway. Knowing he'd never abandon me, I understood his intention. It was that telepathy thing we sometimes do.

When I'd been trapped in a similar situation with Melanie months before, I'd elected to run, with the hope she'd chase me. I'd wanted to create a target for her and force her to come after me instead of focusing on the person she'd already hurt. My plan hadn't worked, and it was something I'd regret every day for the rest of my life.

Watching my friend, I knew he was going to try to create a diversion and make himself a target to buy me some time. The thought made me sick, but it also gave me an idea.

Doob and I locked eyes; I could see the determination through his fear. My voice came out steady, and I was proud of that. "Do it."

Without a moment's hesitation, Doob yanked Sampson's collar, grabbed Jeff, and the three of them darted off into the darkness.

I was gambling on the fact that a control-freak like Big Red—an authority figure, a tough prison guard—clearly expected all of us to stay put and obey his demands. He expected us to cry, stammer, beg and crap our pants. He expected to dole out commands while we remained subservient and scared. That's what he expected.

What *I* expected was he'd be so flustered at my comrades brash departure that he'd have to stagger up to go after Doob and Jeff. And I knew they could outrun him and hide outside in the storm until the police arrived.

But if I was wrong...well, then I was dead.

From his sitting position on the floor, Big Red leaned his head back and roared, "Get back here, or I will kill her! Get back here—"

While his head was tilted back, I twisted and used both my arms to lunge at his left hand—the gun hand—and force it toward the ceiling. We jockeyed for leverage from a sitting position, and even though he was big, he was soft and not all that strong. Still, I was going to be no match for him. Just like it had been in the stairwell with Melanie, the invisible ticking clock boomed in my head. I didn't have a lot of time to fight.

Quickly releasing my right hand, I kept wrangling with my left and reached over his bulk to get the flashlight a foot away. Just as he was moving the gun back toward me, I grabbed the flashlight and pounded it as hard as I could squarely into his family jewels.

He howled like a wounded animal and dropped the gun. I grabbed it and scrambled away just as Gus burst into the room with an entrance that would make Bruce Willis proud.

"Hands where I can see them!" he ordered.

But Big Red was in a fetal position on the floor, cupping his junk and whimpering like a baby.

I looked up at Gus from the floor. "I whacked him in his business," I said with a wavering smile before I burst out crying.

CHAPTER 46

GUS REACTED TO MY TEARS ABOUT THE SAME WAY DOOB DOES, so I pulled myself together while he handcuffed Big Red.

What in the hell was Gus doing with a gun and handcuffs? There was more to this old man than met the eye.

Sirens wailed as Gus led Big Red down the stairs, and I yelled for Doob to come up to make sure I didn't do a second head-dive down the stairs in as many weeks. Doob bounded up the stairs two at a time and crushed me in a hug, crutches and all. Sampson was right behind him, doing his springing, happy dance all around us.

Doob hiccupped, or he might have been hyperventilating, I wasn't sure which. "I...I didn't mean to leave you, Meg...tell me you know, you know I'd never, ever...I'd die first..."

"Doob, you're breaking my ribs," I said, and he backed off instantly. I leaned forward, kissed him on the cheek, and tried not to pay attention to how puffy and red his eyes were. "You followed the plan perfectly! I know you didn't abandon me; I needed you to leave. Big Red was so pissed when you took off he couldn't even think straight. He was all alpha, thinking he was the big man in charge, and you completely unraveled him. You saved the day, Doob, swear to God."

He gave me an *aw shucks* face straight out of the Iowa cornfields and said, "Cut it out. I didn't do anything but run. You and Gus saved the day. What happened anyway?"

"I jammed Big Red in the nuts with a flashlight just as Gus came in like a full S.W.A.T. team."

Doob scratched his head. "Yeah, what's up with that anyway?"

I nudged my chin toward the stairwell. "Only one way to find out. Walk backwards and help me down these friggin' stairs."

Doob and I made our way slowly to the ground level, got me settled on a couch, and watched the chaos. Several patrol cars were parked haphazardly on the lawn, and Gus was deep in conversation with one pair of law enforcement types, while Jeff was engaged with another.

The minute Jeff saw me, he rushed over. "Meagan, I hope you know I didn't want to—"

I put a finger on his mouth. "Jeff, it happened exactly like I wanted it to. You and Doob are heroes."

He raised an eyebrow. "Leaving a girl behind with a murderer doesn't make me feel too heroic. I'm gonna get back with these officers, but I wanted to say I'm sorry and I'm so glad you're okay." He enveloped me in a bear hug that also left me breathless.

"The only way you two are going to get me killed tonight is with these hugs," I said with a smile.

We spent the next couple of hours repeating the same story and answering questions from the various law enforcement personnel who were at the house. Weariness washed over me as I watched the last police cruiser drive down the long lane, presumably off to do paperwork until the end of time.

With a quiet house, Gus, Jeff, Doob and I assembled in the main living area, where Jeff addressed the elephant in the room.

"So…Gus?"

Gus had a twinkle in his eye. "Yes."

"I'm beyond grateful, but I've got to ask why in the hell you showed up brandishing a gun like John Wayne."

Gus's amusement seemed to grow. "After I spoke with Meagan, I made some calls about the big prison guard and didn't like what I heard. I decided to come out and make sure you kids were all right."

Jeff's confusion grew. "Made some calls? To who? What does that mean?"

Gus smiled mischievously. "Did I ever mention I was a state patrolman for thirty-five years?"

Good grief.

We spent the next few hours talking about Gus's exciting life as a state trooper, and I had a delicious thought before retiring to bed.

"Gus, with all of your connections, do you know any judges in the state of Rhode Island?"

He cocked his head. "I know several, why?"

"Do you know any of them really well? As in, they-might-do-you-a-favor-really-well?"

"I do," he said. "I take a trip to Florida with one of them every winter."

I beamed. Handing him Officer Hurley's business card, I relayed all my suspicions about Malcolm Gage Johnson and the finial. It was possible Gus knew about Charlie and Malcolm's history because his face became a deep shade of red the longer I talked.

"So, if you could call in a favor and maybe give Officer Hurley the credit in the process..."

"Consider it handled," he said and pocketed the card. "I think there's a pretty big reward out there for the recovery of the items. I assume you want in on that?"

"If it gets that far, I'll take a couple of bucks, sure. But the bigger reward would be that I'd like Mr. Asshole Johnson to know who brought him down."

Maybe the prick would even come up with a name for his jail cell.

CHAPTER 47

Sunday, November 17th

AFTER SPENDING HALF THE NIGHT TALKING WITH GUS and the boys, I was glad the Jeff-drama was over so Doob and I could get back to Boston. Even though Jeff had an amazing house, I missed my life. And I was determined to make things right with Moira if it was the last thing I ever did.

We got up early, and Doob loaded up the Mercedes with our belongings while I watched from my perch on the couch. Staring at my cast, I never thought I'd actually long for manual labor.

Once Doob had the car all packed, we went in for a final breakfast with Gus and Shelley. After promises to stay in touch through email and phone, I gave both of them the best hugs I could while on crutches, and think I saw a bit of mist in Gus's eyes. I thought about razzing him and then realized—who was I kidding? It was all I could do to not break down over leaving these people I felt like I'd known for years instead of just a couple of weeks.

Doob and I went back to Jeff's to pick up Sampson and were headed north by eleven o'clock. The good-bye with Jeff was somehow easier, and I found myself wondering if something could ever spark between Moira and him. Thinking of my sister, I grabbed my phone and punched the speed-dial button to call her at work. My mother had texted—like Uncle Larry, my old-fashioned mother was texting—Moira had gone back to work, and I was hoping she'd join me at the apartment for dinner tonight. Truth be told, I was actually hoping she'd *stay* at the apartment tonight. But I knew that was wishful thinking. Baby steps, I reminded myself.

"Moira Maloney," announced the crisp voice over the phone.

"Hey sis!" My voice came out in such a forced cheery screech it sounded ridiculous. "Working on a Sunday?"

Her tone dropped about two octaves. "Oh. Hi, Meagan. I have a lot of catching up to do."

My heart sank lower than her voice, but I was determined to sound upbeat, so I plowed ahead in my unnaturally perky squeal. "I just wanted to let you know Doob, Sampson, and I are on our way back to Boston."

"Did you finish your *case*?" she asked with all kinds of attitude.

"I did."

"Well, good for you."

"It is good. The guy responsible for Charlie's death is in custody and will hopefully be locked up for the rest of his life."

"Like I said, good for you."

Man, this was awkward. Stubborn as a mule, and she wasn't giving an inch. As I was struck mute for the moment, she kept talking. "So if there isn't anything else—"

My insides were disintegrating. I simply couldn't take this. I couldn't have her mad at me indefinitely. For eternity. For infinity. "There *is* something else. There's *a lot* of something else. I won't pretend to know what you went through, and I know you hate me right now. I hate myself. Ten times more than you could ever hate me. And if I tell you I'm sorry for every waking minute for the rest of my life, it won't be enough. It'll never, ever, ever be enough. Not for you, and definitely not for Ma and Pop, and not even enough for me. But I can't change what happened. I can only change what I do moving forward."

There was a long pause. And by some act of God, I managed to stay quiet until she responded. I knew it could well go into January, but I was ready.

"I don't expect you to change the past, Meagan. I'm not that foolish."

"Of c-course not," I stammered. "I didn't mean to imply—"

"And if you're so worried about doing the right thing in the future, I assume that means you're in for a career change?" she asked.

Ouch. I wasn't ready for that conversation just yet.

"Is that a no? I mean, you're *so sorry*, right? You feel *so terrible*, right? Wouldn't getting a real job—that doesn't put your family in danger—make a whole lot of sense?" Her voice was cold and shrill.

"Meagan?"

My lips clamped shut. I simply couldn't speak, because I couldn't tell her what she wanted—what she desperately *needed*—to hear. Letting her down again wasn't an option, but I was incapable of telling her I'd quit my job.

I heard a huge exhale of breath. "Your silence says it all. If you're not changing jobs, then you'll be changing roommates," she said with a steely resolve in her voice.

More internal flip flops. "Moira, please just do one thing for me. Please come to the apartment after work. For an hour. For *one* hour, not a second more. I'll make dinner, and Doob will pick up something for dessert." I had to go for broke. "And I know Sampson wants to see you. It's been a long time, and he doesn't understand what's going on. You can't break his little doggie heart." I was most certainly not above using a dog to get what I wanted.

"Really, Meg? Using the Sampson guilt trip? I'll be keeping him when we divide up the apartment, by the way. He's *my* dog."

Tears immediately sprang to my eyes, but I wouldn't acknowledge what she'd just said. She was trying to be hurtful, and she'd landed her mark. Still, I was going to take her venom as long as she planned on spewing it. "6:00? One hour. That's all I'm looking for."

"6:30, and I don't know how long I'll stay. Have some stuff packed for Sampson. I'll take him to Ma and Pop's tonight when I leave."

CHAPTER 48

MOIRA ARRIVED PROMPTLY AT 6:30, LOOKING VERY PALE AND THIN, and Sampson greeted her like she'd just returned from war. In a small way, one might say she had. Sampson's springing was brought to new heights as he jumped up to greet her, licking at her face and humming some type of happy dog-whine between jumps. When his paws would momentarily touch the ground, he'd do circle-spin moves around her before springing in arcs again.

Despite her obvious desire to not be at the apartment, Moira couldn't help but smile. When Sampson finally took two seconds to stay on the ground, Moira crouched down and gave him a big hug. He snuggled his forty pounds into her body, and they ended up in a heap on the floor.

Which would have been cute except they were just a few feet away from where Moira had been curled in the fetal position that horrible night. I saw the horror on her face and knew I'd pushed too hard by asking her to come here.

Gently but quickly untangling herself from Sampson, Moira stood up and tears were running down her face.

"I tried," she said softly.

"I know. I'm so sorry," I said, shaking my head. There was nothing else to say. Doob watched from the table, and I didn't need to look at him to know he was mortified.

"I'm going to take Sampson to Ma and Pop's."

Tears pricked my eyes as I nodded. "Sure. After a welcome like that, you can't make him watch you leave."

As I couldn't help carry anything, I watched in helpless silence as Doob and Moira gathered up some food, bowls, toys, and blankets for Sampson. Moira organized everything in a sports bag, and Doob handed her a two-liter bottle just before she left.

"What's this?" she asked.

"Your parents' water is different from ours. You can mix our water and their water when you get there, just so he can transition. I did it for him when we went to Jamestown, and I think it helped." Doob's chin quivered, and I had to look away.

Moira took the water bottle and gazed at it in her hand, as if it were a foreign object. "Thanks, Doob. That's very thoughtful of you. See you guys." With that, she hefted Sampson's bag over her shoulder, put him on his leash and walked out of the apartment.

I stared at the closed door. Doob squatted in front of my chair.

"We'll get them back," he said softly.

Swiping tears at my eyes, I shook my head.

He put his hands on both my shoulders. "We'll get them back," he repeated. "And we're not going to sit around here and mope, so let's decide on something to do."

"I don't want to do anything," I moaned.

"Wanna play hopscotch?" Doob asked as he looked down at my cast.

"You're not funny."

"Movies? Museum? Mall? Restaurant? Tavern?"

"No, no, no, and no. And does anyone still say *tavern* anymore?"

"My dad does," Doob said, as if that settled it. "Anyway, I saw something earlier on TV today and taped it. I was hoping to share it with you and Moira."

"Well, that's not going to happen," I said sullenly.

"I think it'll still make you feel better," he replied, turning on the television and scrolling to his recording.

I actually cracked a smile as I watched the attractive female news anchor announce there was a possible lead in the Isabella Steward Gardner Museum heist. While names weren't yet named, it seemed that state and federal authorities were chasing a hot tip.

Good old Gus.

CHAPTER 49

Friday, November 22nd

"MEAGAN, I'M NOT GOING TO GO THROUGH THAT AGAIN," Moira said, her impatience coming through the phone loud and clear.

"So you're just *never* coming back to the apartment? You're just going to have me box up your stuff? You're going to stay with Ma and Pop forever?"

She sighed. "I don't know what I plan on doing. Maybe you can get a roommate or something. I just can't walk in there and act like nothing ever happened—"

"Five minutes, Moira. I asked you for an hour last time; now I'm asking for five minutes. I think you'll see things in a different light this time."

That was one of the biggest understatements I'd made in a while. After the night Moira had become upset and left, Doob had been really quiet for a few hours. When he finally perked up, he told me he had a couple of cosmetic ideas for our apartment that might make her feel better. Since I was already staying at his place, he wondered if he could work some magic in our apartment. Several weeks prior, I would have never let Doob-The-Designer loose in my place, but at this point, I figured, *why not*. His mini-palace across the hall proved he had to have some taste in his disheveled little head.

Once I gave him the green light, Doob said he'd speak with his lady—yes, Doob has an interior designer lady—about making a few subtle changes and Moira and I could check it out when they were done. He went on to promise if we hated it, he'd pay for whatever changes we wanted. It was essentially a money back guarantee.

So when Doob invited me to my own apartment after the makeover, I was a little apprehensive, but I tried to remain upbeat about the whole thing. I really wanted my sister back.

Doob made me walk in with a blindfold on, and the whole thing seemed ridiculous until he told me to go ahead and take a look at the new digs. My jaw hit the floor in astonishment. Doob's lady had created a beautiful, warm oasis, complete with earth tones accented with some soft reds and greens throughout the large room. All of our furniture was gone, and the woman had created several zones throughout the space.

"How in the world did you do this in five days?" I asked, incredulous.

"It was a busy week for my decorator lady, but money talks," he said with a shrug, and I gave him a huge hug. I didn't know where to look first.

One section had a lovely mahogany framed couch with two large cushions and what seemed to be a million pillows in deep brown, gold and muted red colors. Across from it were two chairs in matching material, and one had the most beautiful dark green throw over it that I'd ever seen. Nestled in between was an antique coffee table with several mismatched candles, books, and pictures of our family settled on top. A black and white one of Moira and me from last year produced a lump in my throat.

The eating area was nearly as nice as the one at the gala, with a formal dining room table and chairs made of dark wood and intricate place settings at each chair. Two crystal vases of fresh yellow roses added a perfect complement to the dark furniture, and she'd even installed a small, but appropriate, crystal chandelier over the table.

Adjacent to the dining area, the designer had somehow managed to fit a gleaming black baby-grand piano. It was stunning, and she'd mounted a tiny spotlight from the ceiling onto the instrument. Moira and I had both taken piano lessons as kids, and on more than one occasion, Moira had commented on how much she wish she still played.

Doob truly hadn't missed a thing.

I moved on to our galley kitchen where the designer had ripped out the countertops and cabinets, and she'd even widened the pass-through. We now had sparkling black granite countertops cohabitating with fabulous white cathedral cabinets with silver hardware. The appliances had all magically been turned into stainless steel works of art, and—gasp—the refrigerator was full.

The outdated blinds had all been replaced with elegant floor-to-ceiling draperies, and the carpet had been removed from the entire area, replaced by dark, sparkling hardwood floors that were so shiny they looked wet.

As I was processing the beauty of my renovated home, Doob explained he'd only changed the main living space and had left the remaining rooms as-is. But he said if Moira liked the changes and wanted more, he'd foot the bill for that as well.

Dumbfounded and on the verge of tears at his generosity, I sighed deeply. That put Doob straight into a dither. "No water works, Meagan, for God's sake. I did this for selfish reasons. What the heck would I do if you two moved out on me?"

I thought about that for a second. "You'd follow us," I said and sniffled.

"I would," he conceded and pointed at a massive armoire back in the seating area. "You missed the best part."

I looked over at the gorgeous piece of furniture. "It's amazing, Doob," I said with a touch of awe.

He went over and opened it up, revealing what I guessed to be a fifty-something-inch television.

"Good grief. We wouldn't want you to just *sit* in the sitting area, right?"

"God, no," he said. "Now call her, and let's see what she thinks."

So I'd placed the call, and we'd spent the rest of the day hemming and hawing about her reaction. And then we finally heard the key in the lock.

Sampson bounded through the door like an escaped prisoner but stopped short when he realized everything was different. He started sniffing all around and then trotted over and looked up at me with his big brown eyes. Cocking his head, he conveyed, *what gives*?

"Do you like it boy?" I asked while ruffling his ears, but we all knew that I was talking to Moira. She stood in the doorway, taking it all in. I couldn't read her face, but she hadn't stomped out, so that was a start.

Resuming his sniffing, Sampson lumbered over to the pantry, and Doob scampered over to get him a treat. "We didn't move the biscuits, buddy. That's one thing that stayed the same."

Moira took a couple of tentative steps inside. "It's hard to believe this is the same apartment."

"That was kind of the point," I said and heard my voice falter.

Doob zipped across the room and pointed out the TV in the armoire. "You want to see the remote for this bad boy? It can do everything except make your coffee, and I might even figure out how to program it to do that."

"Speaking of, you should see the espresso machine in the kitchen," I offered up, my voice back to normal. "Not that I'll ever abandon the coffee house, but this thing is right up your alley, Moira."

She meandered through the sitting area and ran her hand across the beautifully polished dining room table. Doob and I stayed in the main room and watched her examine things. I almost didn't want to breathe. While she didn't actually go into the galley kitchen area, she stood outside of it and nodded her head in approval.

"This place is something else," she said and walked back toward Doob and me. "You two outdid yourselves."

"I can't take any credit," I said. "It was all Doob."

He approached and gave her the most awkward hug I've ever seen. "We just miss you, Moira. We want you home." His voice cracked, and I'd never seen a more sincere, tender moment in my entire life.

"I miss you guys, too," Moira admitted and looked around the space again. "And I really appreciate all of this. It's beautiful."

"We're glad you like it," I said, my tone hushed. How odd it was to feel this inhibited around my sister.

She glanced toward her bedroom. "Is my stuff—"

"All exactly the same," I assured her. "Doob just changed the main area, so...well, you know."

Moira nodded. "I do. Well, again, this looks really nice. Sampson and I should head back before Ma starts to worry. You know how she gets."

"Pa's worse," I said and smiled.

"True." She gave Doob and me quick hugs, and Doob knelt and wrapped his arms so tightly around Sampson I thought the poor dog would burst.

"Doob, unhand the dog. They've got to go."

"Talk to you guys soon," Moira said, and I watched her and my furry little buddy go out the door.

Even though she'd left for our parents' house, I'd felt the chill had lifted just a bit. My sister didn't hate me any longer. I don't know if she loved me anymore; I wasn't completely sure she even liked me, either. But she no longer hated me, and that was progress.

I looked at Doob, and he had a goofy half-smile on his face.

"What?" I asked him.

"She's coming back to us," he said as his grin widened. "And she's bringing our four-legged friend home, too. The band is getting back together." He started to do a little Doob-dance across the gleaming floors.

"Don't jinx it," I said but found myself wiggling around the room with him.

CHAPTER 50

Saturday, November 23rd

"IS SHE REALLY STILL IN CRITICAL CONDITION?" I asked, unable to hide the skepticism in my voice. "It's been a week. Thanksgiving is coming up; give me something to be thankful for, please."

"I don't like it either, Maloney. But she went into the hospital with a massive head wound and two broken legs, and then she got shot and almost died. Her prognosis isn't good."

"Do they have any leads on who did it?"

"Nothing yet. Everyone who's been questioned has been cleared. Whoever did this was a pro."

A vision of Uncle Larry popped into my head, and I did my denial thing and continued talking. "So, if it gets to that point, how long until they pull the plug?"

"How did I know you were going to ask that? She doesn't have a will that anyone knows of, and it's not like she has a health care directive. She's in her twenties. Bragginini is supposedly running the show right now, but he really has no legal say-so if it looks like she's not gonna make it."

"If it comes to that, is it possible Vic will be the one who ultimately has to make that decision?"

"To pull the plug? Yeah, it could possibly fall to him. He's her biological father, however screwed up that is."

The irony of that wasn't lost on me. "She came back to kill him, and he may end up with the responsibility of ending her life. Ho-ly shit. Keep me posted, Burns, and thanks for everything."

"Take care of that leg, kiddo," he said and hung up.

I relayed everything to Doob, and he shook his head. "What a messed up situation."

"It's like the whole world is waiting to see if this monster is going to wake up. Will she live or die? And if she makes it, is she going to get away with murder? Literally get away with murder. *Murders*, plural. I can't stand it."

As he always does, Doob listened to my rant patiently. Then, "It's like watching those *Twilight* movies."

I raised an eyebrow. "What in the world are you talking about? Melanie's gonna come back as a vampire?" Actually, that wouldn't surprise me. It could even be an improvement.

"I'm just saying you'll have to wait and see. Like with some movies or television shows or books, sometimes you have to wait until the next one to see what happens to the bad guy. Or the bad girl, in this case."

Here's hoping.

EIGHT MONTHS LATER

ON A LATE JULY AFTERNOON, JEFF, MARGIE, AND GUS were enjoying some margaritas on Jeff's deck. The view of the garden was spectacular, and the ocean beyond, even more beautiful. The craziness from November had long since passed, but the memories still stirred now and then.

Gus sighed deeply and said, "You two have done an amazing job on that garden. I think there may be hope for you yet, Jeff."

Jeff smiled and said, "Margie gets all of the credit. I just talk her to death while she does the work."

"That's not true," Margie said and swatted him on the arm. "You did a great job with some of those vegetables, and I've never seen the begonias look so pretty. You're a natural."

"I'm trying. Personally, the black-eyed Susans are my favorite. I love how they stand out against all the other vegetation."

Margie studied him closely for a moment and said, "Well, isn't that something? Ava's favorite was the same flower. It's funny, though. She called them her black-eyed Sams."

The moment seemed to freeze in time. Gus's eyes bulged, and Jeff's head snapped to attention. Margie looked concerned.

"What'd I say?" she asked, swiveling around as if she did something wrong.

"Black-eyed *Sams*?" Gus repeated.

"Yes, why?"

Jeff jumped in. "As in Black Sam Bellamy?"

Margie exclaimed, "Oh my God! Ava always used to say that those black eyes would watch over her and never tell her secrets."

They sat in stunned silence for close to a minute before Gus and Jeff leapt up simultaneously.

Gus shouted, "Jeff, go get two shovels, and Margie, go get your digital camera. We've got some flowers to dig up!"

Thank you to my family, friends, loyal pooch, and readers for your support and encouragement.

CPSIA information can be obtained
at www.ICGtesting.com
Printed in the USA
LVHW080200080920
665291LV00019B/2545

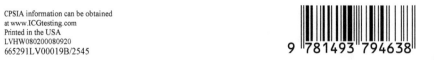